Pat & Stephen

My thanks & best wishes

Michael Parker

(Mick)   DEC 2007

The Eagle's Covenant

The Eagle's Covenant

Michael Parker

Michael Parker

ROBERT HALE · LONDON

ISBN 978-0-7090-8428-0

Robert Hale Limited
Clerkenwell House
Clerkenwell Green
London EC1R 0HT

www.halebooks.com

2 4 6 8 10 9 7 5 3 1

For my four sons
Vincent, Terry, John & Stephen

I would like to thank my nephew Matthew Parker for his invaluable
help in opening up the world of computers for me. But I would
like to say that I have used Matthew's undoubted computer skills
and interpreted them to suit my story, which of course is a complete
work of fiction. So I apologise to him for any technical errors
and claim them for myself.

Typeset in 10¼/14pt Sabon
by Derek Doyle & Associates, Shaw Heath
Printed and bound in Great Britain
by Biddles Limited, King's Lynn

and Economics. She gained her degree, indulged her aggressive opinions and threw herself at life.

In the ensuing four years, Breggie attached herself to the cause of the whites and fought against the ANC, the African National Congress, believing that she would continue the perceived struggle and become a major political figurehead. Such was her hatred of the black people, she was more than just a willing volunteer and agitator, and went on many active missions against them. But in 1994, when Nelson Mandela was elected President of South Africa, Breggie realized that world politics and powerful politicians had rendered her cause useless, so she left her homeland and went to England.

It wasn't long before she found her spiritual home and became involved in all manner of protests and demonstrations where she knew she would meet others of her persuasion. She attached herself to a growing animal rights group and found herself at her happiest when she was attacking animal centres, so called vivisectionists and anyone whom the group considered a legitimate target.

But Breggie found her real calling when she killed her first, innocent victim: a doctor who, unfortunately, was at the scene of an attack one night when Breggie's group raided a beagle farm. He was gunned down and died of his injuries. It was Breggie who had shot him. The group were appalled at the dramatic and unseen turn of events, but such was Breggie's strength and dominance within the group, there were others who rallied to her, elevating her to the role of leader.

Breggie revelled in her new role within the group, but her place as the most zealous among them brought its own dangers and the police finally arrested her. In court she could not be charged with the doctor's murder, nor be held responsible for his death, but she was sentenced to a year in prison and deportation back to South Africa.

When she returned to South Africa, Breggie stayed long enough to see her parents but within a week she turned up in Germany. South Africa was no longer the place where she wanted to be. With her blonde hair, good looks and fine figure, she was a magnet for all kinds of people. But it was her chequered past that attracted the most ruthless, and it wasn't long before Breggie was bound up in another cause.

She looked once more at Joseph and pouted her lips. She was happy, this was where she belonged. This was her strength. Soon it would begin.

7

*

Immense wealth sat comfortably on the shoulders of Manfred Schiller like the well-cut, expensive jacket he was wearing; wealth that had been accumulated by a high intellect, courage, shrewd investments, hard work, plotting, cheating and scrupulous planning, wealth that reached stratospheric proportions and looked down on other billionaires from the lofty plateau of his rightful place as the world's richest man. Wealth that came from armaments, oil, communications, aerospace, commerce and banking. Schiller's wealth was the kind that beckoned presidents and monarchs. It was wealth where others bent the knee and touched the forelock.

If a man's wealth was a measure of his power, then Manfred Schiller was the most powerful individual in the world, and that power meant that although he was now eighty-five years of age, no man, king, president or commoner dared keep Herr Schiller waiting.

On this occasion, however, he was quite happy to wait. And, strangely for someone who was quite used to dealing with the most powerful people in the world, he was as nervous as a kitten.

Manfred Schiller had been waiting in the gleaming lobby of the Schiller Memorial Hospital's private wing for over thirty minutes now. He remained on his feet, refusing the offer of a chair. He was a tall, elegant man without the stoop that often accompanies old age. His hair, thin and white was swept straight back over his head. His features were sharp and chiselled, with a strong, aquiline nose. The good looks of his youth had long disappeared, but he was still a handsome man, and he could remain standing with even the youngest.

The private annexe to the Memorial hospital, built with Schiller's money, had been named in honour of Schiller's only son, Hans, known as Hansi, who had been killed in a flying accident six months earlier. Outside the annexe, beyond the glass doors, which were engraved with the Schiller crest of a golden eagle, a large crowd of *paparazzi* and well wishers had gathered and were waiting patiently with other members of Schiller's security staff.

All out-patient appointments to the private annexe had been cancelled that day to allow complete privacy and security for Schiller's group. Visitors to patients who were already in the private wards had

8

been told to report to the reception desk in the main hospital complex, and from there they would be escorted through the main hospital to the private wing. The complete privacy afforded to this man by the hospital was unprecedented but not altogether unexpected.

The reason for the gathering of the *paparazzi* and changed arrangements for private clients of the hospital, the security for the obvious trappings of serious power in the hands of one man, and for his willingness to wait patiently in the lobby was a one-week-old, infant boy: Manfred Schiller's grandson.

Breggie de Kok loved telling Joseph that it was time to die. It was one of her silly expressions she used when everything had been planned down to the last detail and there was little chance of any of them dying for their cause. As was the case with all terrorists, their cowardly acts ensured almost certain survival for themselves. There were some risks but the dice was always loaded in their favour. And, as was often the case, there were some serious backers financing the group.

Breggie and Joseph were concealed in a slightly elevated position among a copse of pine trees just a metre or so above the road. They were wearing camouflage fatigues, which meant they were practically invisible to any casual observer; certainly to anyone who would not expect them to be there. They had a clear sight of the private road that climbed up the hillside and through the trees to the residence of Manfred Schiller. To their right, about twenty metres or so from them was their American comrade in arms, Karl Trucco.

Trucco was sitting with his back to the road, leaning against a tree. He was quite still, but his mind was working methodically, carefully. He knew what he had to do; what was expected of him. They had rehearsed it all very carefully so that nothing would go wrong and it would all be over in less than sixty seconds.

He let his hand fall to his side until it touched the cold metal of his weapon. Like Schneider, he had an AKS-74 rifle with him, but his was fitted with a Zeiss scope. It had been zeroed at a range of fifty metres. Karl was a crack shot. He needed to be because nothing would happen until he had taken out the lead driver.

Manfred Schiller wasn't alone in the hospital lobby. With him was a small group of people: the director of the hospital, Klaus Beidecke who was the foremost gynaecologist in the country, Dr Schumann and Schiller's private secretary, Michael Strauss. The young receptionist, closeted behind her desk could almost feel the power emanating from the wealthiest man in the entire world and whose presence at the hospital ranked even more importantly than a visit from the Chancellor of the Federal Republic of Germany.

Doctor Schumann and Herr Beidecke were talking quietly together, their conversation almost a deferential hush. Strauss, on the other hand looked quite relaxed while he made monosyllabic comments to Schiller. Occasionally the old man would acknowledge him with a faint smile or a nod of the head, but always his eyes were glued to the internal glass doors at the far end of the lobby, looking for movement.

'Here they come,' Strauss said to him suddenly, tipping his head to one side. He could see the group through the glass doors. Schiller's eyesight was not particularly good, so he was not aware of them until the doors slid open almost without a sound.

He stepped forward as his daughter-in-law Joanna, Hansi Schiller's beautiful young widow, accompanied by her obstetrician and her personal nurse appeared at the doors. Joanna was carrying her week-old baby son, the reason for Schiller's being kept waiting – something he was not used to but quite happy about. Also with Joanna were the baby's nanny, Helga, and other members of the hospital nursing staff.

Schiller held his hands forward. A warm, parental countenance softened the features of his face as he walked across the lobby to the small group. Joanna was beaming, her eyes not leaving the infant for more than a few seconds. She looked up at Schiller and the expression on her face was the same as any proud mother who was leaving the maternity ward with her brand new baby boy.

Beside Joanna, Helga beamed. She was the young, eighteen-year-old family friend who had agreed to defer her university place to spend a year as nanny to the baby. She had been a great comfort to Joanna since the tragic death of her husband, and was almost like a young sister to her.

Schiller smiled at Joanna. 'I am so proud of you.' He kissed her gently on the cheek which she proffered, then he looked at the baby.

'He's lovely.' A small, almost wistful trace of sadness clouded his

10

features for a moment. 'I wish Hansi could have been here to see him. He would have been so proud.'

The reference to his dead son tempered that moment with a deep sense of loss for them both. But it was immediately replaced with their happiness that here at last was Hansi's infant son.

Schiller turned to the obstetrician and shook him warmly by the hand, thanking him for everything his staff had done. Then he thanked each attendant nurse and finally put his arm protectively around Joanna's shoulder.

'Let us take our baby home,' he said warmly.

Outside the hospital, waiting in the sunshine of a warm day, the newsmen held their cameras ready. An immediate bustle of activity started among the Mercedes cars as though there was more to be done than simply open the doors. Schiller had that effect on people. Flashlights began shattering the morning brightness as they bounced off the walls and reflected back in a flickering display from the glass doors and nearby windows. Schiller appeared on the steps with Joanna beside him, his face a picture which would undoubtedly fill the front pages of all the world's leading magazines. Here at last was the new heir to Manfred Schiller's immense fortune and almost limitless power.

Voices called out from the phalanx of pressmen.

'Frau Schiller, how is the baby?'

'Herr Schiller, does he look like you?'

It was a continuation of the usual banal, sycophantic questions one hears from the unfortunate hacks whose task it often is to spend hours waiting for someone without the benefit of being granted a personal interview. And even if they had, it was of little doubt that the syco- phancy would remain. How else would anyone dare interview such a man as Manfred Schiller? How else could they?

The great man allowed them a few minutes of posing, a theatrical but genuine show of thanks to the hospital staff, a wave of the hand and he finally escorted Joanna and her baby to the waiting limousine.

A police car moved out at the head of the convoy as soon as the other cars started to move. Two Mercedes saloons were riding one in front and one behind Schiller's limousine. The convoy swept out of the hospital gates, following the police car and on to the main road. There were no obstructions and no traffic to bar its way as the cavalcade moved swiftly, given its freedom by the flashing blue light on the green and white police car.

Inside the quiet, air-conditioned luxury of the limousine, Schiller took Joanna by the hand and smiled for what seemed to be the thousandth time at her. He lifted her hand and kissed the back of it gently. Because it was a sunny day, the air conditioning worked noiselessly to keep the interior of the car at a comfortable temperature.

'We are a family again, *mein liebchen.*' He said nothing else but just continued to look at her. Many times he had wished he was not an old man. Joanna was so beautiful. Her hair was the colour of obsidian blackness which shone and glittered with each movement of her head. Her eyes were the clearest blue he had ever seen, and she had an Aryan quality about her which belied her Englishness yet somehow strengthened it. No angular features to dull the quality of her face or the smoothness of her porcelain-like skin. Her high cheekbones proclaimed the calibre of her breeding, which was so important to German sensibilities.

Joanna was well aware of Schiller's feelings and quietly thanked him for never imposing himself upon her, particularly now that she was alone. It would not have surprised her if people suspected, or indeed believed, that she was no more than an uneducated bimbo who would soon find herself a sugar daddy in Manfred Schiller to sustain her luxurious lifestyle once the grieving for her dead husband had come to an end.

To her Schiller was the kindest man she had known after her own father who was dead now, and she was quite happy to remain part of his family for as long as he wished.

'Thank you, Manfred,' she responded, and squeezed his hand. 'You are such a treasure to me. We will always be your family. Nothing will ever stop that, ever.'

The fourth man in the terrorist team was Conor Lenihan. Conor had been born in Catholic Belfast and brought up in the sectarian ways of his peers. He was streetwise at a very early age, and had learned quickly how to stone the men of the security forces and bait the Protestants of the 'other side'. Conor had also been fortunate enough to spend many weekends on his uncle's farm in County Fermanagh along the shores of Lough Erne.

It was there that Conor had learned the skills of the hunter. His uncle had taught him how to stalk game, how to set traps. He had shown the young boy how to bivouac at night and live off the land. He became an expert with a shotgun and rifle. Handling a pistol was as easy to Conor as handling a pen.

But these skills were not imparted to Conor to improve his life on the dangerous streets of the city. Conor's uncle was a recruiting officer for the IRA and the boy's tenacity, fearlessness and obvious qualities among his peers had been noticed by the local IRA commander.

Conor, like many of his friends, had always nursed an ambition to serve the Fenian masters in whatever capacity they wished. And it was a massive disappointment to him when he learned that his remit was to join the hated British Army. Much to Conor's surprise, however, he took to the life like a duck to water and it wasn't long before he was nursing the ambition to join the British Army's Special Air Service, otherwise known as the 'Regiment'.

Conor served the army well and his IRA chiefs, and when his career in the army came to an end, Conor was sent to County Kerry in Ireland where he helped train IRA recruits. Conor's time in the Parachute Regiment and with the SAS had been peppered with excitement and adrenalin-charged moments of tension which had honed him into a refined, fighting machine; the complete soldier. But the change from that lifestyle to one of almost total boredom had taken the edge of Conor's skills and had almost cost him his life.

It was a mixture of luck and instinct that helped Conor to escape when an SAS hit team turned up at Conor's farm in County Kerry posing as tourists. Where Conor would normally have been working out in the fields or around the farm at that time of day, he had gone into the farmhouse for a few minutes. He saw the two men from the window talking to his uncle. That had been the lucky bit. The instinct kicked in for some unknown reason and he felt suspicious. For all he knew they could have been a loyalist hit squad.

He slipped out of the farmhouse and tailed the two strangers using the techniques he had learned in the SAS. Within twenty four hours he knew they were SAS, which meant that his cover had been blown. Somehow the British had discovered that he had been a 'sleeper' while in the army, so there was no reason for the soldiers to turn up at the farmhouse other than to kill him.

Twenty-four hours later, his IRA masters had spirited him away to a safe house in Germany and released him from his obligation to the cause. Conor Lenihan was now a free agent.

The drive from the hospital to Schiller's residence was about twenty miles through some of the loveliest countryside in the Eifels Mountains, west of Koblenz. The convoy followed the green and white police car, trailed by a posse of pressmen and *paparazzi*, towards the foothills overlooking the Mosel's route to the Luxembourg border. The towering beauty of this place was never lost on Schiller and he would often spend time there whenever he could.

Schiller's home was set high in the hills of the Eifels. Access to it was by a single road which cut its way through a forest of pine trees. The area around the house, with its commanding views across the valleys and peaks had been cleared of trees for reasons of security. It was bounded by a double fence, the inner of which was electrified. It was monitored by security cameras and patrolled at night by guards with dogs. Another fence had been constructed lower down the slope. This was a standard chain link fence, not electrified, and was there to determine the boundary of Schiller's property. On both sides of the mountain this fence was about six miles in length. It was never patrolled and only checked as part of a standard maintenance programme.

The police car drove past the gates leading to the access road and stopped. Immediately the lead Mercedes turned in towards the gates and was greeted by a security man. The convoy came to a halt. The pressmen and *paparazzi* automatically pulled into the side of the road and leapt from their cars to continue blazing away with their flashlights and TV cameras.

The driver in the leading Mercedes lowered the window. 'What the fuck's going on?' he wanted to know.

The guard was unmoved. He came round to the open window and placed one hand on the roof of the car and the other on the car door. He glanced inside at the occupants.

'Herr Schiller's instructions, said there should be extra security.' He nodded in the direction of Schiller's limousine. 'Make sure them *paparazzi* bastards don't get in.'

As he spoke he placed his thumb at a point immediately below the driver's shoulder. He rolled it against the paintwork, unseen to the people in the car. It was quite an unobtrusive movement, but when he pulled his hand away it left a white mark where his thumb had been.

At that precise moment the driver in the police car rolled his window down. He had in his hand a small transmitter about the size of a mobile phone. He put his arm out of the open window and held it aloft. He made a pretence of waving and let the clutch up. As the car moved away he pressed a transmit button on the transmitter. Then he pulled his arm in and rolled the window up. He smiled at his companion.

'*Frei geld*,' he said and laughed. 'Easy money.'

Karl Trucco saw the red light flicker on and off. The small receiver was propped up against his back pack. The sound had been turned down to a minimum level, but he was just able to hear the intermittent bleep and the sharp, vibrating pulses. He suddenly felt nervous and his breath seemed to catch in his chest. It was no more than he expected. He got up and went through the trees to where Breggie and Joseph were concealed.

'They are coming.' It was simply stated. Nothing more was required. He turned and immediately went back to his own patch, his own killing field.

Breggie held the Uzi tightly as though she was afraid to drop it. Joseph picked up his bag and kissed her swiftly on the cheek. He could literally feel the tension in her body. He kissed her again and then jogged up the road to a position about twenty metres further on from Karl.

The three of them were ready. There was no need to let Conor know the convoy was on its way up the hill. He knew exactly what he had to do.

Schiller was surprised to see a security guard at the gates. These were normally manned by a gatekeeper whose job it was to receive all deliveries of incoming goods, mail and unwanted callers. Anything the gatekeeper was unable to deal with could be handled by the security office established at the entrance to his residence.

He saw the security guard talking to the driver of the lead Mercedes and stiffened. Joanna thought nothing of it but was immediately aware of Schiller's sudden curiosity. He touched the button on the small control panel set into the door and lowered the window. The guard walked up to the limousine and saluted.

'Sorry for the little delay, Herr Schiller.' He stooped and looked in through the open window. 'The boss decided it would be better if we had someone here to keep the *paparazzi* out.'

Before Schiller could respond the guard had stood up and was redirecting his attention to the last Mercedes. Schiller grunted and leaned back in his seat. The window closed noiselessly and the car moved on.

The men in the third car had watched all this with interest and curiosity. The guard walked over to them as their driver lowered his window. He went through the same drill, explaining the reason for the extra security. He waved them through. None of the occupants of the three cars had ever seen the man before.

When the cars had disappeared from view, he then closed the gates and slipped a padlock through them from the inside. He paused momentarily, staring absently at the assembled pressmen, and then went back inside the small gatehouse.

Trucco lifted the rifle and pulled the stock close into his cheek. Nothing obscured his vision as he looked through the 'scope and sighted the crossed hairs on the trunk of a tree immediately across the road from him. He then swung the rifle to his right and waited.

Joseph dropped into position behind a tree on the edge of the treeline. He opened his bag and emptied out its contents; several magazines of 5.45mm hollow point bullets and two hand grenades. He was beginning to sweat and had to wipe his hands down the front of his combat vest. Joseph would not have the opportunity to pick his target as carefully as Trucco would. He had to wait for the car to come to rest.

Breggie's right hand was closed round the trigger of the Uzi. She could feel her heart beating in her chest. She was almost salivating and could feel wetness in her loins.

Conor heard the sound of the cars climbing the hill. He held a limpet bomb in his hand. In the waist band of his trousers he had stuffed a Browning 9mm automatic pistol and around his chest was a Heckler & Koch 9mm MP5 submachine-gun.

Trucco saw the leading Mercedes briefly through the trees. There was very little sound, much of it being absorbed by the forest. Suddenly a vibrant noise shattered the calm; the machine-like rattle of a woodpecker scything through the wood. Trucco closed his eyes and swore softly beneath his breath. His finger had tightened perceptibly on the trigger. Had it not been for the fact that the sound of the woodpecker had been evident since early morning, he would probably have mistaken it for gunfire.

The car appeared, moving effortlessly up the slope. He brought the rifle up to his cheek and peered through the telescopic sight. The crossed hairs danced momentarily on the car, coming to rest on the white mark left imprinted on the driver's door. The mark had been placed immediately below the driver's shoulder. Trucco raised the sights until they were bearing on a point about eight inches above the mark. Although he couldn't see the driver through the darkened windows, he could visualize exactly where his head and shoulders were. It was as though the man's outline was etched on the glass.

Conor watched the first car go by. He was crouched, out of sight, a few metres off the road. The second car came into view, gliding smoothly towards him. He tensed and increased his grip on the limpet bomb.

Joseph had positioned himself on a curve just above the point where Trucco was hiding. They knew that once the car had been hit, it would not make the bend and would probably run into the trees. It was Joseph's task to ensure no one came out of that car with guns blazing.

Trucco moved the gun-sight, following the mark with extreme accuracy. As the car reached the point in the road almost opposite him, he raised the crossed hairs and squeezed the trigger. Through the magnified image in the telescopic sight he saw the driver's window crystallize for a moment and then cave in as the hollow-tipped bullet shattered the driver's skull.

Immediately the car slowed as the dead man's foot slipped from the accelerator. The bodyguards in the back seat knew immediately what had happened and were opening their doors before the car had come to rest. The first one out of the car died in a hail of bullets from Joseph's gun. The second man took a bullet in the chest from Trucco. He was flung backwards by the impact and was thrown from the car like a discarded cloth.

Schiller's driver reacted instantly. His training took control of his movements and he jammed the brakes on, intending to slam the car into reverse. It was almost his last thought as Breggie shattered the tinted window with a long burst from the Uzi. Above the cacophony of sound in the car was the sudden, frightened cry of a baby and the terrified, witless scream from Joanna.

Conor kept his mind on the third car. As it passed him he raced from his hiding place and whacked the limpet bomb on the side panel of the rear door. He threw himself backwards and rolled away from the car. In just a few seconds he heard the dull crump as the car ballooned under the inward explosion of the bomb.

The wheels on the car collapsed outwards and two of its doors blew out. Conor was on his feet instantly. He ran to the car and pushed his Heckler & Koch submachine-gun into the space once occupied by three live humans. He emptied the magazine, spraying it round the car to ensure there was absolutely no chance of anyone surviving.

In less than a minute, all three cars had been immobiliszd and all the occupants except Schiller, Joanna and the infant were dead. It was bloody carnage. An execution skilfully carried out and one from which none of the intended victims could possibly survive.

Breggie opened the door of the limousine and beckoned Schiller to get out. He looked terrified. His skin had lost its colour and he seemed to have aged ten years. The flesh on his skull was like parchment, and the horror in his face was as deep and dark as the most frightening of all his nightmares. He couldn't move his body. He was rigid with fear. Except his hands; they shook violently as he held them up in an ineffectual attempt to protect himself. Breggie reached in and pulled him bodily from the car.

Joanna had stopped screaming. She was intelligent enough to know that these beasts were not about to kill her. For the moment she was safe. Her mind filled itself with all kinds of eventualities; what might become of her, of them. But although she wasn't screaming, she was terrified out of her life. She clung to her baby both to protect the infant and to garner some ridiculous comfort from the baby's touch. The baby was still crying. Its little hands were working the air and sobs racked its tiny frame. Joanna tried to calm the infant, holding it close to her, kissing the wetness of the baby's tears.

'Get out!'

Breggie's command to Joanna was screamed at her. There was urgency in the woman's voice that scared Joanna even more. She hesitated at first but knew resistance was futile. She climbed out of the car, still clutching the baby.

Schiller found his voice at last and started to protest. 'What is the meaning of this outrage?' It was pathetically weak and died on his lips. He couldn't comprehend it all. He was a man used to absolute power and control. Nobody dared challenge him. To do so would have been futile. Yet here were people who had put themselves above his power. They had challenged it with awesome swiftness and terrifying results. He tried to voice his protest again but there was such an aura of evil menace around the figure that stood before them that he could not find the courage. He felt useless and ashamed, and cursed the frailness that old age had brought to his body.

Breggie ignored him and spoke directly to Joanna.

'Give me the baby.'

Joanna couldn't respond. Her maternal instincts were as powerful in her as any mother. The demand from Breggie did not register.

'I said give me the baby!' Breggie held her hand out. In her other hand was the Uzi which was pointing at the ground. She felt relaxed and in control of herself. She knew, however, that time was not on their side. Soon the security guards at the top of the hill would realize something was wrong. They might assume one of the cars had broken down, but whatever they thought, someone would be coming down that road to investigate. If they had been able to hear the gunfire, much of which would have been cloaked by the trees, they would be bringing an army down with them.

'No.' Joanna pulled the baby closer as if that simple act was sufficient to make the woman change her mind.

Suddenly Schiller found his voice. 'Go away. Please. I will pay you anything you like. Anything.'

Breggie ignored him and kept her eyes on Joanna. 'You will give the baby to me. Now!'

'No!' Joanna screamed at her. 'I will not. You have no right.'

Breggie swung her fist at Joanna's unprotected jaw. The blow was so swift and unexpected that Joanna was unable to avoid it. Breggie's fist crashed into her jaw and sent her flying. The baby fell from her arms, but before it hit the ground, Breggie scooped the infant up and clutched it to her camouflage jacket. Then she turned quickly and ran into the forest.

Joanna lay on the ground, not moving. Schiller looked on in horror as the masked figure of Breggie de Kok and his grandson disappeared. He glanced down at Joanna. More in hope than anything else, he looked up the road towards the silent Mercedes. It had rolled to a stop, its bonnet hard up against a tree. Down the road the other car was like a collapsed ball. He knew his men were all dead. The ferocity and speed of the attack left him in no doubt. He bent down and knelt beside Joanna. He took her hand and massaged it gently. He felt hopeless. All around him was death and silence.

All but the stark, vibrant sound of a woodpecker.

CHAPTER TWO

Someone claimed they had reached the scene of the crime within five minutes of the last shot being fired. No one bothered to ask how such an accurate assessment could be made. The police, however, had reached the scene within four minutes of a call being made from the cell phone of the security guard who had reached Schiller first.

Within seconds the senior police officer had called for a massive back-up. All available units were ordered to the area as the hunt for the killers began. The highest priority had immediately been put on this one. As the police units converged, so the wires began buzzing on the news services and television networks. Reuters set up a special desk and ran a dedicated computer link in so that no other low priority news item could possibly delay the smallest gem of information on this most dramatic attack on one of the world's most powerful men.

A world media hungry for information were already setting their satellite dishes up and those fortunate enough to be within 200 miles of the place were driving down motorways eager to snatch the smallest advantage over their terrestrial rivals.

Within twenty minutes of the security guard's cry for help from his cell phone, the senior officer on the scene was Oberkommissar Erich Hoffman, of the *Zentrale Kriminalitatsbekampfung*. This department, the ZKD, was the equivalent of the British CID. Hoffman was thirty-eight years of age and had served in the *Bundespolizei* from his cadet-ship as a seventeen-year-old. All of his service career, with the exception of the first two years out of cadet training, he had been with the ZKD. He was renowned as a hard man and blessed with the patience of Job. All of his subordinates respected him. Very few crossed him.

He stood quietly surveying the carnage. Beside him was Obermeister Uwe Jansch. They had already organized teams to secure the entire area from the media, the public and anybody else who might trample vital evidence in their efforts to get a closer look. While forensic experts began their painstaking examination of the cars, the bodies and the surrounding area, the two policemen stood quietly contemplating the carnage.

The lead car contained three bodies; all male. Schiller's limousine contained just the body of the dead driver. Schiller himself and Joanna were up at the house under police protection and receiving medical treatment. The last car had four bodies inside; three male and one female. It had been quickly established that the female was the baby's private nurse, Helga; a young woman whose life and career had been tragically cut short by the selfish aims of violent people.

Hoffman felt the anger rise up in his chest. Like any policeman, he always made a silent promise to find the perpetrators of any particularly nasty crime, come what may. This, of course, was no different and he made the same promise: whoever carried out this carnage would be brought to book, one way or another. He knew that as a policeman, he could only bring these people to court, but he knew that, given the chance, he would put a bullet in each of them with his own hand.

He turned, his foot scraping noisily on the gravel, and began walking up the slope towards Schiller's limousine. He could hear a woodpecker somewhere among the trees, but ignored it. Jansch followed. They paused beside the car. There was little left that was recognizable as the driver's head. Blood and flesh congealed on the leather upholstery. In amongst it shards of broken glass glittered abominably like small gems on a madman's canvas. They could hear the persistent buzz of the gathering flies.

Hoffman waved his hand across his face to ward of a fly and moved on to the lead car. Its bonnet was pressed up against the trunk of a tree. The driver was still sitting in his seat but had slumped against the wheel. He had been shot through the head. The entry point of the bullet was relatively clean. The other side of his head wasn't there. The three dead passengers, two inside the car and one lying at a crazy angle in the road, had all been killed by machine-gun fire.

Hoffman was already forming a picture in his mind of how the attack had been carried out, but what intrigued him more than the skill, total ruthlessness and speed of its execution was the fact that the act of kidnapping Schiller's grandson had even been contemplated.

He turned suddenly to Jansch.

'Why would you want to kidnap Herr Schiller's grandson?'

Jansch looked at his boss. He arched his eyebrows. 'I wouldn't.'

'I know you wouldn't. But amuse me, please.'

Jansch studied the car for a moment. 'Leverage,' he said eventually.

Hoffman's eyebrows lifted. 'That's interesting. Not money?'

Jansch shook his head. 'Must have cost them a small fortune to set this one up, so they must have money behind them; no doubt about it. It has to be something they want and I don't think its money.'

Hoffman considered Jansch's assessment. He had never met Schiller, but knew enough about the movers and shakers of this world to know that Schiller came out at the very top. The absolute top.

'You are right, of course, Uwe,' he acknowledged. 'But why kidnap a baby? Schiller wouldn't budge on that. Would he?'

Jansch coughed and rolled his shoulders in a shrug to ward off a sudden chill that was seeping into his bones. The sun was still high in the sky, but it made little difference to the sense of horror that Jansch felt. Hoffman's statement that Schiller would not budge was empirical: simply an experienced policeman's observation.

'You believe he would sacrifice the child rather than concede to the kidnappers?' Jansch asked him.

Hoffman nodded slowly. 'Nobody gets to Herr Schiller's position without a streak of ruthlessness in him, and I expect he could be ruthless enough whenever he wanted to.' He sighed deeply. 'But I suppose it depends what the kidnappers' demands are.'

The sound of someone approaching cut through their subjective discussion. They both turned to see one of the forensic team, dressed in a white overall and rubber boots, walking towards them. He stopped, glancing quickly at the car. He was carrying a small evidence bag.

'Sir, it looks like the kidnappers were here overnight,' he said to Hoffman, holding up the bag. 'We found some human excrement.' He pointed a thumb in the general direction. Hoffman curled his lip.

'You are sure it isn't dogshit?' Jansch asked phlegmatically.

The forensic officer was unimpressed. 'The lab will confirm that for us, but I'm quite sure it's human.'

Hoffman smiled. Jansch had a way of ruffling feathers. 'Of course you are. We'll get a DNA sample, won't we?'

In their fight against crime, all well-run security forces world wide were building up data banks of genetic fingerprints gleaned from DNA tests. The data banks were by no means complete, but if a criminal had been arrested and convicted by any of the German Police Forces, his or her genetic fingerprints would be on computer file. Interpol would also have a comprehensive DNA data bank for the use of all European police forces. It would be a major boost to the investigation if this particular killer was on file with their own police force, but, if not, a trace would be put out through the services of Interpol.

'The information should be on your desk by the morning, sir.'

'That will be too late,' Hoffman informed him. 'I want the results on my desk this evening. Understood?'

'Yes sir.' He nodded, wondering just how much the police chief understood about laboratories and testing DNA samples, and walked away muttering to himself.

Jansch watched the man go. 'I have a gut feeling that all we shall learn from that is what the man had for dinner last night.'

Hoffman grinned. 'Pessimist, what makes you think it was a man? It could have been a woman. Someone has got to look after the baby.'

Conor had no idea where they were going. The inside of the van was lit only by the light that filtered in from a curtain drawn between them and Joseph Schneider who was driving. Breggie sat behind the driver's seat. She had the baby with her and had already given the infant a bottle of milk. The child was asleep now. Earlier Conor had lit a cigarette and had been ordered to put it out by Breggie because of the baby. It was ironic, he thought, that she could kill so ruthlessly but consider the health of an infant because of someone smoking.

The rear windows of the van had been blacked out so nobody could see out. Nor, for that matter could anybody see in. Inside the van with Conor and Breggie were the rest of the team: Karl Trucco, Franz, Heinz and Michael. Franz was the man who had impersonated the security guard at the bottom gate. Heinz and Michael were the two police impostors who had led the convoy from the hospital and signalled to

Trucco that the convoy was on its way.

At first the team had been jubilant, still high on their success. The plan had been brilliantly executed. Their escape route through the hillside forest to the perimeter fence had been well marked and meant that they were on their way, inside the van within five minutes of the attack. Now they were sitting silently with their own thoughts.

Conor tried guessing in which direction they were travelling by judging the sunlight filtering through the curtain. He reckoned there would be a back-up car travelling with them in case the van broke down or some other unplanned event compromised them. It made sense that the organization, whoever they were, would have a contingency plan should anything go wrong.

He decided they must be on an *autobahn* now because the van had been motoring steadily without turning for much of the journey. He wanted a cigarette but knew there was no point antagonizing Breggie. It wasn't that he was afraid of the girl, far from it, but inside the back of the van was no place for an argument. And he sensed the others were also offended by the thought of him smoking in such a confined space. So he retreated into his own world and gave up wondering where they were heading or how long it might be before they reached their destination.

It was two hours after beginning their journey that Joseph turned into an estate on the edge of a wooded area. The engine laboured briefly as they followed the road up a hill. At the lower end of the estate, the houses were relatively close together, but as they reached the summit of the hill, the road levelled out and each house had a larger area of land to itself and much more privacy.

They all felt the van turn sharply and then slow to a stop. Joseph got out of the van. They heard a garage door open. Then Joseph was back in the van and it moved with a lurch until it came to rest again. The engine died and they waited in the encroaching silence until Joseph opened the van's rear doors.

Conor led the others out of the van in relief after being cramped up for so long. It was quite spacious inside the garage and there was all the usual bric-à-brac one finds in most suburban garages. He immediately pulled out a cigarette and lit up. Breggie glared at him as she swept by.

'Don't bring that rotten thing into the house,' she snapped at him.

25

Conor gave her a blank look and drew the smoke down deep into his lungs. The others said little as they followed Joseph through an internal door. Conor let them go, enjoying his cigarette. He wasn't happy with the situation by any means because he wasn't in control. And he was used to knowing exactly what the plan was, what the alternatives were and a way out should he need it.

They had been told, by Joseph and Breggie, that after the operation they would be brought to a safe house where they would be paid off. He didn't like that either; he would have preferred to have gone back to his flat in Cologne, lay low for a couple of days, and then pick up his money.

He shrugged; better to remain careful and expect the unexpected, he thought and dropped the cigarette on the floor where he crushed it with the heel of his boot. He then went back to the rear of the van and opened the doors. Inside was an Adidas sports bag. All their weapons were there. Breggie had insisted that they were 'clean' in case they were stopped by a traffic patrol. This had been much against Conor's better judgement but, potentially, Breggie and Joseph were their paymasters and he had little choice but to agree, particularly as Trucco and the others had tossed their weapons into the bag without a murmur. It had been suggested they dump the weapons and have someone else pick them up for disposal, but this had been vetoed by Joseph. Conor knew there was always a chance the weapons would be found and the forensic scientists would garner valuable clues from them. Joseph was right; far better for the organization to remove and dispose of the weapons later.

He pulled his Browning automatic pistol from the bag and stuffed it in his inside pocket. Then he slipped a couple of spare magazines into another pocket. He would like to have taken the Uzi but that would have been rather obvious. He felt a little better now. He zipped the bag up and closed the van doors. Then he went into the house where he found most of the team in the dining-room. The television was on but some of them were reading magazines. Breggie was in the American-style open kitchen area with Joseph. They were talking.

Conor went into the kitchen and poured himself a cup of coffee which somebody had made. They had eaten sandwiches in the van so he wasn't particularly hungry. Nevertheless, he was looking forward to a hot meal. He took his coffee into the room where the others were sitting. They took little notice of Conor as he made himself comfortable in a vacant chair.

He wondered about them. He had no idea how they had been recruited. He had been approached by Schneider in a restaurant. In Conor's world of secrecy and opaque understanding, it didn't surprise him that somehow he had been found by their organization. He assumed it had been his links with the IRA. Perhaps his masters had passed on his credentials because they had no further use for him.

It was academic really as far as Conor was concerned. So long as it was work they were offering and bearing gifts of ready cash, he was willing to listen. And Schneider was promising cash by the bucketful.

Conor assumed the others had been chosen for their respective talents. His was explosives and an ability to kill. He had got to know Karl Trucco, the American, quite well and liked him. It seemed he had been some kind of right-wing militant in the USA and had fled the country for his own safety. But whatever the American's politics or affiliations, the only thing he had in common with the man was this job.

He was introduced to Breggie shortly after his first meeting with Schneider. Something in Breggie's manner made Conor mistrust her from the start. He couldn't put his finger on it but went along with his own instincts. As far as he was concerned she was to be kept at arm's length, and the sooner he was out of that house the better he would feel.

'When do we get paid, Joseph?'

It was Franz who had spoken. The others looked up. Breggie turned round. She was holding a baby's milk bottle in her hand. Conor assumed she had just made it up in the kitchen. She said something to Joseph and left the room. They could hear the sound of her footsteps on the stairs.

'Breggie has to feed and change the baby first,' Joseph replied. 'When she comes down I shall go and get your money.'

Franz looked disappointed. 'You mean it isn't here?'

Joseph shook his head. 'It would have been too risky. The house could have been broken into any time.'

'So where is it?' Conor asked.

Joseph shrugged. 'It's in a safe place. Breggie will stay here with the baby while I'm gone – if that's what you're worried about,' he added.

Trucco went back to his magazine. Conor continued to feel uncomfortable but could do nothing about it. The others seemed to be quite happy with the situation though and Conor wondered, for a moment, if he was worrying over nothing.

Nothing at all.

Hoffman was still studying the wreck of the car which had taken the force of the limpet bomb when he heard a car pull up. He turned in the direction of the noise and swore quietly under his breath. Jansch heard his boss and watched as the car came to a stop. The door opened and a tall, very well-dressed man got out. On either side of the road, the pine trees that stood tall and elegant seemed to pale against the invisible but almost tactile aura that emanated from the man. It was Dr Aaron Kistler, President of the North Rhine-Westphalia Police.

Kistler was more of a politician than a policeman; a man who had little time for the realities of police work and was more interested in the public face of the force and the importance and esteem of his own office and his own person. He held sway over one of the finest police forces in the Federal Republic and demanded total respect from all his subordinates, which he received in public but rarely in private. He walked the short distance from his official car to the wreck by which Hoffman and Jansch were standing.

'Good day, Herr Hoffman.' He ignored Jansch. 'What progress are you making?' It was typical of him not to enquire about the number of deaths that had occurred or how any survivors might be getting on.

'None yet, sir,' Hoffman responded flatly. 'It's a little early. But we do know it was a well-planned and skilfully executed attack.'

Kistler quickly scanned the scene. Even he was aware that he would be more of a hindrance than a help; his visit here was merely cosmetic, more for public consumption than anything else.

'Dreadful business,' he said, looking at the carnage with a deep frown creasing his forehead. Then his expression changed and it brightened.

'I am going up to Herr Schiller's residence,' he informed Hoffman. 'I expect to have good news for him within a day or so, and for that reason I want you to spare no one and nothing in the search for the kidnappers. You must, *must*,' he emphasized with a moving finger, 'drop everything else and draw in as much manpower as you can possibly muster on this. You will have my fullest support. And I want to be briefed daily. Understood?'

'Thank you sir,' Hoffman answered drily, knowing that Kistler's fullest support would not get them one millimetre closer to finding the killers.

Kistler dipped his head in a perfunctory nod and returned to his car. Hoffman and Jansch stood aside as Kistler's chauffeur manoeuvred the car past the wrecks. Despite the obvious ramifications of the attack, Kistler seemed strangely ambivalent and unmoved by it all.

At that moment, Jansch's mobile phone rang. He pulled it from his belt and lifted it to his ear. Hoffman watched him answering in mono-syllables and thanking somebody. He snapped the phone shut and slipped it back into the waistband of his trousers.

'They've found the police car, sir. It was burned out.'

'Crew?'

'No sign yet. Forensic are on it, but they don't hold out much hope.'

Hoffman was thoughtful for a moment. 'Get on to the military,' he said after a while. 'See if we have a satellite scan. From sunrise this morning; anything that passed over.'

'They're not going to like that, sir.'

'Bugger what they like. Probably find Schiller's company built the satellites they're using anyway.'

Jansch allowed himself a smile. Schiller owned satellites and companies that built space rockets. But he didn't own military secrets or anybody else's for that matter. He knew his boss didn't expect miracles though. This idea was a long shot; any still photographs taken at the time of the kidnap might help the experts to identify something that would lead them to the kidnappers.

'Shall I take your car, sir?'

Hoffman shook his head. 'No, I'll have to get up to Schiller's place and start tugging the forelock. Clean up the bullshit Kistler leaves behind. Grab one of the patrol cars. Call me the moment something new develops.' He sighed heavily. 'We've got to catch these bastards, Uwe. Never mind Kistler or Schiller or whoever else pokes their nose in; we've simply got to.'

*

29

It was close to midday when an El Al Jumbo jet landed at Frankfurt Airport. In the business class section, Levi Eshkol glanced up from his copy of *Time* magazine and peered through the window. He looked up at the cabin clock and reset his watch to Federal time. He still had several hours in hand before he was due at his meeting later that evening. He would eat a light lunch first before driving to the pre-planned rendezvous. Later he would dine with his colleagues and maybe drink a little wine; a celebration perhaps.

Levi Eshkol was a native of Israel. He had been born in a kibbutz near Jerusalem forty-five years earlier. He had no other family now. His father had died in the *Yom Kippur* war, one of the children of Israel who had escaped from Nazi Germany to find sanctuary in Palestine. His mother had died a few years after his father.

Eshkol had shown great potential as a scholar and had been widely tipped for a senior role in government. He studied law at Haifa University and completed his doctorate before his twenty-first birthday. He had a brilliant future ahead of him but, to the surprise of many of his close friends, chose not to pursue a career in the corridors of power.

Levi Eshkol became a 'fixer'; a man who worked behind the scenes to achieve a satisfactory conclusion for his clients. In the powerful world of Middle East politics, public deals were merely the gloss on the cake. Politics on the hoof by American emissaries, brokering deals for consumption by the world media, were never possible without men like Levi Eshkol.

It was because of Levi's brilliance, his connections and his knowledge of international law coupled with complete discretion that he was able to move easily among the powerbrokers of this world. But for all the doors that opened for Levi Eshkol, he remained a faceless enigma.

He cleared customs and immigration very quickly and was inside the main terminal building within minutes. He only ever travelled with hand luggage which saved him the trouble of jostling with other travellers at the baggage carousels.

As he passed the news-stands he could see the later editions of the newspapers screaming out banner headlines SCHILLER KIDNAP. He picked up a copy of *Bild Zeitung* and hurriedly scanned the opening paragraphs. A frown gathered on Eshkol's face. To any passer-by it might have appeared that he was naturally troubled by the kidnap and multiple killings. That much was true, but for a very different reason. He brought some change out of his pocket and paid for the newspaper.

The meeting he was attending that afternoon was now about to take on a different agenda. He tucked the paper under his arm and went off to catch his connecting flight to Osnabruk.

Hoffman had seen enough. The place was crawling with forensic experts, detectives, mortuary attendants and official photographers. They would all do their stuff and have all the relevant information on his desk as soon as it was physically and humanly possible. Everybody wanted to score on this one. He walked up to his official car and climbed into the back seat.

For a while he sat there gathering his thoughts. It occurred to him that he should phone his wife and explain that he would probably be late. If he did it now, he wouldn't forget. His driver sat patiently waiting for instructions. The interior of the car smelled of stale tobacco, impinging on the familiar smell of the leather upholstery. He wondered what it must be like, cocooned in a car, fighting to avoid a hail of bullets, knowing there was no escape. He pulled a cigar box from his inside pocket and took out a Canadian Reas half corona. He lit up, blowing the smoke carefully out of the open window.

His wife, Elke, answered the phone almost immediately.

'Hallo, *liebchen*, it's me.'

'Are you on that awful kidnap?' she asked. It was always nice to hear her voice, even if they had only spoken a few hours earlier at breakfast.

He drew heavily on the cigar, pulling the smoke deep into his lungs. 'Of course,' he answered. 'Kistler's poking his nose in as well.'

'He'll be a tremendous help,' she remarked acidly. 'I suppose this means you'll be late again?'

'I'm afraid so. I'll stay at the office tonight, but I'll come home for breakfast.' The end of the cigar glowed again. He expelled the smoke. 'I'll ring you when I can.'

'Good, and when you do finally come home, I'll introduce you to your children again. Just in case they've forgotten who you are.'

She was teasing him, he knew that, but lately the joke was getting a little tedious. He wondered just how much longer it would be before his wife began openly resenting his job. She had asked him more than once to resign from the police and find work in the private sector, but she had never laboured the point. In fact, she was quite philosophical about it.

'I love you sweetheart, speak to you again.'

He switched the phone off and told his driver to take him up to Schiller's residence.

He reached Schiller's sprawling villa after going through a security check at the barrier. What was incredible about this place, he thought to himself, was that all the security was at the top of the hill rather than at the bottom. But then, several kilometres of perimeter fence through the woodland on the lower slope would be difficult to police properly.

He found his boss, Dr Kistler, talking quietly with the billionaire industrialist. They were in a room which had a commanding view of the River Mosel threading its way through the pine covered hills towards Luxembourg in the west. The huge sliding windows to the balcony were closed and outside an armed policeman patrolled. A mite unnecessary now, thought Hoffman.

Kistler looked up as Hoffman was shown into the room. He acknowledged him and spoke to Schiller. The old man turned his head. He looked pale and shaken. Hoffman greeted him.

'Herr Schiller, *guten tag*.' He lowered his head just a little in greeting. 'First let me tell you how deeply saddened I am by the attack on you and your staff, and the kidnap of your grandson.' Schiller tipped his head forward but said nothing. Hoffman went on, 'I can offer you nothing concrete at the moment, but will say that we are doing everything in our power, naturally, to bring the perpetrators of this terrible crime to justice.' He glanced at Kistler. 'I am quite sure we shall have something firmer to work on within an hour or so, and, perhaps, in a few days will be in a better position to bring you news.'

Schiller shook his head slowly. 'You're as bad as Dr Kistler, Hoffman. I would have hoped for something less sycophantic from you.' His voice was firm, demonstrably so.

Hoffman looked at Dr Kistler who appeared to be deeply wounded. Hoffman could have kicked himself; he had dished out that tripe more for Kistler's benefit than Schiller's.

'Then perhaps I should tell you that we stand little chance of finding the criminals, and our only hope for a quick end to this is that they send a ransom demand which you will pay for your grandson's return. Then all that will be left for us to do is to catch the killers as quickly as possible.'

Kistler stood up suddenly like a towering volcano. His dark eyes levelled at Hoffman like the barrels of a shotgun. 'There is little to be gained by that kind of defeatist language, Oberkommissar Hoffman. Your duty is clear; you will find these murderers and return Herr Schiller's grandson unharmed. Is that clear?'

'Perfectly, Dr Kistler,' Hoffman agreed. He turned his attention to Schiller. 'I will need to interview all members of your staff, sir, including yourself and Frau Schiller.'

Schiller waved his hand at the detective. 'Get on with it then, but remember this: if any harm befalls my grandson, someone's head will roll. I trust you understand that?'

Hoffman new exactly what that meant; with Kistler eating out of Schiller's hand like a pet dog, there was little hope of natural justice for him if this kidnap ended in disaster.

They had watched the news reports on television for most of the afternoon. None of them had felt much like playing cards or talking. All they wanted was their money so they could leave. As far as the media were concerned it was the new Baader Meinhof gang. Some had even resurrected the Red Army Faction. They were all at it. For all Conor Lenihan cared it could have been Osama Bin Laden who had organized the whole thing. He was simply a mercenary doing a job of work. Now he just wanted to get back to his flat in Cologne and look around for more work. Maybe the Middle East, he thought.

The sound of the van outside told them that Schneider was back. Breggie had been upstairs with the baby while he had been away. She came down within a few minutes of hearing the car. Conor thought she looked agitated and that familiar gut feeling returned.

As Schneider walked in, Breggie glanced at him quickly. Conor saw the questioning lift of her eyebrows and the alarm bells started ringing. He wondered if he was becoming paranoid about the woman. He had met psychopaths before, served with them in the SAS, and this woman certainly fitted the frame. Signals flashed from her like semaphore when she spoke. She concealed her power behind a mask of overt sensuality, but the latent, psychopathic tendencies were never completely hidden from men of Conor's intuitive reasoning, and he could read the signals clearly. He was not afraid of her but he knew, instinctively, that to tangle with her unprepared would be like tackling a Black Widow spider.

Schneider placed a small, leather holdall on the table. 'Your money's in there. Better count it.'

Trucco took the bag and drew the zip back. He turned the bag over and several bundles of cash spilled out on to the table top. They all reached forward and drew their due towards them. Conor flicked through the bundles that were marked with his name. As he had requested, one bundle contained Euros, the rest American dollars. He had no need to count it; the code, ironically, was honour among thieves. He picked up his jacket from the back of the chair where it had been most of the afternoon and stuffed the bundles into his pockets. Despite the code of honour, he slipped the jacket on.

'You will not see us again,' Breggie said suddenly. 'But I have been instructed to thank you for your part in securing Germany's future.' It was all very wooden, as though she was reading from a script. 'When Joseph and I have left, you may go whenever you like. Please do not leave any trace of your presence here.' She glanced over her shoulder towards the window. 'It is almost dark now, so it will be reasonable for you to wait about thirty minutes. There is a car at the bottom of the hill. The keys are in the glove box. There is a road map in the car. Good luck. Don't get caught.'

'We might say the same to you, Breggie,' Trucco told her. It was Schneider who responded though.

'We won't get caught,' he said, a confident smirk on his face. 'I can guarantee it.' He picked up a small case that Breggie had placed on the floor and winked at them. '*Auf wiedersehen.*'

Breggie was already at the door, the baby tightly wrapped and clutched to her bosom. Conor thought she and Joseph looked just like any young married couple. Nobody would take any notice of them, unlike five men walking through the night to a car that had been parked nearby.

As the door closed on Breggie and Joseph, Conor became troubled by the thought of getting into a parked car and turning on the ignition.

He stood up, restless, thoughts of car bombs trickling through his mind and walked to the window. The vertical blinds had been closed all afternoon. He eased one aside and watched the van disappear from view beyond the end of the driveway. Rain spotted the pane of glass and he let the blind fall back into place.

His colleagues had counted their money and were looking quite happy with themselves. No thoughts of car bombs on their minds, Conor mused. He wondered if he should tell them of his fears; that Breggie and Joseph were not to be trusted. The rain spattered against the glass, pushed by a strengthening wind. He pulled a cigarette from a packet, holding it in his mouth for a while; thinking. Perhaps he would just tell them he had decided to make his own way; leave them to their own fate. Perhaps he was just scaremongering.

He walked into the kitchen and lit the cigarette. At the end of the kitchen a door led into a small utility room giving access to the garage. He had planned to smoke outside but because of the wind and rain he decided to use the garage. It was quite large and it would give him the solitude he needed to think a lot clearer without being distracted by the others. He checked the time. In twenty five minutes they would all be walking out of there, either to their own kind of freedom or death.

Melodramatic, that's what it was, he thought; I'm being melodramatic. He closed the internal garage door behind him and leaned against a bench running the length of one wall. He stayed like that, smoking his cigarette until at last, he made his decision: he would go back in there and tell the others what he suspected and let them make up their own minds. He would leave on his own.

He dropped the stub of his cigarette to the floor and lifted his heel to grind it out when the bomb exploded.

It had been placed beside a wall unit about one metre from the table around which the gang had been sitting. The blast wave shattered everything inside the confines of that room. The four men did not stand a chance as the pressure wave dismembered them piecemeal. The ceiling lifted and shot up through the upper floor as the blast hit the roof trusses and shattered the roof. All the windows disappeared as the force of the blast went through them like a cannon firing shrapnel, and furniture, ornaments, burning bedding and debris shot out in a pyrotechnic display of raining fire.

35

Conor heard and felt the blast, but in that single moment the percussive effect rendered him unconscious as he flew across the empty garage and crashed into the opposite wall. The bench against which he had been leaning was sliced in two as the internal wall caved in under the force of the bomb. Huge chunks of brickwork spun aimlessly and the ceiling of the garage collapsed as the internal support disappeared and the weight of some of the shattered roof trusses bore down on it.

In amongst this terrifying maelstrom a fierce heat burned everything in its path as it seared through the building. Fanned by the pressure wave it scorched everything on the outer edges of the blast, blackening all it touched. A long tongue of flame filled the remains of the utility room and punched its way into the garage where it ignited the traces of oil that had seeped into the concrete floor over several years. Half-empty tins of paint, domestic and industrial cleaning agents, methylated spirits, petroleum based products all started to explode in the small confines of the garage.

The outer steel door of the garage had been blown open but was still attached to the roller guides. The bottom corner of the door was bent out like a dog-eared page of a book and the whole thing hung limp and useless as palls of thick, black smoke funnelled out from beneath it. As the effects of the blast subsided, the flames took hold until they were roaring skywards and pulling in air beneath them, feeding oxygen into the centre of the fire. Within minutes the entire house was a raging inferno.

CHAPTER THREE

The lights from Levi Eshkol's Mercedes cut through the quickening darkness of the Teutoburger Wald as black clouds rolled in behind the hills. The wind whipped up little flurries of debris and the rain pushed hard against the windscreen. The wiper moved back and forth, clearing the rain in a steady stroke.

Eshkol drove without the radio on. He wanted silence, time to think. Beside him on the passenger seat was his briefcase in which he had placed the copy of *Bild Zeitung* which had caused him such consternation. Why had Schiller's grandson been kidnapped? The question had burned itself into his brain and he could only come up with one answer: it had to be the Covenant. It had to be the target. The question of *who?* would be dealt with at the meeting he was about to attend, although Eshkol was quite sure he knew who was behind it.

He drove carefully through the town of Bad Iburg, a charming spa resort that always attracted a multitude of tourists. But in the gathering gloom and darkness, not to mention his own state of mind, Eshkol had no time to think of the picturesque lake surrounded by beautifully tended gardens and the lush, green swathes of the lakeside, now colourless in the evening storm.

He turned left, negotiating the bend that would take him west towards his destination. The trees lined each side of the road and he was careful to keep his speed down for fear of missing the turning he was looking for. When the small junction came he nodded to himself in satisfaction and pulled the Mercedes into a sweeping turn. The road narrowed and took him up the side of the hill until he came to the gateway of a splendid Bavarian-style lodge.

He swung in, the lights from the car picking out the house momentarily. A flicker of lightning raced across the dark sky and Eshkol immediately wished he was back in his beloved Israel.

He parked the car and got out, taking his briefcase with him. He used the remote control to lock the car, leaving his small overnight bag on the back seat. Then he walked up to the front door of the house and rang the bell. Within moments he was ushered in and shown into a room in which four men were sitting. They all rose as he entered and he greeted them politely.

All of these men were known to Eshkol although he had barely met them a dozen or so times in the past. This was the first meeting they would have together. The first man he greeted was Alfred Weitzman, former Security Adviser to the President of the United States of America, now retired and a leading figure among American Zionists. The second man was Avi Binbaum, former head of Shin Bet, the internal counter intelligence agency in Israel, now retired. The third man was Louis Goldman, like Eshkol a native of Israel, now an influential South African businessman. The connection between these three men and Eshkol was that they were all experts in international and industrial law.

The fourth man was Alfred Hess. Unlike the others he was not a lawyer and was relatively young at thirty-five years of age. He was a German banker and member of the German Bundesbank.

The greetings over, Eshkol helped himself to a coffee from a Cona jug and returned to the table around which the others were sitting. He opened his briefcase and pulled out the *Bild Zeitung*. He really didn't have to say anything to the others; he was quite sure they had drawn similar conclusions, but nevertheless, he unfolded the paper and held it up for them all to see.

'Gentlemen, we have to assume the inevitable has happened; they have learned of the Covenant.'

Weitzman nodded his agreement. 'We knew the risks, Levi. Security was damn tight, but if you share a secret. . . .' He made a dismissive motion with his hand. 'I had my team screwed down so damn hard they probably didn't even know what the others were up to.'

'Very commendable, Alfred,' Levi told him dispassionately. 'I'm sure we all believed our security was watertight, but somehow it leaked.'

None of the men in that room would have dreamed of casting doubt on the fidelity of their teams, and it wasn't in their nature to look for a scapegoat. They were pragmatists, all of them, and their only course of action now was damage limitation and a speedy conclusion to their business.

'We discussed this before you came, Levi.' This was Hess, the German banker. 'Why Schiller's grandson was kidnapped and by whom. It has to be the Volkspartei and they want to stop Schiller signing the Covenant.' The others showed their agreement. Hess went on. 'Now we have to protect it. And ourselves,' he added ominously.

In referring to the Volkspartei, or the People's Party, Hess knew they were pointing the finger at one man: the leader himself, Franz Molke. Molke was a political animal, a politician to his well-manicured fingernails. Enigmatic, charismatic, he had carried the German people on a wave of popular support by declaring himself an opponent of the very things that antagonized them. He persuaded the people they were being oppressed by mindless bureaucracy, interfering European Courts, continuing harassment from member governments of the European Union, not to mention the flow of migrants from Eastern Europe. His asides and skilled rhetoric were often aimed at ethnic groups and included blacks, Jews, homosexuals, illegal immigrants, asylum seekers and any other pinko liberal who did not measure up to his idea of Aryan purity. In short he was the antithesis of the modern, fence-sitting politician and was never afraid to voice his Hitler-like opinions at any given opportunity.

The five men in that room were only too aware that Germany was on the brink of achieving everything it had failed to achieve in the previous century: domination of Europe. With the introduction of the single currency in member states of the Union, tacit control would eventually be handed to the Bundesbank, which was to be known as the Central European Bank. Three hundred million souls would be at the fiscal mercy of the bank's masters. Added to that was the certainty that all the European Governments would one day ratify the European Constitution. To control that mechanism would offer unprecedented power to its head. To have that power in a political environment where there was no potent opposition would effectively elevate a strong Chancellor of Germany to a position of supreme power over the new, super state. And the master of that super state would be at the zenith of a power that could equal the might of the United States.

Molke's timetable was perfect. His political ascendancy started with the reunification of East and West Germany. By forming coalitions with whichever party he could deal with, his own party eventually carried almost a third of the seats in the Bundestag, the lower house and main legislative organ in the Federal Republic. By the year 2000 the Bundestag had completed its move to the new Reichstag in Berlin, the traditional heart of German government.

Molke's party was on course to win enough support at the next general election to form a government. It was the belief of Eshkol, his colleagues and Manfred Schiller himself, that Molke would be the head of a new Nazi party. With control of the Bundesbank and domination of weak-minded member states Molke knew they would all fall into line behind his totalitarian diktat. Molke would find it easy to engineer himself into the seat of power as President of Europe, not for the paltry six months allotted to each member state, but permanently.

As it had been so eloquently put: once you have them by the balls, their hearts and minds will follow.

Molke was also a psycho. Running parallel to his party was an organization of thugs, criminals and other psychos. He used these people to eliminate opposition – sometimes permanently, where he believed it would be most helpful. He used all means in the book: intimidation, blackmail, and physical violence; whatever method would achieve results. The man was power crazy, intimidating and very, very clever. None of the crimes committed on his behalf could ever be traced back to him or his lieutenants.

Eshkol reflected for a moment on Hess's remarks, knowing the threat they were under. Now the Covenant had been put together they would all have to take extreme care.

'We have to hope that Herr Schiller will not be frightened off by these thugs.' he shrugged. 'However, we must be careful. Now, if I could have your contributions, gentlemen.'

Each of them had brought the paperwork, bound in ring binders that had been their team's responsibility. Each binder represented over a year's work. Accompanying the binders were computer discs on which they had copied their work. No human value could be placed on each binder or those discs, but the fiscal value of just one binder or disc would make a third-world country go weak at the knees.

They handed them over and Eshkol began the task of reading each one.

*

Breggie de Kok whooped with delight when she saw the house explode. They had driven away and motored out of the limits of the small hamlet, bringing the van to a spot overlooking the house. It had taken them about three or four minutes. Schneider had kept the engine running while Breggie lowered the window. Taking a small transmitter from the glove compartment she had switched it on, then pulled the small antenna out from its recess in the unit. She held it out at arm's length and pointed it towards the house.

At that moment Breggie felt the adrenalin coursing through her veins like a drug and the familiar wetness returned to her loins as she pushed the transmit button. As the house exploded, it changed night into day for several seconds. Schneider gave her no more than ten seconds to indulge her self-serving pleasure. Then he released the handbrake and drove the van away into the night.

Conor tried to open his eyes. One eye felt as though the eyelids were glued together. The other opened to what seemed like an impenetrable blackness. He could hear a roaring sound and was aware of an uncomfortable heat. There was also an acrid smell of burning solvent and paint. At first he did not know what had happened, but as consciousness returned, so too did his memory. He had been standing in the garage smoking a cigarette. There had been an explosion, but not because he had been smoking.

He twisted his body round and tried to sit up, but something was pressing against him. He put his hand up and touched its rough surface. It was like a brick wall and it felt hot. Behind him was another wall but that was cool. He realized then that he was up against the outside wall of the garage. The other brickwork, although he was still not aware of it, was part of the internal garage wall that had been blown across the garage by the explosion. It had come to rest at an angle against the outer wall and part of the bench that had shattered with the force of the blast.

Conor felt anger rising inside him but chose not to dwell on it. If he was to escape the predicament he was in, he needed to concentrate his efforts on finding a way out. There was little doubt in his mind that Breggie and Joseph had bombed the house, but his immediate priority was to get out.

41

He could feel a strong movement of air flowing across his body. The air was quite cool and he reasoned that this was being drawn in from outside. He twisted his body around so that his head was in the cool air stream. With his one good eye he peered into the gloom. He couldn't see anything clearly but he could now feel heat bearing down on him from the wreck of the internal wall. He knew he would die if he didn't get out soon.

He inched his way towards the source of the cool air until he came to the damaged garage door. The air was rushing in through the twisted corner where the metal had been bent outwards by the explosion. Conor was able to squeeze his frame beneath the damaged section until he had dragged his feet clear. His next move was not to stand and stare at the wrecked house in astonishment but to get as far away from it and as quickly as possible.

He turned away from the front driveway as people from neighbouring houses began to arrive, and limped to the rear of the house. There was plenty of cover there because of the trees, but the whole area was flooded in light by the flames from the house. He was desperate not to be seen so he dropped to his belly and crawled beneath the shrubs and ornamental conifers.

Until that moment, Conor had not been aware of any pain apart from the pain in his head. But now he could feel pain from his rib cage and wondered if he had cracked a rib or two. There was also a smell of scorching close to his face. At best he knew he would have been severely bruised and possibly suffering from surface burns.

He gritted his teeth and dragged himself clear of the rear of the house until he was finally in enough cover to stand and make for the trees beyond the rear garden. Once he was there, he dropped to the ground and leaned back against the bole of a tree. He could hear the sound of a siren somewhere in the distance and began cursing Breggie and Joseph for the bastards they were.

'Can you think of any reason, other than money, why anyone should want to kidnap your grandson?'

Hoffman was in Schiller's beautifully designed summer room overlooking the pine covered slopes of the Mosel valley. The light was fading earlier than usual because of the dark clouds coming up from the south west. The lower slopes were still caught in the sunlight, but their

42

colours soon dulled beneath the stormy shadows. The fading light matched the mood of the household in response to the apocalyptic nightmare that had been visited upon them all.

Kistler had left earlier, promising to move heaven and earth in his department's efforts in the search for the kidnappers. Hoffman had been more pragmatic: he had set up an incident room back at his headquarters in Bonn. Jansch was there running it for him at that moment. He had called in a team of officers from department KK11 of the ZKD. This department dealt with serious crimes. He had also drafted officers in from KK13, the organized crime specialists. Other units would be drafted in to help with the investigation, but not until it became clear which elements of this crime needed the particular skills of certain police departments.

He also had a team of officers at the house interviewing the staff. But for Schiller and Joanna, Hoffman would let no one but himself interview them. One other concession to that was a police secretary taking notes while he spoke to the great man and his English daughter-in-law.

Schiller glanced briefly at Hoffman and shook his head. 'That is not a particularly bright question. I am extremely wealthy, so by definition I am a target for every crank in Germany.'

'Nevertheless, Herr Schiller, it is a question I must ask,' Hoffman reminded him. 'And I would say that wealth does not necessarily have anything to do with it.'

Schiller glowered at him. 'What other reason can there be?'

Hoffman wondered if Schiller was being deliberately stupid, or genuinely believed that money was the only reason for kidnapping a one-week-old infant. He ignored the retort and asked Joanna.

'Can you think of any reason, Frau Schiller?'

Joanna looked extremely pale. She had obviously been crying for most of that appalling day and had put in a great deal of effort to come to this interview. Hoffman was in no doubt that she would be unable to tell him anything. But he was wrong.

'She was South African,' she said, not taking her eyes from the floor. It was said in such a matter-of-fact way that it took both men completely by surprise.

Schiller pivoted in his chair. The anger that had been in his face disappeared quickly. Hoffman tensed slightly. He leaned forward.

'How do you know that?'

Joanna looked at him. There was little expression in her face. 'She spoke to me in English. She had a South African accent.'

'She spoke to you in English?'

Joanna shrugged. 'Yes. Why not? Everybody knows I'm English. It's public knowledge.'

Hoffman could see a small, almost incandescent glimmer of hope. It was often the smallest, most innocuous piece of information that broke a case.

'But not everybody knows that you speak German.'

'I don't follow you.'

Hoffman hadn't expected her to. He explained what was causing him a little excitement. 'As far as I am aware, you never give interviews. Is that correct?'

Joanna nodded. 'It's an almost unwritten condition being a member of the Schiller family.' She looked at Schiller who showed his acquiescence by nodding slowly.

Hoffman stood up then. He found pacing the floor helped his train of thought. 'It could mean that she wasn't sure how good your German might be, which is why she spoke to you in your own language.'

'That's a fairly weak conclusion, Hoffman,' Schiller interjected. 'If she was South African as my daughter-in-law suggests, then she was merely talking to her in their common tongue.'

'Unless she was a Boer, then she might have spoken Afrikaans.'

'What does it matter, anyway?' Joanna asked in despair. 'How can it help?'

Hoffman took his eyes away from Schiller who was glaring at him again. He wondered if the old man was upset by the kidnap, or the fact that he was no longer in control. He spoke to Joanna.

'She might have been told to address you in English. Or she might even have spoken to you before.'

Joanna shook her head vigorously. 'No, I don't believe it.'

Hoffman didn't expect her to. 'Could you describe her to me?'

She shook her head. 'Not really. She was wearing a camouflage uniform. Rather like a paramilitary. And she had a ski mask pulled over her head. All I could see was her eyes.'

Joanna stopped there.

Hoffman waited for her to continue, but it was if she had seen something, or remembered something significant.

'What is it?' he asked. Schiller was now caught by this little development. He put a hand out to Joanna, quietly urging her to speak.

'Her eyes.' She looked at Hoffman. 'I'll never forget her eyes.' Neither of the men said a thing. They both waited. 'So sinister and so evil.' She looked at Schiller. 'Didn't you see it, Manfred?'

He apologized quietly. He hadn't of course. Fear had blotted it all out. 'I was afraid, *mein liebchen*, blind with terror I think.' His voice trembled a little as he spoke.

'I will never forget her eyes, never!' Joanna spoke with understated venom which Hoffman found quite understandable. He wondered, obliquely, what would happen if the two women ever came face to face.

'Frau Schiller, if we were able to produce any photographs of women we suspect, would you look at them?'

Joanna made a sarcastic grimace. 'You mean mug shots? Every time you see a picture of some hapless convict staring at the camera, their eyes always seem to be glazed over. I doubt if I could help you.'

'Not even if it was, say, a natural photograph?'

Joanna folded her arms, tucking each hand beneath under her arms. She rocked back and forth, tears beginning to well up. She kept her face down, trying hard not to cry.

'Oh my God, I could kill the fucking bitch. I could, I could.' She started sobbing. Schiller immediately went to comfort her. Hoffman knew the interview was at an end.

'We'll speak again tomorrow Herr Schiller.' He turned towards Joanna. 'Frau Schiller.' Hoffman expected no acknowledgement and got none as he indicated to the policewoman that they should leave.

Hoffman sat in his official car deep in thought as it negotiated the winding road away from Schiller's house. Something teased at his brain. A nagging thought that would not go away, one that made him think that Joanna had kept something from him.

'Do it now Jo-Jo! Now!'

Breggie was fighting with the buttons on Schneider's shirt, her fingers trembling with anticipation. They were sprawled on a long leather Chesterfield. Schneider was astride Breggie. He had been teasing her mercilessly. He knew what state she would be in because she was always the same after a field operation. He loved this moment; Breggie would implore him to make love to her as the lust within her swelled to almost uncontrollable levels. It was an adrenalin rush of pure emotion that drove her to such hedonism, and he knew just how far he would need to go before she became violent. It was a schizophrenic change of frightening proportions when her savagery seemed to be driven by manic lust.

Schneider had allowed that to happen once and regretted it. Breggie had beaten him with closed fists until he had been forced to subdue her with his own strength. When it was over, she had asked him to forgive her. She told him that she had demons inside her and did not know how to control them. Once she had started there was little she could do, if anything, to stop.

Breggie would very soon be at that point and Schneider knew it. As she ripped the last button from his shirt he turned her over and rode her like a rutting lion. Her cries of pleasure tore at his ears until the climax of their lovemaking burst upon them both. It brought them to a collapsed, breathless and enraptured state, leaving them exhausted but immeasurably content.

They lay like that, wrapped in each other's arms for several minutes. Schneider was drifting off to sleep when Breggie heard a sound from the small cot in which she had put the baby. She turned her head and glanced towards the infant. His small fingers moved and then settled. Breggie looked back at the top of Schneider's head, nestled uncomfortably on her breasts. With some effort she eased him off and slid from beneath him. She picked up Schneider's shirt from the floor and put it on. Then she padded across to the cot and pulled back the shawl to check the baby was OK.

Breggie and Schneider were in a small detached house in a suburb of Düsseldorf. They had never been there before. The house had been unoccupied and offered for sale with a local estate agent. An elderly couple had purchased the property and explained, unnecessarily, that they would only use the place occasionally. At other times their family might use it when visiting the area.

The new owners of the property had made no attempt to introduce themselves to the neighbours other than a passing greeting. Indeed, if anybody had asked about the new neighbours, they would have been told that they kept themselves very much to themselves and seemed to be away more than they were at home.

So, when Breggie and Schneider arrived at the house in the late evening, it would not have appeared unusual to anybody who might happen to have seen them. And the plan was that the two of them would be seen, very briefly, out with the baby like any young married couple. A Volkswagen car had been left in the garage for their use. And Joseph had planned to dump the van and use his own car, maintaining, he claimed, his own little bit of independence.

Breggie was quite happy with that arrangement. It was unlikely that either of them would be linked to the kidnap. Their identities were unknown to the police so their photographs were unlikely to appear in the newspapers. Breggie also knew they had powerful forces working for them so they had little to fear.

Conor closed his mind to the blasphemies he was bestowing upon the two evil bastards who had tried to kill him, and concentrated his efforts on getting away from the burning house as quickly as possible. He was still in pain from the battering he had taken in the explosion, but still able to think clearly. The place would soon be crawling with police and he had to be miles away by then.

Conor had no idea where he was, but that didn't concern him. Getting back to his apartment in Cologne was his first priority. The sound of the approaching siren was getting louder so he pushed himself away from the tree against which he had been resting and ran, as best he could, into the darkness.

The thought that was to keep him going, the over-riding aim, his *raison d'être* was to find Breggie de Kok and her twisted lover, Joseph, and make sure they both died in the same way as his late, lamented colleagues.

And to ensure they both knew why before they died.

On the table in front of Levi Eshkol were the four documents. Each document was lengthy and of a fair size. Eshkol had scanned the pages of each document, carefully turning each leaf and speed reading as he made steady and gratifying progress through them.

The four men who had brought the documents to the house were now talking quietly amongst themselves, giving Eshkol the opportunity to browse through the fruits of their labours. They had all played their part in what could prove to be one of the momentous turning points in modern Israel's chequered history.

Weitzman was responsible for the document covering the Americas. His legal team had worked in obsessive secrecy putting together the framework of the document. All members had been sworn to secrecy by Weitzman with the promise of great wealth when their work was completed. He had also promised them an uncertain future if news of their work leaked out.

The second document had been the responsibility of Binbaum. His team had covered Western Europe, but not the Federal Republic. All assets in central Europe had been included too. Conditions had been the same for his team as they had for Weitzman's.

Goldman held responsibility for South Africa and Australasia. His cloak of respectability hid his real politics but opened many doors, particularly in the one party states like Zimbabwe and Zaire. The third document was his.

Hess, naturally, had been in an excellent position to concentrate on Germany. He was able to assemble a hand-picked team from the 50,000 Jews who lived in the Republic. Their allegiance would be total and without question. No need for bribes but promises had been made by him nonetheless.

This left Eshkol. His own document was still in his briefcase. There was no need to scan the pages of course, but it covered Israel and other areas of interest that the other members of the group had been unable to cover. When he had finished reading through the other four, he pulled his own contribution from the briefcase and laid it carefully on top of the others. He felt an almost overwhelming relief even though their task was still not complete. But to reach this stage had been like coming to the end of one part of an extremely tedious and dangerous journey. The rest, God willing, should be relatively straightforward.

He smiled and stretched languidly, then placed his hand almost reverentially on the binders which he had stacked one on top of the other. There, on paper, was Manfred Schiller's entire empire. The others immediately stopped their quiet bubble of conversation and looked his way.

'Gentlemen,' he said. 'I give you The Eagle's Covenant.'

CHAPTER FOUR

It was midnight and Hoffman was back at his desk at police headquarters in Bonn. He had cleared it of all outstanding work, consigning most of it to an ambitious, young graduate policeman who was coming up for promotion. He had phoned his wife to tell her what she already knew, that he would not be coming home that night. A camp bed was made up in the corner of the room just inside the door of Hoffman's office. Jansch had wandered in and out a few times in the last hour and was now sitting opposite him.

'Well?' Hoffman asked, stifling a yawn. 'Is it good news? Have you caught the kidnappers?'

Jansch smiled at his boss's deprecating humour. 'No, but we have the results of the DNA sample.'

Hoffman sat up. 'Do we have a match?'

Jansch slid the file across the desk. 'Chap called Karl Trucco. There's a full profile on him in there.'

'Fill me in.'

'American. Member of a militia group in Michigan. Arrested in connection with the Alfred Murray Federal Building explosion in Oklahoma. That was in April, '95. FBI linked him with the Branch Davidian cult at Waco. Remember the siege? The Alfred Murray explosion was a couple of years after the Waco siege.' Hoffman stifled another yawn. Jansch continued, 'FBI thought he'd perished in the Waco fire.'

'He probably wasn't even there,' Hoffman mumbled. Most democratic police forces held the rather cynical view that the Waco siege had been handled badly by the FBI. Hoffman had concluded that too. 'They were never too sure of who was in that farm building or how many perished. Still,' he observed brightly, 'it gives us a name. Anything else?'

Jansch tapped the file. 'We're fairly sure of the weapons they used, but it's not a lot of use unless we can find the guns. We do know, however, what kind of device was used to blow up the third car.' He turned the pages of the file and ran his finger along a paragraph. 'It was a limpet stun bomb.'

Hoffman had never heard of such a device. 'I've never heard of them,' he said.

Jansch closed the file. 'It's a relatively new device. We got the information from the army. Made by an armaments company in the Czech Republic. The name's in there,' he added, pointing to the file. 'Can't pronounce it though. The device is clamped to the side of the vehicle by a powerful magnet. It has an inner, spring-loaded steel ring which activates the bomb. A shaped charge blows a neat hole in the body of the car followed later, milliseconds I am told, by a stun grenade which explodes about one metre after release. It's a device favoured by specialist forces when dealing with terrorist hijackings.'

'So why were the occupants all shot to death?' Hoffman asked him. 'It seems a trifle unnecessary if they have all been incapacitated.'

'Well, I spoke to an officer in the *Grenzschutzgruppe*.' This was Germany's crack anti-terrorist unit. 'Apparently it's the way they do things. Take no chances, you see. You have to make sure the terrorists are dead. Incidentally, the device would only be used, normally, when storming an aeroplane. Or a bus, perhaps. So long as it's a thin skinned vehicle. Quite effective I'm told.'

Hoffman considered the implication of what Jansch had just said. It was quite important.

'So the person who used it could quite possibly be a former member of one of the special forces?'

Jansch conceded it might be so. 'It's a possibility,' he agreed, 'but only a possibility; it takes no special skill to use one.'

Hoffman considered the ludicrous situation of advanced technology, as was the case of the stun grenade, having to be applied by the use of old-fashioned bravado. Whoever had whacked that grenade on the car had had to be quick and confident. And ruthless too.

'You'd better get on to Meckenheim. Fill them in on the details. They might have a name or two they can give us.'

Meckenheim was a village just south of Bonn. It housed the top, anti-terrorist clearing house in Europe where over 1,000 officers waged a covert war against militant extremism. All the top security services had a permanent liaison officer there, and all forms of terrorist threats, from whatever source of political and religious persuasion, were filtered through the complex and sophisticated data banks housed in the building.

'I've already done that, sir.'

'Good man,' Hoffman said, and meant it. Jansch was often one step ahead of the game. 'Now, what about satellite photos? Did we get any?'

Jansch shook his head. 'Nothing.'

Hofman's head bobbed up and down: another cul-de-sac. But it was a policeman's lot to wander up plenty of those. He yawned again and Jansch tried not to copy him even though he was just as tired as Hoffman.

'OK, Uwe, here's a little pearl for you. See what you make of it.' There was nothing to make of it really, but he wanted the seed planted in Jansch's subconscious.

'I have a feeling that Joanna Schiller is aware of the identity of one of the kidnappers. But she doesn't know it. Not yet anyway.'

It brought Jansch up like a jack in the box. Before he had a chance to say anything, Hoffman started to describe the interview with Schiller and Joanna.

'I believe that because of her reaction; the way she suddenly stopped, like you do when something occurs to you in conversation that could actually have an impact on what you're saying at the time. The way she stopped when she mentioned the kidnapper's eyes. It was just as if she had remembered that she had seen, or met the woman. It was quite uncanny.'

'It would be a helluva break if she had seen this woman before, but it could be difficult without a positive ID.' Jansch couldn't see any way beyond normal police work that would budge Joanna Schiller's mind. He envisaged an identity parade of possible suspects, but it was unlikely that they could pick up the kidnapper, whoever she was, simply by 'making enquiries'. He said as much to Hoffman.

'But that's how it has to be done, Uwe, although that is something of an over-simplification,' Hoffman admitted. 'We need to talk to lots and lots of her past friends and acquaintances. Find out if any of them have South African accents or connections. Good old police procedures, Uwe.

Put a team on it first thing in the morning. You'll also need the help of the British and South African police. But don't tell them why. Send people over there, and make sure you send some bright lads. Men like you.'

Jansch smiled self-consciously and yawned suddenly. 'God, I'm tired.'

Hoffman smiled. 'Aren't we both? You get off then.' He looked over at his bed. 'I'll get some sleep myself. Back here for six, Uwe. I'll see you then.'

Jansch left the office without being told a second time. The room was now empty except for the police chief. Tomorrow he would have a full, twenty-four hour shift of manpower as officers drafted in from other divisions began work.

Hoffman peeled off his jacket, booked an alarm call with the switchboard, and lay down on the bed. He wanted to mull over a few things about the case, but within a few minutes he was sound asleep.

Moments later, the door to Dr Kistler's penthouse office suite opened and the police president walked out. Instead of riding the lift to the ground floor, he walked down the stairs to the operations room in which Hoffman had his unit set up. He opened the operations room door and immediately saw the quiet figure asleep on the small bed. He ignored him and walked across to Hoffman's desk.

The file which Jansch had left was on top of the desk, unopened. Kistler spun the file, opened it and scanned the contents quickly, untroubled by the fact that the police chief was sound asleep just a metre or so from him.

Satisfied, he closed the file and walked softly from the room.

Conor killed the engine of the Opel and sat there for a moment in the pervading silence, not knowing which part of his body hurt the most. Much of it would be salved by a hot bath, but the bruising around his rib cage, and he was now convinced that's all it was, would take longer to heal. He was quite sure now that he had not been burnt; the scorching he could smell earlier was evident only on his clothing.

He had parked the car in Lonnericher Strasse, close to the Kölner Central railway station. It was about three o'clock in the morning and there was very little movement in the streets. He was content to wait awhile and consider his options. Not that he had many.

Stealing the car had proved easy for a man of Conor Lenihan's skills. When he found himself well clear of the burning house and in quiet, sleepy suburbia, he had set about finding a car. He had waited until about two o'clock in the morning knowing that by then, most of the neighbourhood would be well asleep.

He wanted an old car; one that did not have a sophisticated, immobilizer. He soon found an old Opel Corsa, and within minutes was on his way.

Conor drove for a while and soon found he was leaving a town called Schwelm, where the safe house had been situated. That was an irony, that a 'safe' house should be bombed with the intention of murdering all the occupants. It was situated on the south-east of Germany's industrial Ruhr heartland, the powerhouse of Germany's economy. He continued driving until he reached Cologne and pulled into a side road. He waited for several minutes before climbing out of the car, making sure nobody was about. His apartment was about a mile away off Boltenstern Strasse near the docks, just west of the Mulheimer Bridge. There was no way he could really make himself inconspicuous at that time of night, but by walking in such a manner that he looked like someone going home, perhaps returning from a party, he was quite sure little notice would be taken of him.

He reached his apartment about thirty minutes later. He saw several people on the way; early vendors, street cleaners, vagrants, people going home from night clubs, but no police or someone running at him with a bomb or a gun. Conor's flat was on the first floor of a tenement block. He knew nobody else in the block because he had always kept himself to himself. He paid his rent through an agency and used the alias John Buck.

It was cold in the flat, but not unbearably so. The first thing Conor did was to run a bath. There was a gas water heater in the bathroom so hot water was not a problem. The next thing he did was to make a pot of strong tea and carry it through to the bathroom. He peeled off everything and stepped into the bath. It was all Conor could do to keep awake, but he fought the urge to sleep, promising himself that sublime sanctuary when he was ready. Right then he needed to plan carefully, and had several thoughts germinating in his mind, thoughts that could result in the deaths of a lot of people. And Conor didn't care who he had to kill to get to Breggie de Kok and her leviathan boyfriend, Joseph Schneider.

*

Breggie opened her eyes. It was dark in the room and she lay there for a moment. She wasn't aware of any sound that might have woken her. Joseph lay beside her, his breathing quiet and shallow. They had made love until quite late. It had been as furious as it had been pleasurable. Joseph was exhausted by it all and Breggie had felt physically bruised, but she knew it would pass.

Why had she woken? She pulled back the bedclothes and sat up on the edge of the bed. Joseph stirred beside her, made a noise and turned over. She ignored him and searched for her dressing gown in the darkness. She decided to go to the bathroom and padded quietly across the floor, pausing at the cot in which she had laid the baby Schiller. As her eyes adjusted to the darkness she was just able to make out the figure of the infant. He seemed quiet. She reached her hand into the cot and gently pulled the top cover clear of his face. Then she laid her hand on his tiny chest and could feel the measured rise and fall as he breathed. Satisfied she went through to the bathroom.

When she returned to the bedroom, Breggie climbed into bed and cuddled up to Joseph. It was a little while before she finally succumbed to the beguiling warmth and comfort of the bed and she drifted off to sleep.

In the small cot, the baby lay sleeping, oblivious to the big world and the dramas that dogged it. Unaware of it, his tiny brain sensed the smallest quiver deep inside his chest. As the baby drew warm air into his lungs, a small sliver of mucus covered a microscopic airway until it burst under the pressure. This tiniest of irritations was like a reed in the wind and the vibration carried up to his throat and erupted in a single, explosive cough.

Breggie woke again but there was still no noise. She lay her head back on the pillow and wondered how long it would be before the little mite in the cot woke up for his feed. And how much sleep she would get that night. She drifted off to sleep and, at last, everything was peaceful again.

Joanna lay awake in the darkness, her eyes wide open. Unlike Breggie de Kok, sleep was a stranger to her that night. She had tried reading, watching a late night movie on television, blanking her mind and breathing deeply, but it was all to no avail. Her mind kept going back to the horrific scenes of the kidnap. The noise, the deaths, and her darling Manny being cruelly snatched from her. The woman's eyes floated before her, untouchable and unreachable. The eyes were manic, yet beautiful. Cauldrons of Satanic power, pools of enchantment. Where had she seen them before?

The question had burned a fire in Joanna's soul and threatened to destroy her unless she could find the answer. Joanna knew that if she could put a name to the eyes, the policeman, Hoffman, would find her. But how many people does one meet in a lifetime she wondered? How many people leave some kind of unforgettable impression? The questions rolled through her mind like tumbling balls in a lottery. If only she could pick the right one.

Eventually Joanna threw back the bedclothes and got out of bed. She was aware of the dawn light seeping round the edges of the curtains; another day. She rang through to the night staff for a pot of tea to be sent to her room then took a shower.

Twenty minutes later Joanna was dressed in a loose fitting sweater and a pair of blue jeans. She had no make-up on. It was the first time for as long as she could remember. She put on a pair of flat espadrilles and poured herself a second cup of tea which she carried through to the room in which Hoffman had interviewed her and Schiller the day before. When she got there she was surprised to see the huge curtains drawn back and Schiller sitting in one of the leather chairs.

Joanna put her cup on a coffee table. The clink of the china made Schiller turn in his chair. He was about to stand up, but Joanna reached him first. She took his hand and kissed him gently on the forehead.

'Good morning, Manfred. Couldn't you sleep either?' She sat opposite him.

Schiller sighed heavily. His face looked lined and deeply troubled. The kidnapping seemed to have aged him considerably. Joanna was quite concerned.

'Hallo, *mein liebchen*.' He often greeted her like that; two languages, but they always spoke in German. This was something Joanna had insisted on from their very first meeting. 'No, I couldn't.'

'How long have you been here?' she asked.

He shrugged. 'I'm not sure. I've been sitting here watching the dawn come for some time, wondering what it is that makes man so evil to his fellow creature.'

'It's in our nature,' Joanna told him. 'We all have a degree of cruelty in us. Most of us suppress it; others have no wish to.'

He let his gaze drift back to the panoramic view through the huge window. He said nothing for a while.

'It makes me very angry,' he said eventually, 'that men should treat an infant that way. Such a child. He does not deserve that.'

She reached forward and took his hand. 'Please don't worry. We shall get little Manny back, you'll see.' Joanna found it difficult to believe it herself. 'As soon as they tell us how much they want, we shall pay the money and little Manny will be back here with us where he belongs.'

Schiller looked back at Joanna. There was a deep sadness in his eyes that was meant for Joanna, not the infant.

'Oh my dear, dear Joanna, they don't want money. It's something else.'

Joanna stiffened. 'Have you heard something already?'

He shook his head. 'No, but I know what they want.'

'What?'

He didn't reply in the way Joanna expected him to. Instead, he began to talk about his childhood.

'When I was a little boy, I was very clever. I mean, whatever I had to learn at school, I could without any effort. It wasn't something I postured about, and none of my friends seemed to resent me for it. I was also blessed with a sharp brain and an intellect which could destroy most arguments among my peer group.' He looked up briefly and smiled. 'I could see through anybody. I could spot their deviousness, their trickery, their cunning. I had power and was sublimely happy. But I never used that power to control people, unless they wanted to be controlled.

'I built up a small business, employed a couple of friends and by the time I was fifteen years old, I sold the business at an enormous profit. At sixteen years of age I knew I was going to be rich and successful. The power that God had blessed me with would carry me through life on a golden chariot.'

Schiller paused there and his mood became a little more sombre. 'But then I encountered a power that was not born of talent or God given.

A power that was manifestly evil. A power that destroyed men and nations, took from them their dignity, their roots and their lives; a power that controlled others through fear and intimidation. It was an inimical, despotic, evil power.'

Joanna saw rage in Schiller's mind; an almost uncontrollable ferment burning away at him.

'The Nazis,' she said simply.

It seemed to snap Schiller out of his mood. He sighed heavily, nodding his head as he did so.

'I couldn't believe what they were up to at first. My instincts told me they were no good. Hitler was a supreme orator. His speeches were powerful and commanding; mesmerizing even. But I could see through him. Trouble was Joanna,' and here he allowed himself a little chuckle, 'I was making money hand over fist because of his rebuilding programme. I was also converting most of my money to gold and shipping it out because I knew that no good would come of Hitler's plans. It was that old instinct again. I continued to make money throughout the war and, believe me, I was in torment, but I was a businessman first and foremost.

'Then I met Otto Schindler. Do you know of him?' He didn't wait for Joanna's response but carried on. 'He was a successful Austrian business-man who employed many, many Jews in his factories. And, right under the noses of the Nazis, he was instrumental in shipping a lot of them out to Palestine. He was a truly wonderful, brave man. So, unknown to Herr Schindler, I channelled funds into his underground pipeline. The irony of it all is that I was charged with war crimes after the war.'

'I didn't know that,' Joanna said, showing surprise. 'I can't believe it.'

Schiller laughed gently. 'The War Crimes Commission spread their net so wide that practically every businessman in Germany who survived the war was thought to have something to answer for. But they returned my passport and I went on making more money rebuilding Germany and absorbing as much of the rest of the world as I could.'

Joanna wondered where all this was leading to. 'What has this got to do with Manny's kidnap? Are you saying that someone is seeking revenge?'

He shook his head. 'Nothing like it. What they want is my power. They want control of my empire.'

Schiller's empire as he called it was the envy of all businessmen the world over. It was almost inevitable that whatever anyone touched during their normal day, it would have had some connection with Schiller. He controlled an enormous portfolio in raw materials, communications, shipping, aviation, armaments, space exploration and medicine. There was little on Planet Earth in which Schiller had no involvement.

He stood up and took Joanna by the hand so that she had to stand as well. He wanted her to understand so much that by pure, physical contact he hoped that she would feel what he felt.

'Joanna, what I am about to tell you could be dangerous. But I feel you are entitled to know what the stakes are. It is my belief that Germany will dominate Europe within the next ten years. Totally. We now have full monetary union with other member states of the European Union and soon the European Constitution will be ratified; of that there can be no doubt. The Bundesbank will eventually be in control. We have seen the Bundestag, the German Parliament return to the Reichstag, to Berlin. That is a massive, psychological boost to the German nation. I fear for the rest of Europe and for the rest of the world. My money, my empire and my power could provide the German people with such a feeling of supremacy it would be like a drug. We are a strong nation, *mein liebchen*, magnificently strong, but we must never be allowed control. That is why I have made a covenant; to ensure that not one penny of my money nor one brick of my empire will belong to the German nation.'

He stopped there. Joanna waited for a moment, expecting him to go on, to clarify that last statement. When it was obvious he wasn't about to say anything else, she asked him who he had made the covenant to.

He shook his head. 'I cannot tell you that, Joanna. It would be too dangerous. And you must never reveal to anyone what I have told you. Anyone!'

He paused again as if unsure of what he would say next. For a moment, he was unable to look at her. His eyes focused on the backs of his hands. Suddenly, he looked up.

'Joanna, there is something else.' He paused for a while as though there was a conflict in his mind and what he was about to say he was finding difficult. At last he sighed and his eyes seemed to pierce Joanna deep into her soul. 'I am a Jew.'

Joanna gasped. It was unbelievable. This man was the very symbol of Germanic power; the epitome of Hitler's dream for the Aryan Race.

'It is something I have kept secret all my life,' he went on, ignoring Joanna's obvious expression of astonishment. 'I had to in order to guarantee my survival. My father told me when I was quite young that if I ever admitted being a Jew, it would destroy me. He told me that he had never followed the Jewish faith, or lived the Jewish life because he despised it. But he knew when Hitler came to power that the fate of all Jews in Germany had been sealed. He kept his secret through embarrassment and then through fear. I have kept mine, because of my father's warning to save my life. The few people who knew my secret are all dead. They died in the camps,' he added sadly. 'So, you see, I cannot let them have my power, for as God is my witness, the terror will begin again.'

Joanna felt a cold chill slither down her back. Schiller's manner, his change from an old man reminiscing to one who held such strong views about his own people, showed the fear he had of some awful fate being visited upon the heads of those who had no control over their own destiny.

'And you honestly believe that? In today's modern world?' she asked him.

'You do not understand,' he replied slowly. 'Young people simply do not comprehend the sheer, awful insanity that engulfed the world in those dark days. It would happen again,' he added with a shrug. 'Believe me, Joanna, it would happen again.'

Suddenly his attitude changed. From the prophet of doom he switched to the indulgent father-in-law.

'No more talk of it now, Joanna,' he told her brightly. 'You and Manny will have a happy life. You are both well provided for. Now, let us go and get some breakfast.'

He put an arm around a bewildered Joanna's shoulder and led her from the room. He had told her to think no more of it, but deep in his heart, Schiller was a troubled man.

Hoffman was fast asleep when Jansch walked through the door and turned on the overhead light. It was six o'clock. Hoffman screwed his eyes up against the light and took the offered cup of coffee gratefully. Jansch went across to Hoffman's desk and sat down.

'Did you have company last night?'

Hoffman looked up from the coffee. 'Who'd want to get into a bed this big with me?' he growled.

'I was thinking more of a social visit than an assignation.'

Hoffman swung his feet out of the bed and stood up. As he pulled on his trousers he asked Jansch what he was getting at.

'Dr Kistler, didn't he see you last night?'

'No. You were the last person I saw. Why?'

'Oh. Well, it was just that I saw his name in the log when I booked in this morning. He left about thirty minutes after me last night.'

Hoffman shook his head and wandered away towards the wash-room. 'He was probably working late.'

Jansch thought no more of it and concentrated on his coffee and an attempt to convince himself that he had slept longer than the three hours he'd been in bed. He was still wishing his alarm clock hadn't gone off when Hoffman walked back into the room. Jansch yawned and spun the file towards him that was lying on Hoffman's desk. Hoffman pulled his shirt on. Suddenly, he stopped.

'What did you do just then?'

Jansch gave him a peculiar look. 'I don't know. Yawned, I guess.'

'No.' He shook his head. 'The file.' Hoffman pointed at the desk. 'Have you just started reading it? Just then?'

Jansch nodded, not sure what his boss was driving at. 'I've just this second opened it.'

'You turned it round.'

'I had to; I wouldn't have been able to read it otherwise. Why?'

Hoffman returned to the task of getting dressed. 'Oh, nothing really.' He shook his head. 'Forget it. I think my brain must be asleep still.' He picked up his cup and walked over to the desk. 'Look, there won't be a great deal happening for a while. I think I'm going home for some breakfast. Say hello to Elke. I'll be back in a couple of hours.' He put his empty cup on the desk and started walking out of the office. 'The rest of the team should be here shortly,' he called back over his shoulder. 'Tell them I'll have a briefing at nine o'clock.'

He rode the lift down to the ground floor, but couldn't get the file out of his mind. When he had finished reading it the night before, he had got up from his desk and left it there. This morning, Jansch had been sitting in his chair and had to turn the file round to read it. It could only have meant one thing: someone had been in his office while he had slept and read the file.

He stepped out of the lift at the ground floor and checked the night log at the front desk. Apart from the night staff, none of whom had any reason to enter the incident room (they would have woken him anyway) the only people in that building after Jansch had left were himself and Dr Aaron Kistler.

Conor closed the door of his flat. He was carrying a large, black plastic bag. It contained the few possessions he felt he needed. Not that he had much, just enough to see him through the next few days. The remainder of his possessions he left behind to convey the impression that his flat was still lived in.

He carried the bag down to his car and put it in the boot. Then he drove to a local shopping precinct and parked his car in the free car-park. He then began touring the local estate agencies and reading local adverts in an effort to secure lodgings close to his apartment. By mid afternoon Conor found the ideal bed-sit on the opposite side of the road and about fifty metres from his other place.

His landlady, a jovial little woman by the name of Frau Lindbergh, asked for one month's rent in advance and the promise that he conduct himself with due respect to the other tenants. She assured him that hers was a respectable establishment and everybody kept themselves to themselves. Conor was quite happy about that. He had a key and somewhere to stay. It was all he needed.

Oberkommissar Otto Lechter had just finished reading the signal co-opting him on to Hoffman's team at Police Headquarters in Bonn when the phone rang. It was to advise him of the explosion in Schwelm which was in his district of responsibilities. Lechter was head of a department in KK11, the serious crimes division in Wuppertal. The explosion had thought to be the result of a spark igniting escaping gas, but preliminary investigation by the fire department and gas engineers had resulted in the police being called. The phone call was to tell Lechter that the cause of the explosion had been a bomb.

Lechter replaced the phone. He was now faced with a small dilemma: should he call Hoffman and ask to be excused the new task? Or should he hold out for a few days? He decided on the latter simply because he was a career man and wanted to become a well-known face where it mattered. And Hoffman, at the moment was where it mattered.

He drove out to the remains of the house, parked his police car and ducked beneath the red and white police tape strung round the property. The forensic team was still at it. There was a small fire team getting in the way of the forensic department, and the usual gathering of neighbours and sightseers. Members of the press were also there.

The house was a total wreck. All that was clearly visible were the remains of the garage. Because the house was in about half an acre of ground, the debris had, mercifully, settled largely within the boundary. It was inevitable that some of it would be found quite some distance away. Lechter's quick glance told him that combing through what was left would only reveal clues if the search was concentrated at the heart of the blast. But that was not his remit; forensics would do that.

He saw a face he recognized as Kommissar Baum. The inspector was already walking across to him.

'You senior officer here?' Lechter asked him.

'Yes sir,' Baum replied and gave Lechter his name.

Lechter asked him to bring him up to date with all the relevant information.

'Explosion caused by a bomb. So far we have recovered four bodies – what's left of the poor sods. None of them is intact, but it's fairly certain we will not find anyone else in there.'

'Is it the family?' Lechter asked him.

'Apparently not,' Baum replied, sounding surprised himself. 'The owners are away on a world cruise. We are trying to contact them.'

'Poor buggers, this will spoil their holiday. Anything else?'

'There's evidence of a lot of cash; Euros and American dollars mainly. Most of it burned and charred, but quite a lot was scattered all over the bloody place.'

Lechter allowed that to sink in and found himself jumping to conclusions. Much the same as Baum would have done, he decided.

'So what's your hypothesis, Inspector?'

'Empty house, four people and a stack of money. They could have been dividing the spoils of a scam. It might have been money for laundering. Whichever way you cut it, sir, it looks like a gangland killing. With the bomb, I mean.'

Lechter felt inclined to agree with the inspector, but reserved his own judgement. He began walking up the long drive towards the house. Baum fell into step beside him.

'Better get on to Thirteen.' This was Department KK13, the department responsible for investigating organized crime. 'See if they can come up with an angle. If it is an underworld job, they'll get a whisper.'

They reached the house, what was left of it. Lechter would have to wait around for a while, answer any questions put to him by the press and TV people. Not a lot else he could do otherwise.

'You get everything wrapped up here,' he told Baum, 'and have everything on file, on my desk as you get it. Oh, there's one other thing.' He told Baum about Hoffman co-opting him on to his specialist team, the FuGrBP. This was the Fuhrungsgruppen Bereitschaftpolizei. These groups were formed when national security was threatened whether by inimical forces or natural disaster. Anything that could endanger the well-ordered infrastructure of the German Nation. 'I'll be asking the Police Chief to leave me in Wuppertal for a few days. With a bit of luck I'll be able to pass this down to you. OK?'

Kommissar Baum was more than happy with the arrangement. As far as he was concerned this case would be left to gather dust in the filing cabinets once they had established it was an underworld feud. And of that he had no doubt.

Breggie de Kok had finished feeding the baby and was now writing out a small shopping list. Most of that day she had been tending to the infant who seemed to demand her constant attention. Breggie was not the sort of woman who felt entirely comfortable with babies. Although she was not lacking in common sense, she found the whole business just a little tiresome. Her lack of expertise accounted for the frame of mind she found herself in, and Joseph's total lack of interest only resulted in stupid arguments. Now the baby seemed settled, Breggie was grabbing the chance to get out for a spell. Joseph had been given no option but to remain in the house and look after the infant.

Breggie drove the Volkswagen Golf into Düsseldorf and parked in a multi-storey car-park above a shopping mall. She planned to do a little window shopping, spend some time drifting from shop to shop and then visit the supermarket for items she had on the list. It was a small pleasure she had been looking forward to, and the two hours she had allowed herself would fly by, she knew that.

Until she passed a newsagent and saw the headline on a late edition of *Bild Zeitung*.

At first it didn't really register other than as a heading announcing a fatal accident. FOUR DIE IN HOUSE EXPLOSION. Breggie picked up the newspaper from the stand where it resided with other dailies. She began reading the article.

Four people died today in a house explosion in the town of Schwelm. Police say the blast was the result of a gas leak. The four bodies recovered. . . .

Breggie read no more. She folded the paper and paid for it. Then she walked swiftly from the shopping mall. It was all she could do to stop herself flying into a raging fury. Four bodies; the article had reported four bodies. There should have been five, she muttered to herself. Five of the bastards! Which meant one of them had got away, but who was it?

Breggie knew from that moment if she didn't find him, her life was as good as terminated.

Conor lifted *Bild Zeitung* from the rack and read the same article. It had been inevitable, he thought to himself, but now they knew. It was odds on they would find out one of the team had escaped the blast, and it wouldn't be long before they knew which one. Then they would come looking for him.

And Conor intended they should find him.

CHAPTER FIVE

Franz Molke enjoyed a great deal of popularity as Shadow Minister of the Interior. It was something not enjoyed by all politicians in opposition to the elected government. His ascendancy in the brutal world of politics had been nothing short of meteoric, and it would have been difficult to believe that although outsiders only five short years ago, Molke's party had been elected to the Bundestag as the minority party.

At the October elections in 1998, Molke's Volkspartei had polled just over one million votes. The two big parties, the SDP and the CDU had polled thirty two million votes between them. A betting man would not have given Molke a cat in hell's chance of making it to the top. But a betting man would not have reckoned for Molke's political skills, his cunning and his field craft.

The Volkspartei, and its youth arm the Junge Demokraten had worked their collective butts off between the election years, and Molke's field generals had never wasted an opportunity to offer 'sound bites' to hungry media people. The right words at the right time to the right people. In the intervening four years, Molke's party had grown in popularity, stature, and credibility. He had presence and charisma. You couldn't buy it, you couldn't create it; Molke didn't have to try: he was winning hands down.

After the results of the 2002 General Election were declared, the Volkspartei were returned to the German Parliament with fourteen million votes, enough to put them in second place behind Chancellor Kohl's party. Molke had 265 seats out of 672. With his support, Chancellor Kohl was re-elected for a further term of office by two votes. Now, six months after the election, Kohl's popularity was waning as was his health and Molke was poised to take over.

Literally, Franz Molke had the world at his feet. Germany was the strongest power in Europe. It had control of the fiscal heart of the European Union. It had moved its seat of government to Berlin, to the glorious, new Reichstag building, in the year 2000. If they secured power at the next election, the Volkspartei would have control through the office of Chancellor. And the hidden agenda that Molke intended to pursue would make Germany the strongest country in the world.

But, at that moment, Molke was not a particularly happy man. He had just left a private meeting with the President of the North Rhine Westphalia Police, Dr Aaron Kistler.

Molke was sitting in the back of his official Mercedes. Beside him was an aide, a young man whose beautifully tailored suit just about hid the bulge of the holstered gun beneath his arm. Outside the warm interior of the car, a cold wind was sweeping up off the Rhine, pushing little eddies of debris in circles along the gutters and pavements. At that moment, Molke's heart was as cold as the wind itself.

Molke's chauffeur drove the car up to the government building opposite the Chancellor's residence and deposited Molke and his aide at the front entrance. He drove away as the two men hurried into the building.

They took the lift up to Molke's office on the second floor. When they entered, the aide closed the door behind him as Molke went to his desk. He sat down and waited while his aide swept the room with an electronic detection device. It was unlikely that Molke's office was bugged, but he was a careful man and this check was always done if he had been away from his office for any length of time. Normally his secretary would come into the office occasionally, putting files for his attention on the desk, or retrieving files he had signed. When she knew the office would be unattended for some time, she would always lock it. But Molke still took no chances.

The aide finished checking the office and nodded his satisfaction. It was also customary for the two of them to remain silent until this check had been completed. Molke dismissed him and walked across the room to his safe. He dialled the combination and turned the steel handle. This powered up an electronic keypad with an LED display. He tapped in a number, inserted a key in the lock and opened the safe. There was very little in there, but all Molke wanted was the single computer disc that lay on the shelf.

He took the disc to his desk, switched on the computer and inserted the disc in the drive. When he asked for access to a particular file he had to enter a password. Having done this the file opened up to a list of names and addresses. Molke typed in the surname of the man he wanted. When it came up on the screen, he pulled a digital phone from his jacket pocket and dialled a number. There were two phones on Molke's desk, but he did not consider them secure enough for this particular call.

It was some time before the phone was answered. Molke had to wait while he listened to various changes in dialling tone until his call found the man he wanted.

'Hallo.' The voice was heavily accented.

It was all Molke expected to hear.

'Have you seen the late editions of the *Bild Zeitung*?' he asked. After the reply came, he spoke again. 'There should have been five. Find the fifth one and deal with it.'

He put the phone down. It had been a swift, definitive instruction. A lengthy conversation could have resulted in professional eavesdroppers picking up the transmissions. The digital technology used in mobile phones made them almost secure, but such was the advance of electronic espionage, Molke always considered it wise to err on the side of caution, hence the brevity of the conversation.

But his instruction to the voice on the phone had been crystal clear. Molke, who was almost certainly going to be the next Chancellor of Germany, had just issued the order to find the fifth member of the kidnap team and kill him.

Breggie came through the door in a highly agitated state. Joseph was sitting in a chair watching the television. He could see she was excited about something, and because he hadn't expected her back for a couple of hours yet, he knew it couldn't be good news. As he started to rise from the chair, she flung the paper at him.

'Read that!'

Joseph caught the paper and opened it. The front page headlines leapt out at him. He looked up at Breggie and, for a moment, there was little change in his expression.

'I don't believe it,' he said at last. 'It's not fucking possible.'

Breggie's face distorted into an angry grimace. Now in the privacy of the house, she was able to vent her anger, and fear, on the incredulous Joseph.

'Not fucking possible? Read the fucking paper, Joseph.' She stabbed a finger at the article. 'There were only four bodies. That means one of the bastards isn't dead.'

She struggled to get out of her coat, like fighting to get out of a straightjacket. She flung it into a chair.

'How the fuck could it have happened?' She screamed. 'We saw the house go up. No one could have survived that.'

'Well someone obviously did,' Schneider said unhelpfully.

'He must have known. It's the only way. We've been stitched up, Joseph. The bastards have sold us short.'

'No.'

'Yes! Fucking yes!' She was beginning to tremble and hyperventilate. Joseph had never seen her like that before. 'You know what this means?' she shouted at him. 'It means we're fucking dead if that bastard gets picked up by the pigs. We don't stand a chance; our own people will make sure of that.'

Her outrage looked almost uncontrollable. Spittle was flying from her lips as she cursed and raged. Joseph dropped the paper and hit Breggie across the face with the open palm of his hand. The blow sent her reeling across the room. She backed into a chair and fell awkwardly. Joseph took two steps towards her and hit her again.

The effect of the two blows was to literally stop Breggie in her tracks. She flung a protective hand up to her face but, at the same time, she had stopped shouting and spitting. Joseph took hold of her by both arms. He held her upright and shook her gently.

'Listen, Breggie, we have a little time. We also hold a trump card.' He glanced over his shoulder towards the room where the baby was sleeping. 'We'll be OK.'

Breggie put her hand to her face and fingered her cheek. It was stinging from the fierce blow Joseph had struck. She looked puzzled, as if she had witnessed something quite unbelievable.

'What do you mean, we hold a trump card?' she whispered.

'The baby. If we feel we are under threat, we can move to another place. They'll never know where we are.' He shrugged and smiled. It was meant to reassure her. 'They will never find us.'

'We would never get away with it,' she protested. 'Once all this was over we'd end up in the Rhine with concrete for company.'

But because she was calming down, Breggie started to think more clearly. 'Unless we can find whoever it was that survived and dispose of him.' Her eyes brightened. 'If we can do that, we'll be OK.'

'And how are we supposed to find out who it was escaped the blast?' he asked her. 'And if it was a stitch up, they'll never let us find him.'

Breggie sat down at the dining-table. There was a small bowl of fruit in the centre. A couple of magazines lay open. Around the room were all the normal signs of domesticity. A baby's pushchair took up one corner. In another was a clothes drier with a few items drying and waiting to be ironed. The television was on, but the sound had been turned down low because of the baby. A radio burbled in the background, coming from the kitchen.

'We have to be very careful, Joseph,' she said suddenly. 'But you are right; we do have a little time yet.'

Schneider sat down at the table too. He could see the dilemma they were in. The organization might consider they had failed and would have to be taken care of. On the other hand they might be given the opportunity to redeem themselves. It was the least likely option.

He opened a small box and took out two hand rolled cigarettes from among several that were in the box. He put one in his mouth and gave the other one to Breggie. She took it without a murmur.

'I think we'll have to move the baby.' He didn't want to say that. It came out like an unwanted decision. 'It would be a fallback position. We could say we chose that route to protect the baby.'

He lit the cigarettes. Breggie took the smoke down greedily into her lungs. The sweet tasting tobacco sent little stabs of sparkling pain around her body which quickly transformed themselves into a pleasant, comforting sensation. She exhaled the smoke.

'Protect us from what?' she asked. 'The organization? Whoever it was escaped the blast?' She shook her head. 'We'll have to make a contingency plan. Find another place close by in case we need it. We can take the baby there.'

The marijuana was having the desired effect, which Joseph expected it to. Although Breggie had shown abhorrence to the smoking of the usual Virginia tobacco cigarettes, she had never objected to one of his 'funny fags' as she called them. He reached out a hand and placed it on Breggie's arm.

'It wouldn't be long before they found us, Breggie. The organization is so well connected . . .' His pessimism was obvious. He shrugged. 'It might be better to leave the baby and take our chances by getting out of the country.'

She shot him a sideways look. 'Who was the initial contact with the organization?'

'The Dutchman.'

She considered that for a while. The Dutchman was the head of their cell, or group. None of the group knew who the Dutchman's controller was, and the Dutchman ran his own group so that his controller had no idea of their names or identities. It was a standard procedure amongst subversive organizations.

'You might as well contact him, Joseph.' She drew nervously on the cigarette. The end glowed bright red and reflected off her pale skin. 'He may be our only hope.'

'Counterfeit, the whole bloody lot!'

Oberkommissar Otto Lechter was listening to Kommissar Baum on the phone. He was being told that the money recovered from the house destroyed in the explosion, the American Dollars and the Euros were all forgeries.

'I've been in touch with twenty-one sir. They'll be getting back to me as soon as they know more.' Department KK21 was the section responsible for investigating, among other things, fraud and forgery.

Lechter was beginning to get an uneasy feeling about this. It was messy. It was starting to look more than just a straightforward falling out among thieves. With a mass of counterfeit money like that, coupled with the bomb, this seemed like the big pay off. Like all successful detectives, Lechter often relied on hunches to solve cases. The hunch now pressing to be followed up seemed a little too preposterous for him to take seriously.

He thanked Baum and put the phone down. Then he picked it up and dialled Hoffman's number in Bonn.

The phone was picked up almost immediately.

'Hoffman.'

'Hallo sir, Chief Inspector Lechter here.'

'Good day to you Chief Inspector. Are you phoning to tell me you will be joining my team earlier?'

'Not exactly sir. I want to try something out on you: a hunch.'

Hoffman grinned. 'We all have those. Go on then.'

'It's about the bomb explosion in Schwelm; the house that went up.'

Hoffman knew about it but had been quite happy to let Lechter's department handle it in view of the Schiller kidnap. 'What about it?'

Lechter explained briefly the result of his and Baum's conversations and conjectures, and the resultant find that the money was counterfeit. 'It could be the typical double-cross.'

'And?'

'The owners of the house were not killed in the blast. They are away on a world cruise. We will almost certainly find that those killed had no right to be in that house and were only there for the pay off. It was being used as a temporary safe house without the owner's knowledge.'

Had that supposition been put to Hoffman as a standard scenario presented to him at police college, typical of underworld organizations, he would have gone along with it and thought no more of it. But, significantly, Lechter was telling him about a crime that did not require his opinion. He was telling him because he, Lechter, felt there could be a link between Hoffman's investigation and the bombed house.

'You feel there's a possible link between it and the Schiller kidnap?' Hoffman put to him.

'I think it's worth running the two investigations in parallel until we can discount it one way or the other,' Lechter told him.

Hoffman felt that old familiar excitement when a case begins to open up, and little fragments fall into place as the picture emerges. There was no evidence yet and no conclusive proof, but he liked the feel of this one.

'Right, we'll run this as you say. I still want you on my team but I want you to stay there. Anything you get, download it on to the Schiller file here. I'll read it every day, whether there's a development or not. Anything else happens, phone me.'

'Yes sir. Oh, one other thing: I'll need access to the Schiller file.'

Hoffman knew it would be pointless asking Lechter to feed all his information through without being able to do a comparison himself. He agreed to Lechter's request.

'I'll have Jansch give you the code.' He thanked Lechter for his intuitive guesswork and put the phone down. Solving cases was all about a number of things: hard work, luck, evidence, hunches and mistakes. But the mistakes had to come from the bad guys. And so far, Hoffman believed they had made two. Issuing the counterfeit money was just one of them. He hoped the other would be as fruitful.

They came that night. There were two men, coasting up silently to Conor's other apartment in a dark BMW. Conor knew they would come but not quite so soon. He had to admire the efficiency of the organization in acting so quickly. No doubt the same scenario was being acted out at the addresses of the others who had been killed in the explosion. Although the organization knew one of them had escaped, they weren't to know which one.

Conor had dressed completely in black with a black ski mask pulled down over his face. He was sitting behind the window of his bed-sit. There was no light in the room which meant he would be invisible to all but a well-trained observer. He had a night sight with him, which he used to observe the two men get out of the car and walk up to the tenement building.

Conor immediately left his bed-sit and went down to his own car which was parked in the road beneath his window. He turned the key in the ignition and let the engine idle. He knew what the two men would find because he had left the flat looking as though it was still lived in. The gear that he had removed and carried out in the black bag was all he considered as essential for comfort and safety.

He had disposed of the money Breggie de Kok had paid them with. Conor was no mug; he just couldn't believe the organization would use anything other than counterfeit bills when they intended blowing the bloody place apart. The money he had used to pay Frau Lindbergh for his room was from the same source, but he knew he would have to live with that.

Five minutes after Conor had started his car, the two men emerged from the building. They climbed into the BMW and pulled away from the kerb. Conor followed. They drove down the west bank of the Rhine along Adenauer Strasse, cutting into Bruhler Strasse and under the motorway. Conor's knowledge of Cologne was not exemplary, but he was happy with the way things were going.

Eventually the car turned into a side street and deposited its passenger. He waved at the driver as the car pulled away. Conor made a note of the address and continued to follow the BMW. About fifteen minutes later it pulled into a driveway on the outskirts of Brühl. The driver parked but didn't bother to put the car away in the garage of the moderately sized house. Conor was satisfied. He drove past, made a turn further along the road and headed back to Cologne.

Conor could hear the sound of a television filtering through the closed door of the apartment. It was late, but the noise was loud enough to cover the sound made by Conor as he picked the lock. He pushed the door open gently. There was no light burning outside the apartment, so Conor was not afraid of whoever was in there being aware of the door swinging open.

Conor didn't know which apartment the skinhead was using, but by solid reasoning and the general condition of the door and graffiti on the walls, he figured that the occupant of this particular place didn't give a toss about cleanliness.

As the door swung open, he could see general litter along the passageway. A pair of designer trainers lay on the floor and a carelessly flung coat had fallen from the coat hooks on the wall and lay among some newspapers and magazines. The smell that drifted down the hallway was a mixture of alcohol, drugs and an unclean toilet. He was confident he had found the right apartment.

The man whom Conor had seen go into the place had decided to watch some late night pornography on television. He was happily engrossed in the pulsating body movements on the screen and was into his second can of Grolsch lager when he felt the press of steel on the back of his neck. He turned instinctively and saw the edge of Conor's open hand flash towards his face.

The crunching pain of his broken nose was mercifully dulled for a moment by his loss of consciousness. When he opened his eyes, he was spread-eagled in his armchair and the silhouette of someone dressed all in black standing over him. The figure had a gun pointed straight at him. On the end of the gun was a silencer.

'*Wer sind sie? Was wollen sie?*' The fear was evident in his voice.

'Never mind who I am,' Conor told him. 'But what I want is for you to answer a few questions.'

The man, or youth really for he couldn't have been more than about 18 years of age, looked pathetic. His head had been completely shaved and he had tattoos on his forehead and cheeks. He had ear-rings through both ears and a silver loop through his nose.

'Fuck off!' he snarled.

Conor moved the weapon closer. 'Careful. I have the gun, remember. Now, who sent you to the apartment tonight?'

'I told you, fuck off!' He spat the words out, blood mixing with spittle.

Conor shot him in the knee cap, the plop of the silenced gun barely audible above the noise of the television. The youth came off the chair in a scream, clutching his shattered knee. Conor whipped the end of the silencer across his battered nose.

'Answer my question. Who sent you?'

The youth started crying. The words fell out in an unintelligible rattle. Conor leaned closer without touching him. He pressed the gun against the boy's temple.

'Slowly.'

He wept and told Conor that he didn't know who gave the order. All he knew was what the driver of the BMW had told him.

'What's his name? Where can I find him?'

The address was the house to which Conor had followed the driver of the car.

'His name,' Conor insisted.

'Oscar Schwarz.' The name was given reluctantly through clenched teeth.

'Does he live alone?'

'Yes.'

Conor stood up. 'Thank you,' he said pleasantly, and shot him in the head.

Conor left the dead man's flat and gunned the Volkswagen into life. He had planned to drive to Brühl, but now he wasn't entirely sure how he would play this one. Killing the skinhead had meant nothing to him. It was dog-eat-dog; the skinhead would have thought nothing of killing him, and probably having a bit of sport into the bargain. They were all the same, he thought to himself; hard as nails when in company of others. Thick as two short planks most of them. As far as Conor was concerned he had done society a favour.

No, the next move would have to be different. The skinhead's partner was likely to be Conor's link to the next member of the chain, likely to be the person who issued the orders. He made up his mind, killed the engine and went back to the apartment where the unfortunate skinhead lay dead.

Conor wasn't in there long. He found what he wanted and headed back to his bed-sit in Cologne.

Breggie yawned and put the baby back in the cot. She looked and felt awful. She had smoked too many of Joseph's 'funny fags' the night before and that, coupled with the frustration of not finishing a job properly was enough to put her on a downer the morning after. But the baby had been a little bugger during the night. Despite feeding little Manny and changing him at the right times, he didn't want to settle. He just kept crying, sleeping, crying.

Joseph had got irritable too. Eventually he moved to a spare room so he could get some sleep. Breggie didn't feel at all sorry for him because she would need to catch up on lost sleep soon and he would simply have to look after the baby.

She went downstairs and made up another bottle for the infant. Then she made herself some coffee and sat down at the table to drink it.

The baby started crying. Breggie groaned and put the cup down with a loud clatter. She looked up at the ceiling, praying he would settle, but after a couple of minutes she knew he wouldn't. The crying persisted.

Breggie went upstairs and lifted the little fellow out of the cot. He stopped crying as soon as she cuddled him in her arms. His little cheeks were red and he was quite hot. She decided he had too many clothes on so she removed his babygro. Then she held him close and rocked him gently until he was fast asleep. She put him back in the cot and lay down on the bed. Very soon she was fast asleep.

*

As Breggie was falling asleep, and Hoffman was driving home to see his wife and have breakfast, Levi Eshkol was waking from a troubled night. He had discussed the Covenant at length with his colleagues at Hess's sumptuous house in the Teutoburger Wald and their conclusion was that they had underestimated Molke's intelligence network. But far from worrying how Molke's agents had penetrated their own security precautions, they were more concerned with protecting the Covenant.

Eshkol had originally planned to spend some time in Germany before returning to Israel, but now he had to abandon his plans and return home immediately. By midday the house was empty and closed up. The men and the Covenant were gone, and by nightfall, they would all would be out of the country.

CHAPTER SIX

Hoffman was standing in Dr Kistler's palatial office wondering wether to leap across the sprawling mahogany desk and throttle the President of the North Rhine Westphalia Police or turn and walk out. They had been having an argument about the right of access to Hoffman's inquiry by Kistler. Hoffman had challenged him about the file on his desk. Kistler's brutal answer was that he had every right to all information relevant to the kidnap and had made that abundantly clear from the outset.

'I chose not to wake you because you were obviously tired out from all the effort needed in compiling the few notes in the file,' he commented acidly.

Hoffman had attempted to impress upon the man the principle of 'need to know' but was failing miserably. He was also labouring under the weight of Kistler's authority.

'It is now two days since the kidnap and you have made no progress at all. You have the entire Federal Police Force at your disposal and yet you are not one single step closer to catching the perpetrators.' Kistler rose up out of his chair. The dark hair on his head was oiled and swept back revealing the widow's peak at the centre. The lines on his forehead furrowed into deep trenches above his abundant eyebrows.

He balled his hands into fists and leaned menacingly on the desk. His knuckles gleamed white as they took his weight. His bulk seemed to shut out the light from the large window behind him. Hoffman was aware of the Rhine disappearing behind Kistler's silhouette.

'Why?'

Hoffman deeply resented the man's arrogance and ingenuous

approach to policing, but fate had cast him in a subordinate role to this postulating overlord; it was a burden that went with the job.

'I can only act on evidence received and positive leads from inquiries. I can't go running around the countryside busting down doors and arresting every person who I think might have something to do with the kidnapping.' He could feel his words spilling out with shards of venom among them. He took a mental step back and paused for a moment.

'Dr Kistler, you know as well as I do that an inquiry of this nature will not yield anything until we can collate all the detail we have available. And at the moment it is pretty scant. There has been no contact by the kidnappers with Herr Schiller; nothing but silence.' He shrugged. 'I can't make things happen unless we have something concrete to work on, and there's precious little of that.'

He stopped then. No point in trying to ram down Kistler's throat the words he did not wish to hear.

Kistler remained still for a while; digesting Hoffman's pointed remarks about the little progress he was making. He knew there was nothing to be gained from what was basically a standoff. He would have to let his senior police officer manage the inquiry without too much interference, but at the same time he did want to know exactly what was going on and what progress was being made.

'That will be all, Hoffman,' he said at last. 'Just continue to have a report on my desk each morning whatever the state of your inquiries.' He sat down. The interview was over.

Hoffman left and closed the door behind him. He felt better now. He had let Kistler know that he brooked no interference and was not happy about Kistler's sneak reading of the file. One thing he hadn't told Kistler though was that he was a little further down the road than he had made out, but not as far as he would liked to have been.

The incident room was full of officers beavering away in front of computers, typing furiously at their keyboards. Some of the officers were in uniform, others in plain clothes. At the end wall was the usual board depicting a family tree of clues, but only Karl Trucco's photograph adorned the tree. He was one of the unfortunate terrorists who had perished in the bomb blast, now identified by his DNA profile. This had been the kidnappers' other mistake.

Hoffman took all this in as he swept through to his office at the end of the room. Jansch spotted him as the police chief lifted a full cup of coffee from the desk of an unsuspecting junior detective. The hapless individual looked pained as Hoffman crooked a finger at Jansch and went through to his desk.

'I have just received the equivalent of a massive bollocking from Herr Dr Kistler.'

Jansch watched his expression change from an affected downcast look to a wry smile.

'The man's a bloody menace. However,' Hoffman went on brightly, 'he's not on the team.' He drank some of the stolen coffee as the victim of his smash and grab went across to the vending machine for another cup. 'What do we have so far, Uwe?'

Jansch flipped open a file he had brought with him. 'Not a great deal, sir, I'm afraid. We know of Trucco, and inquiries with the FBI and Interpol are still progressing. We are still conducting discreet inquiries into Joanna Schiller's background and circle of friends and acquaintances to see if we can identify any South African connection.' He paused and ran his finger down the page. 'We have supplied the Czech manufacturer of the limpet bomb with the few details we have. Perhaps we can open up a line that way.' He muttered under his breath. 'Nothing on the counterfeit money yet.' He closed the file and looked up at Hoffman. 'And no word from the kidnappers either.'

'Naturally.' Hoffman felt that Schiller would hear quite soon but wondered if Schiller would tell him. He had doubts about the man's willingness to work with the police and wouldn't be surprised if Schiller attempted some sort of deal with the kidnappers. Or perhaps put an army of private investigators on to the case. 'We need to push this Trucco thing. If we can pin him down it's possible we'll make a link with the other terrorists. Make that a priority, Uwe.'

There was nothing else to be discussed so Jansch went back to his desk and began making calls on the secure police computer network. Hoffman finished his coffee and phoned the front desk for his official car to be brought round. It was time for his daily round with Herr Schiller.

Hoffman decided on an attempt to prise open Joanna's reluctance and find a short cut to her possible association with the woman who took her baby. It was a line he had been considering during the drive out to the Schiller residence.

'When did you meet your husband?'

Joanna looked much better than on that terrible first day. She appeared calmer, but Hoffman was no mug; he knew she would still be in quite a state, and would probably continue to be until her son was returned to her.

'At Cambridge University.'

'You were at college together?'

She shook her head. 'No. Hansi was there on a post graduate course. I was in the second year of my degree. It was a Christmas party. Apart from the occasional glimpse of him, that was the only time I saw him.'

'Why did he go to Cambridge?'

'I'm not sure. He completed his degree at Hamburg. The year at Cambridge came later. Why?'

'Nothing. It's not important,' Hoffman admitted. 'When did you meet him again?'

Joanna considered that for a moment, her mind going back to the moment she saw him and knew that she wanted to go on seeing him.

'It was about two years after I had completed my degree. I gained an honours degree in Computer science and found a good position with Siemens. Part of my training meant going to Germany. I had an A level in German, so it was a good opportunity to improve my knowledge of the language, particularly in colloquial German.'

She paused and looked wistful. Hoffman could see in her expression a warm recollection tinged with sadness.

'Hansi was working on a project with Siemens on behalf of the Schiller Corporation.' She smiled. Hoffman thought she looked quite lovely. 'He persuaded Siemens to bring me in on the project. The rest, as they say. . . .'

She left it at that, and Hoffman could understand why.

'Did you ever go to South Africa with the company?' he asked.

'No. Why?'

'You said that the woman who took your baby had a South African accent. I just wondered.'

She looked down at her fingernails. There was no varnish but they were still beautifully manicured.

'I have been trying to think of where, if anywhere, I might have met a South African woman.'

'What about England?' he asked. 'There must have been a number of South Africans at university there.'

She nodded. 'Certainly, I had friends who were from South Africa while I was there. But none who had eyes like that woman. I wouldn't forget that.' She made an attempt at a shiver.

'If you had met this woman, do you think she might have been a fanatic about something?' Hoffman was clutching at straws.

'How do you mean?'

'Well.' He put his hands together and massaged his palms slowly. 'People like that; we remember them. That man or that woman from our childhood who stood out. Perhaps they were very tall or very beautiful. Skilful at something. Always able to achieve more than their peers. If they were fanatical we would often think of them as' – he tapped the side of his head with his finger – 'not quite right.'

She put her hand up and shook her head. 'Tell me where there is a university that doesn't have a hundred zealots. Most of us were on some sort of crusade. Environmentalism, animal rights, left wing socialism, the whole melting pot. We were all going to save the world.'

Hoffman could see he was getting nowhere. Joanna was not suddenly going to spring up and declare that she remembered who the woman was. The only glimmer of hope for him was that he could direct Jansch to a specific area of Joanna's background. Perhaps he should get Jansch to concentrate his efforts on Joanna's university background and her subsequent first year in Germany. After that, her more recent past, he believed standard police procedures would turn up any undesirable South African woman who had come into Joanna's circle.

'Well, I don't think there's anything else I need to know at the moment, Frau Schiller, so I'll leave you alone. But you will let me know if you remember anything, no matter how insignificant it may seem, won't you?'

Joanna assured him she would. She stood up and offered her hand to him. He shook it gently, thanked her and showed himself out.

When he had gone Joanna picked up the internal phone and rang through to Schiller's central control room where she knew he would be working. He answered the phone almost immediately.

'Manfred, this is Joanna. I have decided to go home.'

She heard Schiller gasp. *'Mein liebchen*, are you sure? To England?'

'No, to Bad Godesberg.' Bad Godesberg was south of Bonn. It was the home Joanna and Hansi shared as man and wife. Joanna had not been in the house since her husband had died. 'I cannot wait around like this with nothing to do. That policeman comes each day, we talk and he goes away. It's driving me crazy; I need something to occupy me.'

'So why are you going back to Bad Godesberg? You haven't been there for so long.'

'That's why I'm going. I need something to do.'

'Very well, Joanna. I'll phone through to our Bonn office and have them take the guards off the house and open it up for you.' When his son had died and Joanna had left the house, Schiller had put a security team in place on full time surveillance. 'How will you travel?'

'By helicopter please, Manfred. I don't want the press to know where I'm going.'

So it was done, and Joanna was the happier for it. She was sorry she had to be so deprecating to the policeman, for it was something Hoffman had said that had made up her mind. And perhaps one day she would thank him for it.

Conor was ready. It was early evening and he meant to be at the skin-head's flat before the dead man's partner turned up. On the way down the stairs of the house where he had his bed-sit, he bumped into Frau Lindbergh. As ever she was polite and enquiring. Conor was polite back to her and took his leave. No need to antagonize the old girl, he thought as he gunned the Volkswagen into life.

After Conor had killed the skinhead he had searched the man's wallet for a name, and the possibility of a connection with Breggie or Joseph. He found the man's name – it was Krabbe – but there was noth-ing in the wallet or the apartment to connect him with anybody that Conor knew. He took the front-door key with him too because he intended to return there.

Conor parked his car some way from the apartment and walked. He let himself in with the key, checked the dead body was still there, and set about making himself as comfortable as possible.

He found what he needed to make a cup of coffee and settled down to watch some television. It was about two o'clock in the morning when he heard the sound of footsteps coming up the stairs. He got up, switched the television off and went to the front door as the bell sounded.

When he opened the door, he saw the man who had been with the skinhead – the driver of the BMW. He was quite tall and was wearing a leather jacket over a sweatshirt and jeans. He looked a great deal smarter than the skinhead.

'You Oscar?' Conor asked, pointing a finger at him. The stranger looked taken aback and not too sure of himself. He nodded.

'Yes. And who are you?'

'John Buck,' Conor lied. It was the name he used on his forged passport and normally when dealing with people who had no need to know his real name. It was just another measure of security for Conor. 'Jürgen can't make it tonight, asked me to help out.' He stepped out of the door and pulled it to behind him. 'It's OK,' he reassured the man who was looking decidedly unsure. 'I know what we've got to do.'

'You're not German.'

As an observation, it wasn't particularly bright, because Conor's German was heavily accented.

'I can still do what Jürgen can do.' He walked to the stairway. 'Come on then, Oscar. There's work to be done.'

Oscar wasn't moving. 'I want to see Jürgen.'

Conor gave him a look of exasperation. 'He can't talk right now,' he told him truthfully. 'He's tied up.'

Oscar hesitated, and then seemed to make up his mind.

'OK,' he said at last. 'We can talk on the way.'

They went down the stairs to the BMW and were on their way to Conor's place within minutes.

The talk was mainly of Oscar trying to figure out why Jürgen had not let him know of this change of plan and the fact that he didn't know Jürgen had any English friends.

Conor did not wish to disabuse him of the idea that he was English, so said nothing. Instead he concentrated on trying to glean as much information from Oscar as he could.

Presently they pulled up in the street outside Conor's apartment. All it needed now, Conor thought, was for Frau Lindbergh to look out of her window and glance down the street. He put the thought from his mind as they walked to the flat and up the stairs. When they got to the door, Oscar looked at Conor and put his fingers to his lips. To Conor's amazement, Oscar shoved a picklock in the keyhole and opened the door.

Conor then followed Oscar in who was holding a silenced pistol in his hand. Conor followed suit. He went through the motions with Oscar of checking every room in the flat and coming to the obvious conclusion that the flat was empty.

Oscar dropped into a soft chair, obviously pissed off with the lack of a target.

'He's not here,' he said unnecessarily.

'How did you know he would be here?' Conor asked. 'Who told you?'

'The Dutchman.'

'The Dutchman? Who's that?'

Oscar seemed to be a mile away. He suddenly looked up. 'I don't know. He's just a voice on the phone.'

In the darkness it was difficult to see any expression on Oscar's face. A thin light from the windows pierced the gloom. The familiar things in the room were picked out in soft relief; shades of grey and black.

'Perhaps he doesn't live here anymore.'

Oscar reached over to a chair and picked up a discarded newspaper. 'This wasn't here last night. It's today's, so he must have been here.'

It was truer than Oscar realized. Conor had been back to the flat and left the newspaper. He had also made himself a drink, opened a tin of beans and thrown the beans down the toilet. The can he had dumped in the rubbish bin in the kitchen. He had done enough to let them think, if they took the trouble to look, that the flat was still occupied.

'He must be out on the town, nightclubbing. We can wait till he comes home.'

Oscar shook his head. 'We could be here all fucking night. It wouldn't do to be seen leaving the flat in the early hours of the morning.' He stood up. 'No, come on, we're off.'

He was walking out of the flat before Conor realized what was happening. It wasn't quite the way he had planned it. He had hoped he could learn more from Oscar, perhaps a direct link to Breggie or Joseph, by working his way into the man's confidence. But judging from Oscar's desire to leave the killing to another day, Conor had blown his chance.

He followed him down to the car, his mind working furiously on how best to gain an advantage out of this dismal situation. He reckoned no more than a few hours could elapse now before the skinhead was missed and someone found him.

If he hadn't got something from Oscar by then he would have to go back to his old apartment and wait for them to come to him. That would mean giving them an advantage because by then they might have guessed who had killed the skinhead. If so, Oscar would come back packing more than just a single gun.

Conor still hadn't really made up his mind what to do when Oscar pulled up outside the skinhead's place.

'You want off here?'

His thought processes were working furiously now. In a few seconds Oscar would ask him again. He had to make a decision which would be irrevocable.

'There's something in Jürgen's flat I want you to see,' he said suddenly.

Oscar looked puzzled. 'What?' he asked.

Conor affected an apologetic air. 'I should have showed you before we left tonight. It's important though. I know Jürgen would like you to see it.'

'Can't it wait till tomorrow?'

Conor shook his head. 'I don't think so. It may be gone by tomorrow.'

Oscar sighed heavily and killed the engine. 'It had better be worth it,' he warned.

Conor got out of the car and led the way to Jürgen's flat. He opened the door with the key he had taken from Jürgen's body and ushered Oscar in.

'Down there,' he said, pointing towards a door at the end of the hallway, turning on the light.

Oscar began moving down the corridor, avoiding the trainers on the floor and the coat. Conor remained behind him. When Oscar reached the door, Conor urged him to open it. He placed his hand on the door handle and let the door swing open on its hinges.

The light from the hallway fanned across the interior of the room as the door swung open. Oscar saw the familiar impedimenta of Jürgen's lifestyle coming into the light. The long settee on which he and Jürgen had shared many a beer came into view, followed by Jürgen's feet, his legs sprawled at an unusual angle. One of them was covered in blood from a massive wound at the knee.

The door stopped swinging and Oscar edged it open. Jürgen lay there. Even in the half light Oscar could see the whiteness of the skinhead's flesh, blanched by the spectre of death against the obscene blackness of his dried blood.

Oscar knew, at that moment, his own life was over. He had walked into the hangman's pit where death was the inevitable companion. He turned and looked at Conor who had pulled his gun and was now pointing it at him.

'You did this?'

It was a croak. The words cracked and scattered across his dry tongue. Beneath his jaw he felt his heart pounding inside its prison. There would be no release from death row.

'Sit down.'

Oscar was now looking at a different man. Gone was the 'Englishman' he had taken little notice of. Now he was staring at a killer. One who, like himself, showed no mercy nor feeling for his victim. But now he would know what it was like to feel the fear; to drink from the chalice of insanity and suffer its pitiful harvest.

His legs started to tremble. Their strength seemed to wilt until he feared he would fall. The shaking rippled through his body and blurred his vision. Tears formed behind his eyes and unseen fingers gripped his loins.

In less time than it took him to walk the length of Jürgen's room, Oscar had become a nervous, bumbling wreck.

'On the settee, next to your friend.'

Conor had to push him. Oscar stumbled across the floor and collapsed on to the settee next to the lifeless form of the skinhead. He tried to edge away from the body as though fearful that some contact might unleash a plague on him.

'What are you going to do?' he clamoured forlornly.

Conor pulled an upright chair around and sat astride it, still pointing the gun at Oscar.

'You know what I'm going to do, Oscar.'

'No, please. Let me go. I'll do anything. I'll pay anything.' Oscar's pleading was a rambling coward's attempt at begging for mercy. Conor hadn't really expected it.

'I have some questions for you.'

'Anything, anything.' He had his hands up like a priest blessing a congregation. 'Ask anything you like.'

'Who's the Dutchman?'

Oscar slumped back in despair. 'I don't know. I swear.'

Conor believed him. It would have been most unusual for the foot soldiers in a well run terrorist organization to know their commanders. Or at least, know where they lived and have direct access to them. It did happen though, but often through a lack of disciplined control.

'How do you contact him?'

'I don't. He contacts me.'

'How?'

'By phone.'

It seemed reasonable to Conor. The Dutchman would issue his orders when necessary. The troops would always be waiting around for those orders. Otherwise they would get on with their lives.

'Is there a code word you both use?'

Oscar nodded. 'He gives me the new code word each time he phones. I use it when he phones again.'

'So the next time he rings, you repeat the code word he last gave you?'

Oscar nodded again. He wasn't looking so wretched now. Probably, mused Conor, because he feels a little less threatened.

'What's the next code word?'

Oscar lifted his head but was reminded by Conor waving the gun at him that resistance was futile.

'Gullit,' he said weakly.

'What?'

Oscar drew a deep, painful breath. 'Gullit. He was a famous, Dutch footballer. He uses Dutch footballers all the time.'

'So when he phones, you simply say "Gullit"?'

'Yes. There's nothing else.'

Conor waited.

'Then what?'

Oscar shrugged. He made a small movement with his hands. 'That's it. He tells me whatever it is he wants me to know or do. I repeat it. He gives me the next code word and hangs up.'

Conor nodded thoughtfully then stood up and shot Oscar twice in the chest. The force of the bullets threw Oscar back into the settee. His arms opened out and fell by his side and his chin dropped on to his chest.

Conor went across to him and put his fingers on the side of his neck. There was no sign of a pulse. He went through Oscar's pockets, took his wallet and car keys and walked out of the flat.

While Oscar died, Breggie was nursing a very unhappy child. Throughout the previous day and through the night, the baby would only sleep for short spells, after which it would wake up crying. Feeding the baby did not always pacify him, and his temperature was giving Breggie cause for concern.

Her own problems were pushed to the back of her mind as she fought to control her temper and alleviate her tiredness by snatching sleep whenever possible. Joseph had proved to be quite unhelpful and had no patience at all.

It was about four in the morning when Breggie laid the infant Manny in his cot, gently pulling her hands away and almost holding her breath for fear of disturbing him. She laid the back of her fingers very lightly on his cheek and could feel the worrying heat from his soft skin. She yawned and lay down on the bed beside the cot. Within minutes she was fast asleep, but not before promising herself that she would seek advice when day came.

Luckily the baby slept until about eight o'clock. When he woke Breggie, she was quite pleased to think she had got four hours of unin-terrupted sleep. The baby's tears were through hunger, and Breggie was much the happier for that. She got Joseph out of bed and told him to make coffee and sort himself out, and then she tended to the baby's needs. One hour later, Breggie was ready to seek the advice she had promised herself.

She drove herself to the shopping mall she had visited two days earlier, intending to take advantage of Joseph, and leave him longer than the thirty minutes she had promised. Breggie had no intention of staying out too long though because she did not feel she could trust Joseph enough to leave Manny with him for more than an hour.

She found a large chemist store and waited until she caught the assistant's eye.

'Could I see the pharmacist?' she asked, glancing towards the dispensing end of the counter.

'Of course.'

The assistant brought the pharmacist over. She was a tall woman, bubbly hair, blonde. More like a dancer than a chemist. Breggie felt unusually nervous. If she had been pulling an Uzi out to gun the woman to death, she would have had that familiar adrenalin rush and sexual emotion she enjoyed at the kill. But now she was a kitten.

The chemist smiled. 'Can I help you?'

'Yes. I need some medicine.'

'Is it for you?'

'No,' Breggie replied, 'it's for my son.'

'What's wrong with him?' the pharmacist asked.

Breggie could feel her hand trembling. She pushed it into the pocket of her coat. 'He isn't sleeping too well. He has a cough.'

'A cough,' she repeated. 'How old is he?'

Breggie had to think. 'He's three weeks old,' she lied.

The woman straightened. She blinked and stared at Breggie. 'Three weeks old. Well, goodness, why haven't you taken him to your doctor?'

'Oh, it isn't that bad,' Breggie blustered. 'Not bad enough to see a doctor.'

'Well you should, you know. I can't prescribe anything for a child that age.' She let it sink in. 'Who is the baby's doctor, anyway?'

Breggie wished she had never asked. It would have been much easier to have purchased a child's cough mixture from the counter.

'We don't live here. We're from Munich. We're on holiday.'

It was all going to pieces and Breggie knew it. Other customers at the pharmacy counter were beginning to take an interest in the conversation.

'We have a data base on computer of all registered practitioners,' she informed a bewildered Breggie. 'I'll get the phone number for you and you can ring his practice. Or, if you like, you can ring the hospital where the baby was born. It will be in the best interests of the baby if you contact someone.'

Breggie was shaking her head even before the woman had finished. 'No. I haven't got time. It doesn't matter anyway; we're going back tomorrow.'

The woman put an admonishing finger up at her. 'That may be too late. A baby that young must be treated as soon as possible. He simply must.'

Suddenly Breggie had had enough. She muttered a disgruntled remark to the poor woman and walked away from the counter.

The pharmacist watched her go and continued watching until Breggie was no longer in sight.

'Strange woman,' she said to the assistant who had been beside her all the time. 'Such silly behaviour. Still, what can you expect from a foreigner?'

'Was she foreign?' the girl asked.

The woman nodded, quite smug. 'Oh yes. She was South African.'

At six o'clock that morning, Franz Molke was being woken in the usual way with a cup of coffee. By 6.30 he had showered and dressed and was sitting at his breakfast table with the early editions of the morning press. It was his habit to read the sports pages first before getting down to the headier contents of the newspapers, suitably highlighted by his press secretary.

Molke's private residence was situated on the outskirts of Bonn. He had started the Volkspartei from a room in that house, but now the party headquarters were in the old capital itself. It was Molke's intention to transfer party HQ to Berlin as soon as the Volkspartei's rise to power had been completed. He was also having a splendid residence built in Berlin on a prime piece of land in the old eastern sector.

Molke would normally breakfast alone, unless some urgent government business needed his attention. Then he would usually have his press secretary at the table briefing him along with his ministerial private secretary. That morning he was alone, and the phone rang.

He picked it up from the table, still reading of Borussia Dortmund's exploits in the league cup.

'Molke,' he said abruptly.

'Morning, Franz. I thought you should know the Covenant may no longer be in Germany.'

Dr Aaron Kistler never introduced himself on the phone when talking to Molke. There was no need because his booming, bass voice was so distinctive.

Molke stopped reading. 'What makes you think that?'

'I cannot be too sure, but my sources believe the Covenant is complete. It's my supposition that it would be unwise to keep the document in Germany.'

'Do you think it has been signed?'

'No, but Eshkol left the country yesterday after his meeting with the others, and we are not sure which of them has it, but we do know they have all left Germany.'

Molke felt his heart sink. Losing sight of the Covenant was a blow, but not insurmountable. They had expected difficulty in tracking down the document and had only learned of Eshkol's group at the eleventh hour. In fact, kidnapping Schiller's grandson had been a last resort for Molke's people. Had they been able to identify Eshkol and the others in time, they would have taken the Covenant from them. Molke had little doubt that the Covenant would not be brought back into the country until Schiller was ready to sign.

'Do you have people working on it?'

'Yes.'

'We must find out where it is whatever the cost.'

'I know. I'll be in touch.'

The phone went dead and left Molke staring into space. He switched his phone off and put it on the table. The exploits of Borussia Dortmund Football Club were no longer of any interest to him and he pushed the paper angrily to one side.

The flaw in Molke's plan was Schiller's grandson. The great man might view his personal empire and its future stewardship more important than the life of an infant barely two weeks old. He could still sign the Covenant and live with the consequences; in which case Molke's vision of a mighty Volkspartei at the head of a new super state would be little more than a pipe dream.

The key now was to apply pressure to Schiller. And Molke knew a way that disturbed even his own sensibilities.

CHAPTER SEVEN

Conor parked the BMW a couple of blocks away from Oscar's house, and walked the rest of the way. Before approaching the house, he did a complete survey of the immediate area and the house itself as inconspicuously as possible. When he was satisfied it was reasonably safe to do so, he let himself in but exercised a great deal of caution. Jürgen's submission that Oscar lived alone did not necessarily mean there would be no one else in the house.

He slipped in through the front door using Oscar's key and closed it behind him, pausing first to listen carefully for any sounds that might tell him that somebody was in the house. He remained still and quiet for about five minutes before venturing forward to carry out a thorough search of the likely places he would find Oscar's personal documents and anything that could lead him further into the heart of the organization. To that end he was to be disappointed. There was no obvious evidence of any links Oscar might have had to any subversive group or extreme political party.

Conor wasn't really surprised; most people involved in such a criminal activity would take great care in concealing any incriminating documents. It was likely that Oscar had a safe or some other secure place to put anything sensitive. Conor could find no safe in the house so he assumed that there might be something on computer file, but not being much more than a personal computer man, and not a hacker, he felt it would be a waste of time even looking.

Having completed his cursory and not too thorough search, Conor left the house, and the car, and walked back towards the city. It was a cloudy night and dawn was struggling to put some light into the eastern sky. There was no rain and just a slight breeze so the walk was not a problem. There were people about; early starters, road cleaners and the like. He found a taxi rank and had a cab take him back to Jürgen's place. He paid the taxi off and walked up the street to where he had left his own car. Thirty minutes later he was back in the bed-sit, thankful to have avoided the early morning prowling of Frau Lindbergh.

But before settling down for the night, he bundled all his outer clothing, including his shoes into a large bin bag. His intention was to dispose of it the following day because Conor was only too aware of the forensic evidence on his clothing that could link him to the deaths of Krabbe and Oscar. Within thirty minutes of arriving back at the bed-sit, he was tucked up in bed and was soon sound asleep.

Joanna flew back to Bad Godesberg that morning. Schiller was sorry to see her go, but understood her reasons. The helicopter took her from Schiller's residence to a private airfield near Godesberg. She completed the remainder of the journey by chauffer-driven car.

She was welcomed at the house by her own staff. Most of the security guards had been removed, but at Schiller's insistence some remained. It made sense too because they all knew it wouldn't be long before the press were camped outside the gates.

Joanna had wondered if returning home to the house she had shared with Hansi would be too painful. She had so many happy memories of their time there together. Now, however, the pain of Hansi's death and the pain of little Manny's kidnap were coupled together and she found herself walking round the rooms recalling some of the moments they had shared together.

She ate a light lunch and watched the midday news on television. Then she went through a short work-out in the private gym, showered and changed into a pair of jogging bottoms and sweatshirt. By the middle of the afternoon, Joanna was feeling in a relatively better frame of mind and set about the task she had come home to do.

As a young girl at school, Joanna had always kept a diary. It became so much a part of her adolescent life that she took her diary-keeping habit to university. The problem there, of course, was that keeping a diary seriously interfered with studying and socializing, so the diary took a back seat. Although some entries did appear they were so short they hardly merited their own appearance in the pages.

After leaving university, Joanna took up her diary again, but because she spent a great deal of her time working with a computer, progress made her pen redundant and all her entries found their way on to computer file.

The advent of photo scanners for computers revolutionized Joanna's records and she began working back through her past, lifting those special moments and editing in scanned photographs for each of those occasions.

She brought this hobby with her to Germany while working for the giant Siemens Company and found it extremely useful; many of her business presentations included scanned photographs and, while not unusual, it always added an element of pragmatism to her style.

When she and Hansi became serious about each other, Joanna encouraged him to adopt her way of keeping personal records. Although Hansi was not particularly interested in keeping a diary – in fact he was quite happy to let Joanna do that – he did endeavour to use some of her ideas when compiling his own files and references.

It was her own records, and those of Hansi, that Joanna wanted to look at; for she was convinced that somewhere in those records, she would find the woman who had kidnapped her beloved Manny.

She worked steadily on her own files, searching back through her own happy memories. At times she would find herself remembering those memories and dwelling on them. It was almost a pleasure to sit and reminisce.

Then, suddenly, Joanna's heart skipped. Hansi was on the screen. She was still going through her university records and hadn't expected to see her dead husband so soon. He looked so young and happy. Tears came into her eyes as she looked at the images before her. It was a Christmas party. There were others in the scene too, but she really only had eyes for her husband.

Reluctantly, Joanna moved on. When the light began to fade and hunger prevailed she was forced to break off for a while. She had dismissed most of the staff earlier that afternoon so decided to find something to eat herself. An hour later, after a microwaved meal for two (she was that hungry), she had made a pot of tea and was back in the study and in front of the computer.

She resumed her trawl through the memories and found that her entries were getting less and less frequent. And the less frequent they became, the more she could recall people and faces she had met. And she was satisfied there was no South African woman among them.

She turned then to Hansi's records, but to get those meant going to his safe. Nobody had been in that safe since Hansi had died because she had expressly forbidden it. There had been talk of legal moves to gain access to the safe by his business colleagues, but her father-in-law had blocked them. So Hansi's secrets, if there were any, remained locked away, and Joanna had promised that those secrets would remain so until a year after his death.

Hansi had always believed he was the only one who knew the combination to his safe. What he didn't remember was that one evening when he was very drunk, he had taken Joanna into his study to give her a present and had opened the safe in front of her. In his drunken state he had dialled the combination while speaking the letters out loud. The numbers had stuck in Joanna's brain and she had never forgotten them. Not that she ever needed to know because she had never wanted to go into Hansi's safe.

Until now.

She dialled in the combination and opened the heavy safe door. There were several papers in there, but she ignored them. What she was looking for was his box of computer discs. As she pulled out the box, she inadvertently dragged out an envelope which fell on to the floor. As it hit the parquet flooring, a computer disc slid out from inside the envelope. She put the box on the desk and picked up the envelope and disc from the floor. There was nothing in the envelope, but on the disc were the two initials VP.

Curious, she put the disc into the computer and asked for a file directory. The directory list came up on the screen. There were several but as soon as Joanna tried to access one, the screen went blank and an instruction appeared that she should enter a password. Joanna ejected the disc and checked the label to see if a password had been written on either side. Inevitably there was nothing other than those two initials. She put the disc back in the computer and tried again but each directory yielded the same result. They all needed passwords to access them. Joanna tried the obvious like family names, nicknames, birth dates etc., but all came up with a rejection.

Determined now to try to gain access to the files on Hansi's disc, Joanna pulled her own box of disc files towards her. She ran her fingertips through them until she found the one she wanted. On the label was the title 'Party Games'. She smiled at the memory.

When Joanna was in her final year at university, she and her undergraduate colleagues would write programmes and challenge the others to run them without knowing the passwords and defences that had been written in to each programme. Naturally each challenge became tougher as they all fought to outdo each other. Joanna cracked all the challenges with a programme she devised and called 'Detective'. She was now about to try it on Hansi's files.

Joanna's programme ran on a method of spinning groups of letters instead of just regurgitating endless words in a hope that the programme might find a match with the passwords locked into the target file. Because the password would more than likely be fairly short and not more than eight letters anyway, the groups of letters would be in pairs initially, then in threes and finally five letters.

The idea was to check the target file's access parameters for matching blocks of two, three, and five letter groups. Whenever matching groups were found, and they could be in any order, the programme would begin to pair groups at random until it found a match or several matches.

Because passwords were often eccentric or personalized, they were not always found in any dictionary, so Joanna's programme would come up with matches that could trigger a recognizable group of up to five letters and put these up on the screen. It would then be up to the operator to add either a prefix or suffix of their own. The programme avoided groups above five unless it came across a direct match in the file's password dictionary because this would result in an unnecessarily long list of possible matches. The programme worked on the odds that passwords would more often than not be less than eight letters.

The advantage of Joanna's programme was that it would run in any language that used the Roman alphabet but was kept to blocks of letters rather than complete matching to reduce the memory required. It could never do a direct comparison to passwords because they were always 'fenced' in such a way that the host computer would detect illegal interrogation and shut down.

She set the programme running and went off to make herself a cup of coffee.

Hoffman put the phone down and curled a finger at Jansch. The detective got up from his desk and came over. Hoffman was chewing the end of a pencil.

'That was Lechter,' he said, taking the pencil from his mouth and tossing it on to the desk. 'He's investigating the explosion at that house.'

Jansch nodded. Hoffman looked away, lifting his head to stare at some imaginary spot on the ceiling.

'They found some counterfeit money there, remember?' Jansch said he did. Hoffman lowered his gaze.

'Well, some of the bloody stuff has turned up in Cologne.'

Jansch stiffened. 'Cologne?' He digested that for a moment, and then shrugged. 'Must mean it's being distributed then.'

Hoffman screwed his face up and shook his head, but not too emphatically.

'Well, Lechter has been on to Twenty-one, but they are not aware of any forgery operation going on.' He held his hands up in a gesture of submission. 'Doesn't mean there isn't one going on, but. . . .'

'So what's that got to do with us?'

Hoffman swung back and forth on his swivel chair. He stopped and pointed a finger at Jansch. 'Remember Lechter had a theory that it might have been a pay-off? We've identified Trucco as one of the victims of the bomb. So, if the kidnappers were paid off at that house, and their employers intended silencing them permanently, there would have been no point in handing over genuine bills.'

Jansch was ahead of him. 'So someone is using the same counterfeit money as the kidnappers. Assuming it was the kidnappers.'

'And they are in Cologne.'

Jansch stood up. 'I'll get on to it. I'll ring Lechter first, and then I'll get some men out there asking questions.' He turned to leave, but Hoffman stopped him.

'Jansch, go yourself. But remember, this is Otto Lechter's pitch; don't queer it.'

Jansch smiled. 'I'll be diplomacy itself, sir.'

Hoffman grinned back at him. Then his expression changed. If it was the kidnap group, then this could be the single, oddest break they would get.

Breggie had got back from her disastrous trip that morning in a worse state than when she had left. She realized she had acted naively and stupidly. By letting the chemist question her about the baby, Breggie had virtually walked into a trap of her own making. She knew it would not have taken much more to have roused the woman's suspicions and have her calling for the police. Not that Breggie thought the chemist would have connected her to the Schiller kidnap on such a flimsy display, but it would have provoked a great deal of thought from any policeman worth his salt.

If Breggie was to be truthful to herself, it had frightened her. So much so that she had driven straight back and not dared go into another pharmacy, even to buy a child's medicine off the shelf. Joseph was not too pleased when Breggie insisted he go out to a chemist somewhere in the city and buy a bottle of child's cough mixture. He rolled her a cigarette before he left.

Most of that day was then taken up with pacifying the baby, fretting over it, coaxing it, loving it and screaming at it. Whatever Breggie did, the baby just seemed to get worse. The medicine Joseph had brought home was little more than flavoured linctus by the time she had watered it down, and Breggie knew they were getting close to point where they would have to get professional help.

'If the baby is no better tomorrow, Joseph,' Breggie told him, 'we must send for a doctor.'

Joseph was reading. He looked up from the magazine and gave Breggie a peculiar look. 'Lot of good that'll do,' he muttered. 'It will just bring the police down on us like a ton of bricks, you know it will.' He went back to his magazine.

'Joseph!' Breggie shouted despairingly. 'Little babies like this can die very easily if they get unwell. We mustn't let that happen.'

Joseph put the magazine down again. 'Then don't let it happen. Look after him. That's what you're here for.'

'That's not what I'm here for.' Her voice notched up a pitch. 'It's what *we* are here for, Joseph, you and me.'

He picked up the magazine again. 'You just get on with it, Breggie. He's your responsibility.'

Breggie ripped the magazine from his grasp. 'He's our responsibility,' she screamed and flung the magazine across the room.

Joseph jumped up from the chair but Breggie grabbed him as he walked past. She spun him round.

'Nothing must happen to that baby, Joseph. Nothing!'

'What if it does? It's no great loss.' He shrugged.

She slapped him hard across the face. 'You bastard; it's Hansi's baby you're talking about, Hansi's baby! Nothing must happen to him.'

'Then don't let it.' He brushed past her and retrieved the magazine from the floor. 'And if you hit me again, Breggie, I'll break your fucking neck.'

Breggie slumped into a chair. She seemed beaten. 'It should have been my baby, Joseph,' she cried. 'Do you know that? My baby. If that English bitch hadn't come along it would have been me that Hansi married.' The tears were flowing freely down Breggie's cheeks.

Joseph looked down at her forlorn figure. 'Don't kid yourself. That English bitch has class. All you have is a pair of legs that opens at the first sign of a prick. You're OK for screwing, Breggie. Pretty good screw too. But the English woman' – he paused and made a circle with his thumb and forefinger – 'she's class. Hansi would never have married you. You were always going to be his rough trade. For him, it had to be someone he could show off, someone elegant. She had it, Breggie, and you know it.'

'He loved me, Joseph,' she wept softly.

He shook his head. 'No, Breggie, he fucked you, that's all.'

He looked at the magazine then changed his mind and flung it on to the table. 'I'm going out.' He put his hand in his pocket and brought out his tin of hand-rolled cigarettes. 'Here, have one of these.' He put the tin on to the table next to the magazine. 'We'll talk when I get back.'

He left her there weeping and shut the door, closing his mind to the problem. But whatever Joseph Schneider was, it wasn't stupid. If the baby died, they were both in trouble. Tomorrow they would have to find a doctor.

*

The programme had come up with a host of matching sequential groups, filling the screen in columns. Joanna saw some names come out at her as instantly recognisable but almost certainly perfectly useless. Feeding a batch of Russian letters or other East European languages would have been pointless. She sat at the computer and began the next stage of the search.

Joanna began scrolling through the text a page at a time and highlighting what she considered were possible key words for access to Hansi's files. Each word she thought she could use was highlighted and saved to a memory bank. After thirty minutes she had reduced the columns to one containing about twenty or so words.

Joanna separated these into four groups of five and began concentrating on ways of identifying the passwords. One was quite obvious to her. It was the word *Kampf*. It was a complete word meaning conflict, or struggle. Other words began to impose themselves upon her until she saw the word *Keile* in one of the groups. It meant 'key' in German. Joanna suspended the programme and tried to access Hansi's files with the word *Keile* but it was rejected. She went back to the word search again.

After several abortive attempts at coming up with the right words, Joanna instructed the programme to run the groups with pairs of consonants and vowels attached as prefixes and suffixes. It spewed out many, many more words and, finally, put a list of matches on the screen. Joanna could feel her pulse quickening; she was getting closer. Her next step was to get through the first door to the files' directories. She would need a key to open the cabinet.

Cabinet!

'I wonder,' she muttered beneath her breath. The word *Schrank* was on the list. She tried that but she was still denied access. Seven letters. Hansi could have used an eight-letter word, she thought, and typed the letter 'e' on the end. The new word, *Schranke* meant 'barrier'. It seemed apt. She entered it into the password dialogue box and held her breath.

There was a momentary pause as the programme checked the word. Joanna tensed. Suddenly the screen changed and Hansi's list of files appeared. Joanna felt a ripple run through her and she banged the desk softly with her closed fist. She was in! She had opened the door and was looking at a screen asking her to select a file.

At this point Joanna felt quite weak. She remembered often feeling like this at university when she had cracked open a particularly difficult programme. Then she would feel elated and punch the air.

She stood up and walked around the room for a few minutes, letting the blood circulate and getting the stiffness out of her limbs. She could feel the excitement beginning to filter back, but at the same time she was also feeling nervous. Cracking Hansi's files had never been something Joanna thought she'd ever want to do. Now she had done it and was about to look into her dead husband's most intimate secrets. It scared her.

Coffee first, she thought. The pot of tea was still there but it was cold and now she needed coffee. She went out to the kitchen and made a pot, bringing it back to Hansi's desk. She poured a cup, drank it straight down and refilled the cup again. Then she looked at the screen. Which file, though? Which one to look at first?

Because the files were listed alphabetically, Joanna decided to go in that sequence. The first file was titled *Abwehr*. It meant 'defence'. She opened the file and found herself looking at what appeared to be a breakdown of special groups working within an organization. It was headed *Gegenintelligenz*, 'counter-intelligence' operation. It listed sections of the Volkspartei working as a military arm of the party, and gave details of those units, their leaders and where in the Federal Republic they were stationed.

Joanna scanned the pages quickly, speed reading her way through each screen and uncovering the details of a secret army assembled to undermine the freedoms enjoyed by the German Nation. Details of how the groups worked to spread disinformation in key areas such as the press and the big workers unions, government employees and the unemployed revealed a deliberate plan to mitigate any opposition to the Volkspartei.

With her disbelief growing by the minute, Joanna realized she was reading a document that was inspired by right wing extremism culled straight from the pages of Nazi history. That it belonged to her dead husband was even more disturbing and she was beginning to think she should never have broken into the files in the first place.

But Joanna knew that was nonsense; she had made the first, tentative steps into her husband's innermost sanctum and needed objectivity and pragmatism as her companion, not emotion or fear. Somewhere in those files, Joanna believed, she would find the name of the woman who had kidnapped her baby son. She owed it to him to find her.

It was midnight and Breggie de Kok was still awake. Her head ached and her eyes felt as though someone had poured sand in them. She wanted sleep; quiet, uninterrupted sleep. A sleep in which there were no dreams. A sleep in which she could drown and wake refreshed. A sleep that would last a full dozen hours or so. One without worry. One without fear. One from which she would wake and not have to think about anybody else.

But that richness was no longer part of her life. Beside her bed in his cot was the infant Manny. He was sleeping now, but for how long? How long had it been, she wondered, since she had finally rocked him off to sleep? And how long would it be before he woke again, crying and choking for breath?

When Joseph returned with the small bottle of linctus, he had found Breggie asleep, so, naturally, he woke her. The effects of the cigarettes had left her with a deep, throbbing headache which did nothing to improve her temper. The inevitable argument followed which had resulted in blows. Breggie had come off worse, but what the hell, she had thought to herself, it was at least a way of letting the frustration out.

And, of course, the baby had woken up because of the noise and the inevitable cycle began again. Breggie wondered how much longer she could stand it. She wasn't cut out for baby minding on such a scale. The maternal instinct in her was more forced than natural which made her task so much more a chore than a pleasure.

She swung her feet off the bed and went through to the kitchen, made herself a cup of coffee and sat at the breakfast bench drinking it and contemplating her future.

Breggie could see nothing but failure as the inevitable outcome. The baby's health was deteriorating fast. It meant he would need specialist treatment. Joseph had reluctantly agreed to ask the organization to send a doctor which meant they would have to reveal their where-abouts to Joseph's controller. It went against their meticulous planning and the principle of the need to know. The only other people who knew of the house were the elderly couple who obtained it for them. They had been specially hired by Joseph, and no one in the organization knew of its whereabouts.

Breggie finished her coffee and made up her mind. Once the doctor had seen the baby and prescribed something more likely to help the little chap, she would leave the house for a place nobody knew about. Not even Joseph. She hadn't been there for almost a year now. Somewhere she had spent some of the happiest moments of her life in Germany.

She felt better now that she had made up her mind. She put the empty coffee cup in the sink and turned the light out. On the way back to bed she paused beside the cot where Manny was sleeping.

'Not long now, little fellow,' she whispered. 'Soon you will be where you really belong.'

Joanna woke with a start. She was still at the desk, sitting in the luxurious captain's chair Hansi liked so much. The computer in front of her was still running but a screen saver was decorating the screen with psychedelic patterns. She shook her head and rubbed the sleep from her eyes. Then she stood up and went though to the bathroom. The clock on the wall told her it was four o'clock in the morning. She freshened up and went back to the computer, hit a key and contemplated the file that had returned to the screen.

Joanna had come a long way since breaking into Hansi's files. It was a road of surprises, shocks and disappointments. A whole gamut of emotions had swamped her until she thought she was no longer capable of being touched by each new revelation of Hansi's past.

She had made copious notes, gone from one file to another and cracked passwords that barred entry to some small files. In doing so, Joanna had lost her way a little. The original quest had been to track down the South African woman, but she had diverged from that route so often as she followed Hansi's devious, secret world of revolution, disinformation, plotting and intrigue against the established order in Germany. It was almost beyond her comprehension that in today's sophisticated Europe such devil's work could still be contemplated. But in front of her were the facts.

104

What Joanna had uncovered was the blueprint of the New Germany and its role as Europe moved into a closer union as a United States of Europe. At its head would be Franz Molke and the Volkspartei. Behind it would be the might and strength of Schiller's empire with Hansi holding supreme power.

What had shocked Joanna to her core was the line from a letter to Franz Molke, the leader of the Volkspartei, from Hansi in which he had declared that it was 'unlikely' his father, Herr Manfred Schiller, would still be alive much beyond the year 2000. If he was then he, Hansi, would find a way of terminating his father's influence. It would mean *complete, unchallenged control of my father's empire.* What was unwritten but clearly meant was that Hansi did not intend his father should live long enough to stop his murderous plans.

At that moment, Joanna stopped loving her dead husband. All feeling, all residue of love, any sadness at his death was washed away by a sense of revulsion and contempt. And she felt soiled. It did nothing to prevent Joanna feeling immensely sad though. She had loved Hansi and believed there could never be another man with those qualities that she found so endearing. How wrong she had been.

The remainder of the search through Hansi's files became automatic; a robotic march through pages of transcript, columns, meaningless jargon. She seemed to have lost the will to carry on, but she felt there was nothing to lose now; she could no longer find anything that would hurt her.

Until she came across a list of names which appeared to represent some kind of inner council or committee. The names were alphabetically listed with a short profile alongside them.

Except one: the name of Breggie de Kok. It leapt off the screen at her. Attached to the name was the simple statement: 'see file'.

Joanna found her interest had suddenly returned. She closed the file she was reading and began searching the file list until she saw the name, 'Breggie'. She accessed the file. It opened with a personal profile.

Breggie de Kok. Born Johannesburg, South Africa, 1970. University of Witwatersrand. Left South Africa 1994 for England. Joined militant animal rights group in east England. On trial for murder of doctor. Not proven, returned to South Africa. Short stay, arrived Germany 1996.

First contact with Breggie, Christmas 1995, Cambridge (not the university). Recognized potential recruit. Cultivated strong friendship. Continued again when Breggie arrived in the Federal Republic. Despite marriage to Joanna, considered Breggie's friendship and participation in Volkspartei work too valuable to lose. Established address at Koblenz. . . .

Joanna closed her eyes and shuddered. Here, virtually in her dead husband's own hand, was an admission that Breggie de Kok was his mistress and had been probably as far back as Cambridge.

Cambridge! Joanna stiffened, sitting bolt upright in the chair. Cambridge. What was it that was significant? What was it that was leaping off the screen and shouting at her?

She kept saying the word Cambridge over and over again in her head. Joanna never knew a Breggie de Kok at Cambridge, so why should that period impinge on her now? Why should it strike a chord?

She pulled a large scribbling pad towards her and wrote: *Cambridge, Breggie de Kok. Why?*

She went back to the file and forced herself to continue reading through her dead husband's perfidious and treasonous admissions.

It came to Joanna, not in a flash of sudden recall, but in a moment of tiredness, when she didn't seem to be able to think, such was her state of mind and her fatigue. It was then she realized where she had seen Breggie de Kok.

She smiled and closed Hansi's files down. She ejected his disc and inserted one of her own. One she had been looking through so many hours ago it seemed like a lifetime away. She went through her personal diary until she came to the period at Cambridge and the Christmas party. The first time she had been in the same room as Hansi.

The photograph came up on the screen. Her and Hansi laughing and posing for the camera. As with so many photographs of that kind, other people always appeared in the background. She enlarged the picture until it filled the screen.

Even allowing for a slight deterioration in quality, there was no mistaking those eyes; the same piercing eyes that had stared out at her from behind the ski mask. In the background, looking towards the camera was Breggie de Kok. Suddenly the emotion of it all was too much and she began to sob bitterly.

Joanna had finally identified the terrorist who had kidnapped her son.

CHAPTER EIGHT

Levi Eshkol sat on one side of a long table in a vacant room in the Israeli Parliament, the Knesset. Facing him was the Israeli Prime Minister, Benjamin Kossof. There was nobody else in the room. Between them was the Covenant. Kossof had agreed to see Eshkol after receiving a message through an intermediary. The urgency in the message was implied rather than pronounced, but the prime minister knew Levi Eshkol would not waste precious time on non urgent matters.

'Thank you for giving me the opportunity to read your brief, Levi,' the prime minister was saying. 'I must say it's an intriguing document. And this, I presume, is the Covenant?'

'In its entirety, sir, all it needs is Manfred Schiller's signature.'

'Then why did you bring it to Israel if Herr Schiller is in Germany?'

Eshkol shook his head. 'He will not sign it until the kidnap of his grandson has been resolved. I couldn't risk leaving it there.'

Kossof was aware of events in Germany. 'You think the people responsible for the kidnapping want the Covenant, and would kill to get it?'

'No question, sir.'

The prime minister closed his hands together. 'Tell me, why should Schiller want to sign this now? Why didn't he simply make out a will?'

Eshkol shrugged. 'He has his reasons. I asked him that when he first contacted me. He told me old age is a weakness; it brings a sharp mind to a feeble end. He was afraid that he might not have the ability to oversee such a transfer of power, and that it would require strength.'

'But why us?' the prime minister asked. 'After all, he is a German. He

108

faced the War Crimes Commission at Nuremberg. Is it atonement?'

Eshkol shook his head. 'Schiller was never a Nazi, but they made him extremely rich and very powerful. I got the impression from the conversations I have had with him that he does not want that power to fall into the hands of the Neo Nazis.'

Kossof frowned and shook his head slowly. 'The Volkspartei. Sad bastards.' He brightened a little. 'So, what legal challenge can be mounted to the Covenant?'

'None, sir; the Covenant is secret. Only five men have seen the document in its entirety.' He pointed at the folders in front of the prime minister. 'Once you have read it you will be the sixth person. But remember, Schiller will sign this document in the presence of lawyers. He will not be under any duress. He cannot be declared insane. And it is his creation.'

Kossof was trying hard not to get excited. It wasn't in the nature of experienced politicians like him to show their hand in public and it was difficult to relax that position in private. But here was a gift from the gods and it was being bestowed upon the people of Israel. It was difficult not to show some emotion.

'Suppose Schiller changes his mind after the Covenant has been signed. Say, a year or two later?'

Eshkol had deliberately held something back, but now he was about to reveal the jewel in the Covenant's crown.

'The legal position cannot be challenged. All the mechanisms have been put in place by the Covenant to complete the transfer across the globe. But there is another aspect to this: Schiller runs his empire, not just through company presidents and corporate lawyers, but through a system of linked satellites. The satellites are owned by the company and have all been put into orbit by the Schiller Aerospace Industry. They are activated by codes through two master satellites which, naturally, only Schiller and his immediate subordinates have access to.' Eshkol was warming to the subject; it made him feel quite good. 'When the signing has been completed, Schiller will instruct the satellites to accept new codes. These will be encrypted codes which we will supply. The satellites will ask him for confirmation once he has put the new codes, *our* codes, in. The satellites will then automatically transfer control to the new codes. Once they are in, we will instruct the satellites to accept a new set of encrypted codes, *ours*, of which Schiller, nor his lawyers, will have any knowledge.'

He shuffled in his chair. 'Now, all this has been agreed with Schiller's co-operation. There will be no change of heart or mind. Once those new codes have been logged into the satellites, Israel will control the single biggest industrial and commercial empire, the world has ever seen. With our ability to scan the globe our potential will be almost limitless. We would be able to react favourably to the volatile financial markets, maintain armament production in less politically sensitive areas, handle a third of the globe's raw materials and precious metals and, if it was in Israel's interests, we could influence important decisions by foreign governments. We will be at liberty to intercept what might be considered as low grade military traffic between most governments, including the Americans, although high grade traffic will not be too difficult to access using new, sophisticated technology. We will "see" most of the communication links used by terrorists. We will have considerable power. We will, literally, become a super state.'

Kossof drew in a long, deep breath. The reality of Eshkol's revelations was not lost on the prime minister. If he had just been told that this kind of power was being handed to an Arab state, he would have moved heaven and earth to prevent it. He would have risked an all out war and all its consequences to stop it.

But how different it was that a country such as Israel, a country whose history was covered in its own blood, a country born out of violence, a country that wanted to live at peace and not at war with its Arab neighbours, should now be on the brink of such power.

The possibilities were endless and teased his mind like a temptress. If he stopped to contemplate the rights of such ownership, or if he consulted with his advisers on the morality of what was being offered, he would find objection. He would pit sanity against insanity, open the gates of Mammon, and bring the Arabs into their midst baying like scavenging dogs. It would bring its own holocaust.

These thoughts had flashed through Kossof's mind and brought him to the inevitable conclusion that he wanted the Covenant for Israel, but it would have to be a closely guarded secret, open to but a few of his most trustworthy colleagues.

'How long will it take to complete the signing?' He tapped the fold-

110

ers on the table in front of him.

Eshkol considered it for a few moments. 'Probably a couple of hours. Schiller will read each page carefully with his lawyers before signing it. They won't be too happy about him transferring complete control to us, but they will have to go along with it. They'll all be getting a very handsome bonus anyway. So, with Schiller, his lawyers and our lawyers all reading each page. . . .' He turned his hands palm up. 'It'll be a lengthy session.'

'Where will the transfer take place?'

'At Schiller's home in Germany or his company head office in Frankfurt. He has a central control room at each site, both identical. Each control room has a shift of satellite control officers working there when he is in residence.'

Kossof pushed his chair back and stood up. He stretched and rubbed the cheeks of his backside. Eshkol watched him walk the length of the room, deep in thought. He returned to the chair, sat down and ran his hand across the top of his head.

'You appreciate the position this puts me in?' Eshkol nodded. 'Israel cannot be seen to be partner to something like this. It's political dynamite.'

Eshkol had anticipated this reaction. Politically the Covenant was a hot potato; Israel could be accused of collusion, malpractice, obsessed with the idea of absolute power. In short, anything the world wished to throw at it.

'I do. But I am not asking your government to sanction the Covenant publicly.' He paused. 'However, privately you might find there will be a great deal of support for it.'

Kossof smiled. 'My colleagues would be falling over themselves.'

Eshkol laughed. 'To get control, no doubt.'

The prime minister became serious. 'Who will run such a huge corporation, Levi?'

'I've set up a private holding company,' Eshkol told him. 'In my name.'

'You paid for that?' Kossof asked in surprise.

'Schiller.'

'I see. But you don't intend holding on to control of the company, do you?'

Eshkol shook his head. 'In time it will become the sole property of the Israeli Nation.'

'Administered by the Israeli Government.'

'It's a wonderful opportunity, Prime Minister.'

Kossof's expression became fixed. His eyes stared out at Eshkol without showing any sign that he was concentrating on anything in particular. It was vacant. Then he blinked several times and ran his hand over his balding head.

'I find myself between a rock and a hard place, Levi,' he said. 'I am glad you've brought the Covenant here, but I wish you hadn't. As prime minister, I want nothing to do with it, but as a citizen of Israel, I want it badly. However, seeing as you have presented me with a virtual *fait accompli*, I applaud and thank you for it.' He stood up. 'But I want that document off Israeli soil the moment the German Police have found Manfred Schiller's grandson.'

Sergeant Tobias Kowalski of the Dade County's Police Department, North-west Division in Miami, Florida wasn't expecting a day any different to other days in the sunshine state – the usual spate of assaults, theft and drug-related crimes, tourists losing their credit cards, passports, whereabouts and anything else they were capable of losing. So, when he got a call from the dispatcher's office, it pulled him up sharp.

'Got a call from Officers McNab and Gonzalez. Something pretty bizarre going down. Mac wants to talk to you. Should I patch him through?'

'Yeah, do that.'

The voice came through clearly on Kowalski's speaker phone.

'Found a body, Sarge, out in the 'glades.'

Kowalski shifted irritably in his chair. 'So, why call me?'

'Well, we reckon this one's gonna be a bit different 'cos we found him hog tied like a roasting pig, Sarge. Figure he was meant to be meat for the 'gators, but we got to him first, seems like.'

'Is he black?'

'No, sir, he's white. And he's been drawing his pension some time, I reckon.'

'Where d'you find him?'

'Like I said, in the 'glades, 'bout ten miles north-west.'

'Want me out there?'

'Reckon so, Sarge. Something 'bout this one that don't figure right.'

Kowalski allowed himself a moment for a silent curse. Usually his officers dealt with homicides in customary fashion, calling the Homicide division and handballing it quickly to the detectives. A call like this often meant a great deal of extra paperwork which meant his officers spent more of their valuable time in the office instead of on the road.

'Where are you?'

The patrolman gave Kowalski the exact location and within five minutes the sergeant was motoring along the turnpike out of Miami.

The scene wasn't pretty. Deep in the everglades where sawgrass grew over one metre high and mangrove roots clutched deep into the swamp, the body clung to the earth in a parody of prayer. The old man, whoever he was, had died in the kneeling position. His chin had sagged on to his chest, and from the marks on his naked body, he had been severely tortured before being shot in the back of the head.

'How come you found him out here?' Kowalski asked the obvious question because it wasn't exactly the place to bring a patrol car.

The officer looked across the 'hammock', or islet, pointing with his clean-shaven chin. 'Had a call 'bout a still. Someone's bootlegging. Probably sold a cheap cut. One or two run maybe. Customer didn't like it, reckon.'

Good hooch had to pass through the distilling process at least three times to make it nearly pure. 'Four run' was quality stuff. One or two run was dirty.

'We were over there. Saw the body.' He moved his arm in a loop. 'Had to make a pretty big detour.'

'Did you call Homicide?'

'On their way.'

Kowalski looked at the body again. The poor wretch had been tied round his hands and feet. Whether he had been carried to his place of execution like that or not was for the detectives to decide. Not that it made much difference; the poor bastard had died in a very nasty way.

When Joanna woke, it was about twelve noon. Her trawl through Hansi's files had been so traumatic that she had finally cried herself to sleep. Joanna had cried not because she was unhappy, because she was anyway, but for the way in which she had been misled and cheated. Her sense of values had always meant fair play and honesty in dealings with people who were very close to you. She felt now that she had been duped and used by a man who saw her as nothing more than a decorative bauble; a useful appendage to accompany his quest for power.

Joanna did not want to find satisfaction in Hansi's death; no woman could bear a man's child willingly and wish that upon him, but she discovered an uncomfortable sense of relief that he would no longer be around to impose his will upon so many unsuspecting people. It upset her so much that simple tears could not justify her reaction and she wanted to assuage her own guilt and loathing by making amends to Hansi's ingenuous enemies. But that would have meant exposing Hansi's fraud to his father, and she was afraid that such revelations would kill him.

Joanna needed to confide in someone. A man or woman she could trust. But there was nobody in her life she knew who could help her with whatever choice she made. She could tell Hoffman, show him the files. But how long before it reached the ears of the press? And wasn't Hoffman a policeman whose career was determined by results? A coup like this for him would elevate him to something like a national figure, but the publicity would kill Manfred Schiller. And, at the very least, it would still not guarantee the return of her beloved son.

Joanna could only see one solution at the moment: let the police know she believed she knew the identity of the kidnapper. If they could arrest this Breggie de Kok and find her son, there would be no need to reveal any of her dead husband's involvement in covert Volkspartei matters. The details of their schemes could be fed to the police as 'leaks' which would effectively stop the party in its tracks. Molke would never be elected to a position of power. And, as a result of that, Hansi's father need never know of his son's traitorous games.

She picked up the phone beside her bed and asked the operator to put her through to Herr Doktor Aaron Kistler, President of the North Rhine Westphalia Police at his Bonn office. And, yes, she told the operator, she would be happy to wait.

Conor had grabbed a good night's sleep and was feeling quite chirpy despite having bumped into Frau Lindbergh that morning. She had asked him if he wanted her to cook for him, or take care of his laundry. No extra charge of course. Conor had thanked her politely and waived the offer. The last thing he wanted was Frau Lindbergh getting her feet under his table. He had made an unconscious note to find other accommodation just as soon as it was convenient. No more than a couple of days he hoped.

He was back at Oscar's house. Before going in he had waited outside for well over an hour observing the place. There had been no callers nor had there been any movement from inside. Now he was inside and sitting at Oscar's desk waiting for the phone call he was convinced would come. When it did, it was on Oscar's mobile phone.

'You did not answer your phone yesterday.' The voice was fairly lightweight and a little husky.

'Oscar is dead,' he told the voice. There was no immediate reply. Conor could hear the man breathing. He gave the codeword.

'Who are you?'

'John Buck,' he lied. 'Jürgen's dead too.' This time he heard the little explosion of breath. 'They're in Jürgen's flat.'

The breathing became controlled again. 'Tell me what happened.'

'I don't know. I was supposed to go on a job with Oscar and Jürgen. I had to meet them at Jürgen's flat. They were both dead.'

'How did they die?'

'They were shot. I didn't know what to do. I took Oscar's phone because I knew you would contact him.'

Conor found it remarkably easy to lie and invent a foundation for his imaginary involvement with Oscar.

'Who are you?'

'I told you. I'm John Buck.'

'You are not German.'

'No, I'm an American. I came over with Karl Trucco. We were part of Oscar's team.'

'Have you seen Trucco?' the voice asked.

Conor shook his head unnecessarily. 'No. He was on some job couple of days ago. I haven't seen him since.'

He was gambling on the chance that Oscar chose his own cell members. Security within the organization would demand it. But he couldn't be sure that Oscar was involved in any way with the kidnap. The team assembled for that was a bit special. He hoped the voice would not be too closely informed of who was actually on the kidnap team.

'What was the job you were supposed to be going on with Oscar and Jürgen?' the voice asked.

Conor shrugged. 'Not sure. Think we were going to waste some guy. Oscar told us to be tooled up. Why?'

The question did not get answered. 'And you have no idea who or why Oscar and Jürgen were killed?'

Conor heard a phone ring somewhere in the background. He sensed rather than heard the voice move as his caller lifted the other phone. A movement and sound like the mouthpiece being covered was quite clear. Conor decided the voice was answering another phone. After a lengthy silence, Conor realized the voice was still waiting for an answer to the question.

'No, I don't know why they were killed. It's like I said, I just found them.' He paused, waiting for a reaction. It didn't come. 'What do you want me to do?' he asked.

'Do?' The voice sounded surprised. 'What do you mean? What can you do other than keep well clear of poor Oscar and Jürgen?'

'No, I didn't mean that.' Conor affected a little urgency in his voice. 'I was working for Oscar. He's dead and you're his boss, so I'm working for you now, right?'

'In your dreams, Mr Buck.'

Conor was afraid he would be cut off. The trail would be dead. 'Wait! Can we meet? I need an angle, something. Oscar was my pay check.'

'Correction: Oscar *was* your pay check. Goodbye, Mr Buck.'

The phone went dead.

Conor automatically moved his head away from the phone and looked at it. Then he put it back against his ear. It made no difference; the phone was no longer connected to the voice. He put the phone back on the desk.

At that moment, Conor heard a sound. It was a small, intrusive sound that was out of place in the undisturbed silence in the room. Only the distant, muffled noise of occasional traffic passing the house could be heard in the room. To Conor's well-tuned instincts, it was a warning. And, as he moved to rise from the chair, he saw a movement on the extreme periphery of his vision. He ducked forward and pushed himself away from the movement, but he was too late. He felt the blow strike him on the side of the head and immediately everything went black. He was aware of the impact as his body hit the floor and then he lost consciousness.

Joseph had kept his word and contacted his controller. He arrived that afternoon with a doctor. Breggie came down from the bedroom where she had been struggling with the baby. Mercifully the little soul was finally asleep. Joseph did not introduce the doctor to Breggie. All three of them knew what the score was and expected nothing less.

'Where's the infant?' the doctor asked.

Breggie took him upstairs. Joseph remained where he was, his part of the job done. The doctor examined little Manny very carefully. Fortunately the boy did not wake.

'Tell me as much as you can about his condition,' the doctor asked Breggie.

She told him everything, including the effect it was having on her. The doctor listened without interruption. When she had finished, he looked down at the baby and then back at Breggie.

'First of all I have to tell you that the baby is quite ill. But I think you know that.' Breggie nodded. 'And he should be in a hospital, but you know that, too.' Breggie nodded again. The doctor went on, 'Because I am aware of the circumstances, I will have to treat the baby now. However, I cannot return here because of the distance I have to travel. If his condition has not improved in two days he will have to go into hospital.'

He opened his bag and brought out a pre-packed syringe together with a phial. 'I am going to give the baby an injection which should help. Then I'll write out a prescription for him.'

He injected the contents of the syringe into the baby's arm and put the empty syringe on a table and told Breggie to dispose of it. Then he opened a prescription pad and began writing.

When he had finished he looked up. There was no expression in his face.

117

'Don't forget, if his condition has not improved in two days, he must be admitted to a hospital.' He closed his bag. 'Or he will die.'

Breggie took the prescription from him. 'He must not die.'

The doctor gave her a peculiar look. 'That, I'm afraid, is in the hands of God.' He pointed to the prescription. 'And by the way, don't get that at a local pharmacy, go to a big store.'

Naturally, Breggie was curious. 'Why?' she asked.

He stood up, ready to leave. 'Local drug stores get used to handling prescriptions from local doctors. Better to have it filled out by the bigger store.'

The doctor had a coffee before he left. Breggie felt a little easier now the baby had been seen by him. She hoped she wouldn't have to send for him again. It had taken four hours by the time Joseph had picked him up and brought him to the house. Two hours each way.

She was in the kitchen thinking about preparing an evening meal when it hit her like a bomb: it was late afternoon and Joseph would not be back until late evening. If she wanted the prescription filled at a big drug store, she could not wait for Joseph to return. She would have to go herself.

She swore out loud and leaned back against a cabinet, tossing her head back in disgust. She had to have the medicine today. If she waited for Joseph he would have to find an emergency chemist. It would be a local and that would be against the doctor's express wishes. There was nothing else for it but to go herself. And that meant taking the baby.

Breggie's dilemma now was that she had no real option but to drive to the shopping mall she had visited with such disastrous results if she wanted the medicine before the shops closed. She wasn't too happy about showing herself and the baby at the store because of her cock and bull story about visiting from the south. The nosy pharmacist might ask awkward questions again.

In the end Breggie knew she had little choice but to worry about getting her priorities right. There was only one and that was the baby. He needed that medicine. She went upstairs and lifted the infant out of his cot, wrapped him up well and put him in a chair while she manhandled the collapsible pushchair into the car. She then piled her hair up on top of her head and wrapped a headscarf round the blonde locks. With a fairly nondescript coat on, Breggie figured she wouldn't draw too much attention to herself.

Before leaving the house, Breggie put a bottle of milk in the pushchair and crossed her fingers she could make to the drug store and back without little Manny waking. She gunned the Volkswagen into life and headed for the centre of the town.

Much of the precinct was emptying now which made Breggie feel more exposed. That heightened sense of exposure unleashed little demons inside her and she could feel thousands of eyes upon her. In reality, of course, no such thing was happening. Breggie was simply another shopper.

She approached the supermarket drug store attempting to relax and act normally. Her efforts probably made her more abnormal than ever, but she was not aware of it. The dispensing counter appeared like an obstacle to be overcome, looming large in her waking nightmare. There was no sign of the nosy pharmacist which gave her much cause for relief.

She put the brake on the pushchair, praying that the baby would not wake. All she needed was two or three minutes and she would be out of there. Little Manny could scream his head off then. An assistant took the prescription from her and passed it through to the pharmacists working behind screens at one end of the long counter.

Breggie tried to act casual but her head flitted from one object to another. Her movements were spasmodic, affected almost. She could feel her pulse rate rising. People stared at her. Or did they? God, she thought, get on with it. Get that bloody prescription filled!

The assistant returned, took payment for the medicine and handed it across the counter. Breggie thanked her and left. She had only taken two steps when she realized she had left the pushchair. She went back, grabbed the pushchair and practically ran from the store.

The assistant watched her go, and then went back to the dispensary where she spoke to the chemist who had just filled the prescription.

'Remember that South African woman who was in here a couple of days ago?' she asked.

The chemist thought for a moment. 'Oh yes, had a problem with her baby.'

'That's right. Well, she was just in. That prescription you filled, that was hers.'

The woman stopped what she was doing and went to the clip of prescriptions she had hanging beneath a label with her name. She took it down and studied it. After a while she handed it to the girl.

'Look, see if you can decipher that doctor's signature. Then check it against the list of local practitioners.' She looked up. 'She said she was up from the south for a day.' Then she shrugged. 'Check it anyway. I'm curious.'

The girl, happy to be relieved of counter duty for a while, departed quickly and the chemist went back to making up medicines. Meanwhile, Breggie was climbing into her car thanking her lucky stars that the baby was still asleep. Soon she would be back at the house and everything would be fine. Panic over.

Conor woke in darkness. He could feel the blindfold tight around his eyes and an unyielding hardness beneath him. His hands had been tied behind his back. He listened for some time before attempting any movement. If he heard a breath, a cough, or voices, it would mean he wasn't alone. If there was someone there with him, he wanted them to believe he was still unconscious. He mentally ran the rule over his body, but, apart from a pain on the side of his head where he had been coshed, there didn't appear to be any other damage.

Conor thought back to the phone conversation he had with the Dutchman. Whatever he may have thought and however he had planned to tackle the man, he had seriously underestimated him. The Dutchman knew who he was talking to. At least, Conor presumed that. But how had he latched on so quickly? He remembered hearing the phone ring and the Dutchman answering it. Perhaps that was the call to tell the Dutchman where Conor was phoning from. A line trace perhaps? Would the organization have that kind of power?

The suppositions were academic: they had picked him up as easy as taking sweets from a child. All Conor could do now was wait, and hope there was a way out of his predicament.

He didn't have to wait long. He heard a door open and the sound of music in the background. The sound was cut off as the door closed. Hands lifted him to his feet and took the blindfold off.

He was standing in what was obviously an office. There were the usual accoutrements one associated with such a place: large desk, swivel chair, telephone etc. Against a wall was a computer station. The decor was heavy and masculine. There were framed photographs of people; probably celebrity photographs. Behind the desk were heavy drapes. They were closed and presumably covered a window. From the sound of the music he had briefly heard, Conor assumed he was in some kind of club.

Standing either side of Conor were two men. In front of him was one of the fattest men he had ever seen.

'The Dutchman, I presume?'

The fat man moved and walked behind the desk. To Conor's amazement he sank his massive frame into the swivel chair.

'So, you know my name.'

Conor shook his head. 'No. I only know what they call you.' He sensed the two gorillas beside him tense up. The Dutchman made a small, sideways movement with his head. The two men relaxed.

'What are we to do with you, Mr Lenihan?'

That disappointed Conor. He had hoped, for a while anyway, that he could maintain the pretence that he was a certain John Buck. Evidently the Dutchman knew otherwise.

'My name is John Buck,' he told him, hoping the lie would stick.

The Dutchman shrugged. 'Fine, if you want to be John Buck, you can. I just happen to know you are Conor Lenihan. And it was you who dispatched poor Oscar and Jürgen.'

'You don't know that,' Conor argued. 'You're making it up. I told you, I worked for Oscar. I was supposed to go on a job with him.'

The Dutchman interrupted. 'Stop it, Lenihan. You are wasting your time and mine. I know who you are and that you killed two of my men.' He adopted a condescending look. 'The question is, what am I to do with you?'

Conor didn't give much for his chances of getting out of this alive. He had been trained for such a scenario by the SAS. All he could do was maintain some kind of dialogue and hope some small chance or opportunity might present itself. A chance he would willingly take with both hands – if they weren't bloody tied!

'What makes you think I was in Oscar's place?' he asked the Dutchman.

The fat man pushed out his bottom lip. 'We saw you go in.' He

121

moved and his flesh wobbled. 'You see, Lenihan, we knew there was trouble when Oscar didn't answer his call yesterday. You weren't too careful, you know.'

Conor gave a rueful smile. 'So what now, are you going to shoot me?'

The Dutchman shook his head. 'I don't know yet. If I had time to finish this conversation, it would inevitably end in your death.' He stood up, with a great deal of effort, from the chair. 'As it is I have more pressing business to deal with, so you will have to wait.' He gave a quick lift of the head to the two gorillas beside Conor. 'Put him downstairs. We'll finish this tomorrow.'

The two heavies took hold of Conor and marched him unceremoniously from the room through a door at the rear. They took him along a passageway, through another door and down some steps into what he presumed was the basement. Without a word they shoved him on to a packing case and left him there. He watched them disappear up the stairs, the door close and the lights go out. There was nothing around him except complete blackness.

CHAPTER NINE

Hoffman had finished eating breakfast and was drinking a cup of coffee, his thoughts on the latest football results which were in the paper he was reading. His wife, Elke, had removed the dishes from the table and was back at the table, pouring herself a cup of coffee.

'You're not making the news anymore,' she told him. The coffee pot was put down with a flourish and movement of the shoulders which Hoffman was quite familiar with. It was a kind of 'I told you so' movement.

'It's because we are not making any progress,' he answered and went back to his paper. He didn't make a habit of discussing cases with his wife unless he felt he could tap the treasure trove of feminine logic. Then he would leak little pieces of information to her and wait for the gem that the entire police force had failed to come up with. Naturally he would go back to the office and claim all the credit. 'The kidnappers are being unusually quiet.'

'Why, because they haven't spoken to you?'

He put his cup down. 'They haven't contacted anyone, I can assure you.'

Elke thought about this for a while. She watched her husband put his head down to the paper again and wondered how she would react if she had a child kidnapped.

'The police always get in the way,' she said.

'Mmm?'

'Well, it must be obvious that all Herr Schiller would want to do is pay up and get his grandson back.' There was no immediate response, so she went on. 'All you lot want to do is flood the place with police and frighten the kidnappers away.'

He put the paper down. 'This is not a straightforward kidnap.'

'Are there other kinds, then?' she asked. Her eyes hooded over for just a fraction of a second. 'Schiller is a powerful man, but if you lot get under his feet, you'll just annoy him.'

'Are you suggesting we give up and go home?'

She bridled at that a little. 'No, of course not, but it must be obvious: Schiller has more people working for him than you do, and more resources. He could be in touch with the kidnappers right now and you wouldn't know about it.'

He disagreed, shook his head and went back to his paper. 'We'll find them,' he said without conviction. Then he looked up again, quite suddenly. She caught the expression on his face.

'Well?

'Oh, nothing,' he lied. 'Something I have just remembered.' He finished his coffee in one gulp and wiped his mouth with the napkin. 'Must go,' he told her, getting to his feet. 'I'll ring you later about dinner this evening.'

He came round the table and kissed her on the lips. 'I love you, sweetheart.'

Elke smiled, perhaps a little smugly, and went to the door with him.

Hoffman climbed into his car, waved back at his wife and reached for his portable phone. He had Jansch on the end of the line within seconds.

'Uwe, Hoffman here. I want you to put a tap on Schiller's phone. Now.'

'I'll need a court order—'

'You won't get one,' Hoffman interrupted. 'Schiller's too powerful to be trifled with. The court will never agree.'

'I could go to the minister.'

Hoffman shook his head and started the car. He was moving when he spoke again. 'That would mean Kistler knowing. He would block it. Just do it Uwe; I'll accept full responsibility.'

It was Elke who had triggered the thought. With Joanna Schiller away from the house, Schiller could be using her to communicate with the kidnappers. He could have kicked himself for not thinking about it sooner.

He put the car into gear and rolled out of the drive.

When Hoffman arrived at Police Headquarters, Jansch was waiting for him. Hoffman went through into his private office, beckoning Jansch who immediately followed him and closed the door behind them.

'Well?' Hoffman was impatient to hear that Jansch had carried out his order.

'I've had to invoke Special Powers as a matter of State Security, sir. I passed it down to Eleven. They weren't happy but, seeing as your signature will be all over the document. . . .' He left it at that.

Hoffman was satisfied. 'Good work, Uwe. I want twenty-four hour surveillance on the line and all messages recorded. If that bastard starts talking to the kidnappers, I want to know about it.'

Jansch was surprised at Hoffman's choice of words and his reasons. 'What makes you think Schiller is in contact with them?'

Hoffman looked away. 'I don't. But it didn't occur to me that Frau Schiller's departure from his residence may have been a subterfuge.' He looked back at Jansch quite suddenly. 'I take it there has been no contact?'

Jansch shook his head. 'None yet sir; as far as we know.'

Hoffman relaxed, sinking back into his chair. He indicated to Jansch that he should sit down. 'Good. Now, what have you got for me, anything new?'

Jansch held up one hand, splayed his fingers and with the other hand began ticking off each point as he made it.

'The counterfeit inquiry has dried up a bit. Oberkommissar Lechter might downgrade it. I couldn't find anything in Cologne that might implicate the kidnappers. However' – he moved on to the second finger – 'two stiffs have turned up in a flat in Cologne. One of them is a local hood. Both shot to death. No reason at all why this should have anything to do with us, but I spoke to the chief on the phone last night. He said he would take it on board as part of the counterfeit investigation in case there is a link.' Third finger. 'The limpet bomb – the one that was used in the attack?'

Hoffman's mind was already drifting away to the reasons why Joanna Schiller had left. He dragged it back.

'What about it?'

'Well, forensics identified part of a serial number on the casing. It has been traced to a shipment dispatched by the Czech manufacturer. The Czech Government were very helpful on this. They had to be.'

'Oh, why?'

'It was a consignment for GSG9, sir'

GSG9: Grenzshutzgruppe; the Federal Republic's Specialist Anti-terrorist Force, recruited from, and answerable to the Federal Police.

'Shit.'

'I had a phone call during the night from them. They carried out an inventory check. One bomb is missing.'

Hoffman shook his head. 'Not any more it isn't. It's in pieces at forensics. God, the shit will hit the fan when this gets out.'

'They'll keep a lid on it, sir. But there will be an internal enquiry.'

Hoffman knew how keen the Special boys would be to keep this quiet. If the Press got hold of it they would have a field day. He waved a dismissive hand across his desk.

'Just put it on file and keep it in the back of your mind. If they can tell us who took it, we'll be on a winner. Otherwise. . . .'

Jansch put his hands down. 'That's all, sir. Apart from pushing on with inquiries there's little else we can do.' He stood up. 'I'll go and see if the line tap has produced anything.'

Hoffman agreed. His job now was to stir things up.

The phone rang. He picked it up, listened and turned a pale colour. He then put the phone down and cursed quietly.

He stopped Jansch. 'That was Schiller's secretary. They received a child's finger in a special delivery package this morning.'

Joseph Schneider had slipped out for a couple of hours. Breggie had been quite edgy, but the baby seemed to be responding to the prescription. Joseph wanted no part of it and was getting tetchy himself. The original plan to play happy families simply wasn't working. Neither he nor Breggie could handle it. More to the point, he was getting frustrated at acting as nursemaid to a sick baby and an increasingly neurotic woman.

Once upon a time he would have spent the best part of the day in bed with Breggie and then gone out partying through the night with her. She had always been fun to be with. Now she was dull and morose.

She seemed to have lost that wild edge and her zest for life. It was obvious to him that she was preoccupied with the baby's illness, but she was also afraid of the organization; something that he would have said, once upon a time, was impossible. Breggie laughed in the face of authority.

He drove into the city, parked up and ate breakfast in a fast food restaurant. He used the time to read the morning papers and see that there was virtually no news of the kidnap. Whatever there was had been consigned to the inner pages. The sports section offered more serious reading for him and he whiled away the time in relaxed harmony with himself.

When he was ready, Joseph left the restaurant and found a public telephone box. He dialled a number, checking his watch to ensure it was the correct time, and waited for someone to come on the line. He heard the phone line click and the sound of music in the background.

'Yes?'

'It's Joseph.'

'Ah, good morning, Joseph. I'm afraid I have some painful news for you.'

Joseph chuckled. 'What could be more painful than living with a sick child and a neurotic woman?'

'Well, it won't be for much longer. We want you to terminate her.'

To say Joseph was stunned would be an understatement. He was mortified. So much so that his reflex reaction was not to believe what he had just heard.

'Say that again.'

'Terminate her. She has been compromised.'

Joseph felt the needles of fear stabbing at his flesh. If Breggie had been compromised, then why not him? In which case the organization would want to get rid of him as well.

'What happened?' he asked. He could feel a tremor in his voice.

'The Schiller woman has identified her. We have about twelve hours grace. She must be dispatched by then.'

'What about the baby?' Joseph had a fleeting glimpse of himself trying to pacify the little wretch until the operation was over.

'Just do the job and let me know when it is finished. We will come for the baby.' There was a pause. Music thumped out beyond the voice.

127

'And, Joseph, don't worry; you are perfectly safe. You have my word on it. Phone me when it is done.'

The phone went dead and Joseph felt a cloak of overwhelming despair descend on him. How on earth could he do this to Breggie? He knew he would have to, that much was quite clear. He suddenly harboured visions of running with Breggie, but he knew the inevitable outcome did not bear thinking about. No, he would have to do it and it would have to be quick.

He put the phone back on the hook and turned away from the booth. A stranger waiting to use the phone gave him a withering look which Joseph did not see. He went back to his car and sat in it for some considerable time before starting the engine and driving back to the house.

Breggie was in a better frame of mind just then. The baby was settling a little better, and she had managed a few hours' unbroken rest. Joseph had gone out while she was asleep. Because they were no longer sleeping together, she didn't know he had gone until she came down to make a cup of coffee.

She spent the morning by herself, only having to feed little Manny once. She did wonder what was keeping Joseph, but didn't dwell on what might be. She did know that he made contact each day with his controller. She hoped he might bring her some news that would point to the end of this insufferable job.

She had decided to cook herself some lunch and had put a saucepan of water on the stove to boil when she heard Joseph drive up. She went to the window and looked through the curtain. Usually Joseph would step out of the car, slam the door behind him and head for the house. But this time he didn't. He sat in the car for some time. Probably no more than half a minute, but from his complete lack of movement, it was obvious something was on his mind.

He got out of the car, closed the door and looked back over his shoulder at the house. His body language was all wrong to Breggie. He looked reluctant to move and there was quite clearly sadness in his expression when she saw his face.

Intrigued, Breggie went to the front door and opened it for him. He seemed surprised to see her standing there and walked towards her as if in a dream. He stopped at the door and opened his mouth to say something, but no words came out. He looked forlorn and childlike.

'What's the matter, Joseph?' she asked.

He shrugged and said nothing. Instead he shouldered his way past her as though he was in a temper. She shut the door and followed him into the room, asking again what it was that was troubling him.

'Nothing!' he snapped and threw himself into an armchair.

Breggie decided it would be better if she left him alone. If he did have something on his mind, it wouldn't be too long before she knew what it was. And because she was feeling in a better frame of mind she might use her feminine wiles on him to find out the truth. She decided to leave him there and went into the kitchen to finish cooking her lunch.

Joseph watched her go. As soon as she had disappeared into the kitchen he went to a drawer in the dining-room unit and took out a loaded, Browning 9mm pistol and silencer. He chambered a round and leaned against the unit to stop himself from trembling. There was nothing else for him but to get it over with quickly. If he dwelt on it, the reasons why, and the reality of it all, he wouldn't have the guts to go through with it.

He took off the safety catch and walked slowly towards the kitchen.

Breggie had just finished chopping some red peppers when she heard Joseph's step. She put the knife down and reached up to an open shelf for the pasta storage jar. As she lifted down the heavy glass container, she turned to Joseph and was about to say something when she saw the gun in his hand.

In that fleeting moment, Breggie saw the heartache in his eyes and the words in his mouth.

'I'm sorry, Breggie, my love,' he cried, and pulled the trigger.

Breggie screamed the moment the gun fired. The noise was nothing more than a champagne cork exploding from the bottle. In that instant, she flinched and turned away from the shot. The heavy glass jar shattered in her hand throwing shards of glass and pasta everywhere. The punch to her wrist was like being hit with a brick. For what seemed an eternity, but was no more than a second, they both stared at each other. Breggie knew that if she waited a moment longer, she would die.

Fortunately for her, she reacted quicker than Joseph. He had expected to see her collapse to the floor otherwise he would have pulled the trigger a second time before she had a chance to move. But what he saw was Breggie hurling a saucepan towards him, its contents spreading out like a bow wave.

The boiling water hit him and with it the pain. He screamed out and clutched at his face, reeling back instinctively. One reflex action was to fire another shot towards her, but because he was unsighted, the bullet went wildly astray. Breggie picked up the knife she had been using and lunged at him. The point went into his chest, skidding off a rib bone and into his heart.

Joseph didn't draw another breath. His eyes opened wide just inches from hers as his hand fell away. The pain in them was not physical but instead, a tormented, emotive pain. Breggie watched him slip to the ground and she instinctively grabbed him, but his dead weight brought her crashing down on top of him, forcing the air from his lungs in one last sigh.

She lay there for a moment, her mind plundered of all reason. Beneath her lay the man she had cared for and almost learned to love; the man who had tried to kill her and whom she had killed in self defence. Why?

She pushed herself away and remained sitting on the floor, her back against a kitchen unit. She began to cry, softly at first. Then she started sobbing and the tears fell unashamedly down her face. She kept rubbing her cheeks and eyes with her hands until there were no more tears to cry. And she looked down at the sorry figure of Joseph through inflamed eyes and with a tortured mind, and kept asking the same question.

Why?

Hoffman made good time to Schiller's place, but not before the press latched on to the fact that something big was going down. The speed of the media grapevine never failed to impress Hoffman, despite his years in the police game. How this had leaked out, he had no idea. He could only surmise that some of the press boys were paying Schiller's staff some kind of retainer. It wasn't illegal, so it wasn't a problem. But avoiding their probing questions as he tried to gain access through the crush at the gate was.

Hoffman found Schiller's doctor was with him. The look on the medical man's face was bad enough to give rise for concern. Before Hoffman spoke to Schiller, the doctor took him to one side.

'He has had an enormous shock, Herr Hoffman. I have given him something to calm him down, so you mustn't tax him too much.'

Hoffman's face was expressionless. 'Does he have a heart problem, Doctor?'

The doctor nodded. 'I'm afraid so. You really must be careful.' He took Hoffman by the elbow and told him he would have to remain during any interview. Hoffman had no choice but to agree.

Schiller was in his bedroom. The room seemed to be inordinately big, but for a man of Schiller's wealth the question of a room's size would be a triviality. He looked dwarfed in the king-size bed, but his pallor did convey the reality of the shock he had received.

'Good morning, Herr Schiller.' Hoffman sat beside the bed. Schiller didn't answer him. Hoffman ignored the man's omission of civility and continued.

'Would you tell me what happened?' he asked.

'You know what happened. A package arrived with the baby's finger in it.'

'Do you know who delivered it?'

'Don't be stupid, Hoffman. I don't receive the mail directly. My secretary does.' He took a deep breath. 'The Bundespost I should think.'

Hoffman already knew that the package had been delivered at the gatehouse by taxi. Naturally the taxi didn't wait. Neither did the security guard on duty think to ask the taxi driver to wait. There was no reason why he should. But Hoffman needed to ask the question in case there had been a message inside the package, which he knew, was not the case. But for his own reasons, he didn't trust Schiller.

'You believe the finger has been cut from your grandson's hand, don't you?'

Schiller gave him a withering look. 'Where else could it come from?'

'Until we have conducted tests, we have to keep an open mind on that.'

He turned to the doctor and mouthed the words: 'Where's the finger?' The doctor put his hand up in a way that signified the finger was still in the house and in a safe place. He turned his attention back to Schiller.

'What do they want?'

'What does who want?' There was no trace of feeling in the question. It sounded almost rhetorical.

'The people who kidnapped your grandson. You must know what they want, otherwise they would not have put pressure on you by sending that package.'

Schiller looked almost bored. 'Oh, you policemen can be so bloody tiresome. It's a week now and you are no closer to finding the people who kidnapped my grandson than you were at the beginning. And now you're asking me what they want. I don't know; it's as simple as that.' He looked away.

'You're lying to me.'

The doctor protested immediately at Hoffman's accusation and stood up in a show of contained rage.

'What on earth do you mean by that? I told you Herr Schiller is not to be troubled.'

Hoffman glanced at the doctor but kept his eye on Schiller. 'If that finger belongs to his grandson, then I suggest Herr Schiller is not going through anything like the pain and anguish the baby is.'

'That's not fair,' Schiller protested.

'Nor would you be going through the same pain as Frau Schiller,' Hoffman put in before Schiller could continue. 'If you do not tell me what they are demanding, and if you still insist they have not contacted you, nor have they contacted Frau Schiller, I can only assume they have no intention of returning the baby.'

The doctor blustered again but Hoffman ignored him.

'I presume you have told the baby's mother?'

'No,' was Schiller's answer, which was shouted almost with fear in his voice.

'She has a right to know,' Hoffman reminded him. 'More than you do. If you won't tell her, then we will have to.'

Schiller had been lying semi prone in bed, his back supported by several pillows. He struggled upright, his thin frame looking even frailer now.

'When you have completed the tests on the finger, and I presume you mean blood tests?' Hoffman nodded. A DNA test would also be carried out if the hospital had a tissue sample from the baby. 'Then I will tell my daughter-in-law if the test proves it is our little Manny's finger. Otherwise I see no reason to upset her further.'

Hoffman agreed. 'Very well, Herr Schiller, I'll go along with that.' He stood up. 'Before I leave, I will ask you again. But I want you to think very carefully before answering. Have the kidnappers been in touch with you? And, do you know what they want in return for your grandson?'

Schiller answered immediately, and he was quite adamant. 'I have no need to think carefully, Oberkommissar. The answer is no on both counts. Now go away and find them. And find them quickly before they take another limb off my poor grandson.'

The door to the cellar opened suddenly, throwing a shaft of light into the darkness. Conor jumped and turned his face away from the light. Footsteps rattled on the stairs as someone came down into the dank basement. Conor squinted through half-open lids, not letting the brightness dazzle him too much. He made no attempt to look at the person who had just come down the stairs, but used the moment to cast his half-closed eyes around the room, identifying anything that might help him, and trying to retain a snapshot in his memory of the layout.

The cellar was, like so many cellars are, no more than a dumping ground for unwanted furniture, impedimenta, packing cases, old cast-offs and the like. Conor was sitting on a chair against one of the packing cases. He was facing the centre of the room. Occupying the centre now, beneath an unlit light bulb, was one of the Dutchman's gorillas. He was pointing a gun at Conor and beckoning him to stand up.

Conor did as he was told and stood. The gorilla, wisely, kept his distance, and waved the gun in the direction of the cellar door. Conor turned and began climbing the stairs. Any thoughts he might have had of trying to make a run for it were quickly dispelled by the silhouette of the second gorilla standing in the passageway outside.

Conor was propelled towards the Dutchman's office and bundled inside to an empty chair facing the gargantuan man. The Dutchman was leaning against his large desk, resplendent in a silk dressing-gown. He was smoking a massive cigar which was dwarfed by his own enormous fingers. When he was satisfied that Conor was sitting and his own men were suitably positioned, he spoke.

'What are we to do with you, Lenihan?'

'I want a piss.'

The Dutchman roared with laughter. 'I expect you do, but you'll have to wait.'

Conor thought the man was grotesque. His flesh wobbled obscenely. The gorillas laughed as well. Eventually the laughing subsided.

'Why did you contact me after you killed Oscar and Jürgen? What did you want?'

'I didn't kill them. I told you that.'

The Dutchman nodded at the man standing behind Conor. He heard the movement and felt the sudden slap across the back of his head. The pain was bearable to a man like Conor, but the humiliation made him extremely angry. He kept his cool. He lifted his head and looked at the fat man.

'I want a piss.'

The Dutchman ignored the statement and this time he didn't laugh. 'What did you want? You killed them and then . . . what?' He leaned forward. 'Were you going to kill me? Is that it?'

Conor ignored him.

'Well?'

When no answer was forthcoming, the Dutchman nodded at the gorilla and Conor felt the stinging slap across the back of his head.

'We could go on like this all day if you want, Lenihan. We can all slap you about. Look.'

With a sudden swiftness that belied his incredible bulk, the Dutchman swung his open hand and caught Conor on the side of his face. The blow was so fierce, and delivered with such astonishing strength, that Conor was thrown from the chair and crashed up against the wall. All he could feel was an acute pain inside his ear canal from the pressure of the blow, and a stupendous numbness all down the side of his head and into his shoulder. He could hear a piercing, ringing tone inside his skull, but beyond that, he could hear nothing else.

He lay on the floor in immense pain for some time, curled up in the foetal position expecting to be kicked, and tensing his body should it happen. When, eventually, nothing had occurred like that, he struggled up into a sitting position. He feigned weakness, wanting to impress his captors with their physical and psychological strength, that they could so easily intimidate him.

One of the gorillas took hold of Conor by his shirt collar and hauled him to his feet. He dragged him across to the chair and threw him on to it. Conor slumped forward, his head down. He could hear the Dutchman moving and tensed himself for another blow. Instead, he felt the tip of a finger beneath his chin, forcing his head up.

'Why did you contact me?'

Conor gagged, dribbling copiously. The Dutchman quickly pulled his finger away.

'I wanted work,' he lied.

The Dutchman nodded to one of the gorillas and Conor felt the slap across the back of his head. Compared to the previous blow, it had little effect, but he made a show of suffering pain.

'Please,' Conor said, putting a plaintiff lilt to his voice. 'I'm telling you the truth. All I wanted to do was find work.'

The Dutchman hit Conor on the other side of the head which sent him flying across the room. Like the first blow from the fat man, this one was just as powerful and just as excruciatingly painful. Conor's involuntary cry was not affected: it was a genuine cry of pain.

He rolled across the carpeted floor, fetching up against the opposite wall and allowed himself to collapse slowly into what looked like unconsciousness. He heard the ringing in his ears and felt the numbing pain, but he drew on all his mental resources to still the screams that threatened to erupt from his throat, and kill the urge to fling himself at the three men in a violent reprisal. Not that it would have achieved anything because his hands were still tied and two of the men in the room were armed.

Suddenly, the Dutchman uttered an oath and waddled back to his chair behind the desk.

'It's not even sport.' He gestured to the prone figure of Conor. 'There's no profit in prolonging this. We'll kill him.' He looked up at the two gorillas to issue his next order when the phone rang. He picked it up and listened for a while. He made one reply and put the phone back on the rest.

'Schneider is dead.'

Conor's ears pricked up despite the pain, but he maintained the pretence of unconsciousness. The Dutchman spoke again.

'The bitch killed him.'

'Has she gone?' one of the men asked.

'Yes; baby too.'

'Where?'

He shook his head. 'I don't know.'

'What are you going to do?'

'I don't know. I've got to think.'

Conor's mind was racing despite the pain he still felt. He had no doubt that the 'bitch' referred to was Breggie de Kok. Why she had killed Joseph was obviously a mystery, but it was academic: Schneider was dead. That's what the Dutchman had said. It looked like the whole thing was falling apart, but Conor wasn't happy; he still wanted revenge despite the circumstances he was now in.

'We've got to find her.'

'And where do we start looking?' Conor heard one of them ask.

There was silence. Then a chair scraping as the Dutchman got up from his desk.

'We've got to look in Hans Schiller's place.'

'In Godesberg?'

'She won't be there,' the other voice said.

'No, but the answer will,' the Dutchman replied.

Unknown to anyone else in that room, the Dutchman was aware of Hans Schiller's propensity for keeping his most intriguing secrets on file. He also knew that Hans Schiller kept a love nest for himself and Breggie de Kok, but not where it was. He was quite sure that he would find the answer to that in Hans Schiller's house at Bad Godesberg, where Joanna lived. He looked down at Conor's prostrate body.

'Throw him in the cellar. We'll deal with him later. Then get back here and I'll tell you what I want you to do.'

Conor felt the rough hands groping for him. He allowed himself to sink heavily as a dead weight and was dragged from the office to the cellar door. There was no courtesy extended by the men who already considered him to be a dead man and he was thrown, unceremoniously, down the cellar steps.

Hoffman had just stepped into his official car when his phone rang. He punched the speak button.

'Hoffman.'

'Kommissar Hoffman, Dr Kistler. Where are you?'

'I'm just leaving Herr Schiller's place.'

'Good. When you get here, I would be grateful if you would come and see me immediately. Thank you.' He hung up.

Hoffman's surprise was etched all over his face. He closed the phone and slipped it back into his pocket.

When he arrived back at police headquarters, Hoffman rode the lift up to Kistler's office suite. Kistler was waiting for him.

'Thank you for being so prompt, Hoffman. Please, sit down.'

Hoffman did as he was invited and said nothing, but his curiosity was ratcheting up several levels. Kistler wasn't seated. Instead his bulk seemed to fill the windows overlooking the River Rhine. It was a while before he spoke and Hoffman wondered if the doctor was composing himself for something. The answer wasn't long in coming.

'Frau Schiller has identified her grandson's kidnapper.'

It was a simple statement, spoken with a certain level of fatalism that Hoffman thought he detected but chose to ignore. The impact of the statement however was like a minor earthquake. It sent tremors through Hoffman's body and caused his stomach muscles to tighten. He was unable to speak for several seconds.

'Would you say that again, sir?'

Kistler turned away from the window and slipped his bulk into the leather chair behind his desk.

'Frau Schiller has identified her kidnapper. She is a South African woman. Her name is Breggie de Kok.'

Hoffman frowned and fixed his eyes on Kistler's poker-like expression. There was nothing in that face to suggest anything other than the conveying of a simple message. But Hoffman could not dismiss the nagging suspicion that his president was acting duplicitously.

'When did you learn this?' he asked calmly.

'Last night.'

Hoffman closed his eyes and opened them again. His temper was rising and he was doing his level best to control it.

'Why have you waited until now to tell me?'

Kistler leaned back in his chair and put up a defensive hand.

'I had to promise her something. When she phoned the department, she specifically asked for me. She told me she had identified the kidnapper, but was not prepared to tell me who it was unless I promised to keep a lid on it.'

Hoffman put his head in his hand and shook it in despair. Then he looked at Kistler.

'That is preposterous. How can you keep something like that a secret? It's imperative we are told everything. Time is always important.'

Kistler nodded. 'I know and I fully appreciate your concern, but!' He made a defensive gesture with one hand. 'Frau Schiller was absolutely adamant: she had her own reasons for wanting it this way. She wouldn't say what those reasons were, but she does not want this getting back to Herr Schiller, which means it must not get into the newspapers.' He shrugged. 'Don't ask me why, but those were her terms. I was to tell you and you were to go about your business, catch this Breggie de Kok woman and Herr Schiller would be none the wiser.' He paused, letting it sink in. 'The reason I haven't told you earlier is because I have been with Herr Molke all morning.' He sat back, explanations over.

Hoffman digested it. He also considered the implications. Keeping it from the press would not be impossible, but it would be tricky. If the newshounds got hold of this it could prove to be a double-edged sword: it would greatly increase their chances of tracing the South African woman, but greatly increase the risk to the baby. It was something he knew he had to consider carefully. He would also have to consider Kistler's culpability; without proof there was nothing he could do to prove the doctor was deliberately impeding the investigation.

'Thank you, sir. Perhaps I should go and interview Frau Schiller myself.' He got up to leave. 'And perhaps, sir, in future you will let me know immediately if you receive any other little gems that might help the inquiry.'

'Of course,' Kistler answered pleasantly, 'of course.'

Hoffman got up from the chair, making a pointed examination of the man's face. The last time he was in this office there had been a look of thunder in the President's countenance. But this time Hoffman was convinced there was nothing but a smug expression planted on Kistler's face.

CHAPTER TEN

Conor opened his eyes and did a quick mental check of his condition. Apart from feeling sore and bruised, he was still intact. He struggled to a sitting position and started moving around the floor until he came to the foot of the stairs. Using this point as a reference, he began to visualize the layout of the cellar using the picture he had retained in his mind from the brief light shown when the two gorillas had opened the cellar door.

He worked his way over to a packing crate, fumbling until he could get his back against a corner of it. The he levered himself up to a squatting position and felt his way up and down the edge of the crate with his bound hands until he found a sharp edge.

He had no way of knowing if he had found a nail or screw head, or even a piece of protective, metal edging. But whatever it was, he began rubbing his bonds up and down against the sharp edge.

It must have taken Conor twenty minutes or so before the last strand of the cord that bound him sprang free. His hands fell apart and blessed relief swamped his burning and aching muscles. The first thing Conor did was to drop his trousers and pants, and defecate. Sweet, merciful deliverance flooded his mind and a wholesome smile broke his scarred features.

When his bowels and bladder were empty, he dressed himself and made his sightless way over to the open plan staircase. He took up a position beneath the stairs and began a patient vigil which he hoped would not be too long. He knew he would have one shot to do what he was planning. If it failed, he was a dead man.

After four hours, Conor heard a footfall beyond the door. He was sitting on the floor, with his back to the wall, beneath the stairs. He immediately stood up so that he was standing beneath the tenth step from the bottom. The door to the cellar opened and the light above him flooded into the cellar. Conor was quite certain that he could not be seen. Not that the Dutchman's gorilla would be looking for him.

The man came through the open door and began descending the staircase. Conor was pinning his hopes of success that there would only be one of them. As the man's foot touched the ninth step, the one now opposite Conor's head, Conor reached through the opening with his hand and grabbed the man's ankle. He pulled it back with such strength that the man was pitched forward into space. The drop to the concrete floor was about two metres. Added to the height of the man's head and shoulders, it was a considerable height to fall.

The cry was muted as his head crashed against the concrete. The gun he was carrying went skidding across the floor. Conor moved swiftly, coming from beneath the staircase and driving his fist on to the man's head. There was no need for anything else; the man was either unconscious or dead.

Conor immediately glanced to the top of the staircase but could see no one else. He then dropped to his hands and knees and searched frantically for the man's gun. Fortunately it had pitched up against a crate. Mercifully not the one Conor had used.

He picked up the gun and went back to his victim, searching his clothes quickly. He found a spare magazine clip, a wallet and a bunch of keys. He could see in the light from the door the unmistakable Mercedes gunsight on the key fob.

He ran to the top of the stairs and glanced carefully into the passageway. It was empty. There was a door at the far end which Conor hoped led out to a yard or something. He ran to the door, slipped the bolts and pulled it open. He was right; it opened on to a backyard.

He figured that this was the rear of a nightclub. The dead man's car would have to be parked somewhere, probably in a staff car-park. He climbed over a fence and dropped into a street. Then he walked quickly but carefully towards what looked like the main street. He soon found himself in front of the club which had the name Pandora emblazoned above it. He thought of Pandora and the Flying Dutchman and wondered if it was significant. Then he went in search of the car.

Five minutes after pulling the gorilla's feet from under him, Conor was driving a Mercedes away from the Dutchman's nightclub.

A short distance away from Frau Lindbergh's boarding-house in bed-sit land, a police Opel was parked. There were no markings on the car to indicate it was a police vehicle, and the two policemen inside were not in uniform. It was close to midnight and they were getting bored. They had been on shift almost two hours and there was little prospect of anything exciting happening for the remainder of their night shift.

'What I don't understand,' one of them was saying, 'is why we have to watch some little old lady just because she spent a few, bent Euros at the local shop.'

His partner shifted in his seat in an attempt to ward off the stiffness that was creeping into his limbs.

'This one's come from the top though.'

'She must be ninety if she's a day,' he complained. 'Probably got the forgeries out of the cash point.'

'Don't be daft; she's too old to know how to use one.'

They lapsed into silence, each one with his own thoughts. The street was deserted save for the occasional car parked here and there. One of them glanced at the dashboard clock; thirty minutes before they would be relieved. He arched his eyebrows and wished he was home in bed cuddled up to the warm, soft body of his wife. He hated night shifts.

A movement in his wing mirror caught his attention. He could see the figure of a man walking towards them. That in itself wasn't even exciting, but it was movement; a break from the grinding boredom of sitting there doing nothing. Their orders were to keep an eye on the Lindbergh place and make a note of any late visitors. They had a list of her current tenants and the local constabulary were in the process of running a check on them. At the moment, none of the tenants was under suspicion.

The figure crossed the road and continued to walk toward them. He passed the unmarked police car and paused outside the Lindbergh place. Both of the policemen stiffened. The figure began searching through his pockets. He stopped and walked a few paces towards a Volkswagen which was parked a couple of metres from him. He put a key into the lock, opened the door and reached inside for something.

Then he shut the car door, locked it and crossed the road. He walked about thirty metres and went into a tenement block.

The two policemen looked at each other.

'Why would he want to park his car that far away?' one of them asked. He didn't expect an answer because the question was largely rhetorical. 'Run a check on it,' he suggested. 'It's something to do, anyway.'

His companion picked up the microphone from beneath the dash and contacted the police control room. He asked for a licence plate check on the Volkswagen. He gave them the number plate details. Within two minutes the licence holder's name and address was being typed out on a small printer inside the car. He tore it off and read it under the map light.

'John Buck, nationality Irish. Lives at. . . .' He looked up. 'Down there. So why has he parked his car outside the Lindbergh place?'

The other policeman said: 'Hang on a minute.' He opened the glove box and pulled out the list of names of Frau Lindbergh's tenants. 'I thought so,' he declared cheerfully. 'There's a John Buck listed here as a tenant.' He showed his partner.

'Perhaps we'd better have a little chat with him.'

'We can't, can we? Our orders are to observe and report.' He shrugged. 'So we report.'

Conor let himself into his apartment. He had been afraid that he'd left his door key in his bed-sit at Frau Lindbergh's. Then he remembered he'd left it in the Volkswagen; now he could enjoy a long soak in the bath and work out his next move.

Breggie wandered around the apartment in a dream. Each room held special memories for her. Each step led to a treasured moment. How happy she had been with Hans Schiller. How they had loved those carefree days, lost in a world so far away from the realities of life.

The baby was comfortable now, responding to the medication, and sleeping. It gave Breggie the time to think about her position, and time to think of what might have been.

The apartment was their secret; one which no other person shared. It was exclusive and discreet. Hans would leave on a business trip for a whole weekend, never questioned by his perfect little wife, Joanna, and spend those glorious moments with Breggie.

The apartment was in Koblenz and overlooked the Mosel River where it merged with the mighty Rhine. Hans had purchased the deeds shortly before his marriage to Joanna and presented the key as a 'wedding present' to Breggie. She had never openly questioned his choice of partner. Reasons in the stratospheric world of Hans Schiller were never without substance, and Joanna's qualities, both from a business point of view and as a partner to Hans had never been open to debate. The glossy magazines loved the union, the international business community approved of it, and the glitterati positively swooned over it. Breggie simply took him into her bed and made him feel like the most important person on the planet.

She wasted no tears on her memories; those days were past. For the moment she could look back and feel a warmth and fondness as she moved from room to room. In the master bedroom she paused and remembered the last time they had made love. It was the night before he had been killed in the plane crash. His passion had burned as furiously on that night as it did the very first time he had made love to her.

She smiled wistfully and went back into the luxurious kitchen. She had made coffee earlier and now needed to sit and think about the situation she found herself in.

Breggie, quite wrongly, believed Joseph had been ordered to kill her because she had failed to eliminate all five of their colleagues. She was not aware that she had been identified. Had she given it serious thought, she would have realized that Joseph was equally to blame as her. Bombing the house had been their joint responsibility.

Breggie's problem now, of course, was how to turn this to her own advantage. She held the trump card at the moment. To play it too soon could prove disastrous. Returning the baby to the Schiller family could net her a fortune. Now that she was no longer part of the organization she could simply demand a ransom for the return of the child. The problem was, how to do that and get away with it?

She resolved to give herself a couple of days and hope she could come up with a foolproof plan.

At the same time Breggie de Kok was considering her future, Levi Eshkol was taking lunch at a pavement café in Tel Aviv. He had walked from his apartment, enjoying the warmth of the autumn sun, and despite the trauma of the kidnap, was feeling in good spirits. He honestly believed that Schiller would complete the transfer of power, and sign the Covenant, within a few days.

He finished his bagel and pushed the plate to one side, drawing his coffee towards him. On the chair beside him was a copy of the *Jerusalem Post* which he had purchased while walking down from his apartment to the café. He stirred his coffee and picked up the newspaper. He hadn't bothered to look at it earlier, leaving that pleasure until now. But as his eyes fell on the lower corner of the front page, he felt small icicles of fear cascade over him like steel needles.

PROMINENT AMERICAN JEW FOUND SLAIN IN MIAMI. *Former Presidential Security Adviser, Alfred Weitzman, was found brutally slain in the Everglades just north of the city of Miami. Florida State Police are not releasing details except to say that the killing had all the hallmarks of a professional execution. The FBI....*

Eshkol raised his head slowly and let the paper sink into his lap. Alfred Weitzman. He shook his head. It couldn't be, not the Alfred Weitzman he knew. He looked back at the newspaper. *Former Presidential Security Adviser.* It was unequivocal; there in black and white.

He stood up, his legs feeling quite weak, and took enough Shekels from his pocket to cover the bill. He scattered them on the table and hurried back to his apartment.

Eshkol's first phone call was to Avi Binbaum, one of the four men who had worked on the Covenant. The former Shin Bet chief came to the phone almost immediately.

'*Shalom*, Avi,' Eshkol greeted him.

'*Shalom.* I think I know why you are phoning.' Binbaum sounded mournful.

'You've seen the story about Weitzman?' Eshkol asked him.

'Ah, yes. I have been in touch with my former colleagues in Shin Bet. They have asked the Americans for details, but they know very little.'

'I fear the worst, Avi. Molke's behind this.'

He could almost hear the old man nodding in agreement.

'I believe that, too. Will you contact the others and warn them?'

Eshkol agreed. 'And I think we should contact Schiller,' he added with a reluctant shrug. 'We must ask him to sign the Covenant and complete the transfer immediately, before Molke's damn thugs get to the rest of us. *Shalom*, Avi. God be with you.'

He put the phone down without waiting for the old man's response. A shiver ran down his spine as he thought of Weitzman's fate. If it was Molke's thugs, and it was almost certain to be, they would have wanted to know the whereabouts of the Covenant. He would have died a painful death before telling them that the Covenant was in Israel with Levi Eshkol.

Conor drove to Bad Godesberg and spent a busy morning locating the whereabouts of Joanna Schiller's place. It wasn't too difficult considering the media were practically camped on her doorstep. His first, cursory inspection of the place told him much of what he already knew; it would be virtually impossible to gain entry without being seen.

The house was a single-storey bungalow, or villa. The wall surrounding the grounds was about two metres high. Two-thirds of the walled area was fronted by public roads, while the remainder bordered other, equally secure properties.

By mingling with the media people outside the main gate, Conor was able to see relatively clearly across the open lawns that separated the house from the wall. His trained eye was quick to spot the security devices around the place and the presence of dog faeces which suggested dog patrols. Had Conor been part of an SAS patrol, well briefed and prepared, he would have had no problem in gaining entry into the house unobserved. But that was not the case; he was armed with only a handgun, on his own, and with no foreknowledge of the grounds and the house. It was painfully obvious therefore that he would have to come up with a solution to what seemed like an impossible situation.

Conor drove away from the house and found himself a restaurant where he could eat lunch and give some thought to his problem. He knew he had to gain access because the answer to Breggie de Kok's whereabouts lay in that house. He didn't know how, but the Dutchman seemed convinced the answer was in there. All he had to do was get in there and find it.

The solution came to him quite suddenly. It was so blindingly simple that he found himself chuckling out loud. It wasn't without some risk and it meant a delay of at least one day. But it was a chance he would have to take, and taking risks was Conor Lenihan's business.

Jansch brought the two polystyrene cups of coffee over to Hoffman's desk and set them down gingerly without spilling the contents. A self-satisfied grin announced the achievement to Hoffman who had followed Jansch into the office.

'So what about this chemist?' Hoffman was asking him. 'What makes her think it's the de Kok woman?'

'Well, she doesn't know that, does she, sir?' Jansch lowered himself into a chair. 'What bugged her was the girl's attitude. And the way she was acting.' He sipped the hot coffee, grimaced and put the cup back on the desk. 'She comes into the pharmacy asking for something for a sick child and then gets hot under the collar when it's suggested she takes the baby to see a doctor.' Hoffman sat down at the desk and lifted the cup to his lips. Jansch went on. 'Claims she's from down south, Munich she said, and then legs it.' He put a finger up in the air to make a point. 'The chemist noticed she had a South African accent.'

'But she didn't know we were looking for a South African woman,' Hoffman reminded him, 'so that's not significant in itself, is it?'

'No, but when she returned a couple of days later, she had a prescription from a doctor.' Jansch was into his stride now. 'The counter assistant thought she was acting a bit strange.' He laughed. 'Even forgot to take the baby with her when she left the counter. Had to run back, quick.' He was digressing. 'Anyway, the counter assistant told the chemist. The woman then asked her to check the signature on the prescription. It turns out the doctor was from the other side of Dortmund which is a long, long way from Düsseldorf, so she called us.'

Hoffman arched his eyebrows. 'Thank you for the geography lesson, Uwe. I take it we are checking the doctor out?'

Jansch nodded. 'The local boys are on it now.'

'Good,' Hoffman replied thoughtfully. 'So if it is our Fraulein de Kok, she will be in Düsseldorf.'

'Possibly.'

Hoffman considered this for some time before reaching a decision. What he had in mind was a formidable task but police work was all about patient plodding.

'I want all the property agencies checked in Düsseldorf,' he said at last. 'Any property sold or rented within the last six months within a ten-kilometre radius of the pharmacy. Eliminate the obvious ones as soon as possible. Discreet inquiries on the remainder.'

Jansch expelled a deep breath. 'That's a lot of footwork. It'll take days.'

'Nevertheless, I want it done. Oh, and ask Meckenheim if there are any known terrorist safe houses in the area.' Jansch picked up his coffee and got up to leave. Hoffman stopped him. 'And I want to see that doctor. If that bastard's involved in this, he'll never practise again.'

'Unless you bargain with him,' Jansch flung over his shoulder, as he walked out of the office, and left the vague challenge hanging in the air.

Schiller learned from the police that the baby's finger was not that of his grandson. It had been established that the finger had been dead when it had been cut off, but more importantly the blood group and DNA taken from the tissue sample kept at the hospital did not match that of Schiller's grandson.

The old man was greatly relieved to say the least, but it did nothing to alleviate his mood and temper. He was normally a controlled man. Years at the leading edge of international business had shaped his character and honed his tolerance level. Losing one's temper in the power game could cost money, and it was something Schiller tried very hard not to do.

But today was different. This was a personal trauma, a conflict of family emotion and personal ambition. Against his great wish that the vast empire he had built should not fall into German hands was the life of his grandson. Should he risk that, the single life, against the millions of lives that would inevitably be influenced by his Covenant?

As a businessman, Schiller knew the answer: the Covenant would

147

win every time, providing the single life was that of an unknown child in some remote region of the world, and not that of his own flesh and blood. How easy it would have been to write the baby off and think no more of it than as a casualty of life. But what roused Schiller's anger was the phone call he had received from Levi Eshkol that day. Although he had never met Alfred Weitzman, he could feel the stomach-tightening terror of the Nazi hand as it reached across the ocean and took the life of an old man.

Schiller's judgement had often been mixed with an element of instinct. The turn of a card might persuade a gambler to raise the stakes, but Schiller's game had rarely been played on such fickle moments. Now his judgement had to be right, his instinct reliable. He didn't believe Molke would order his thugs to kill the baby once the Covenant had been signed, although he vowed to expose the man if that happened. So he gave Eshkol his word: if his grandson had not been found within forty-eight hours, he would instruct his lawyers to start proceedings which would end with the signing and transfer of control of his empire to the Israeli people.

Of course, the real reason for his anger was that he would have to tell Joanna of his decision. She would not understand, he knew that, but his decision would be irrevocable. He understood the pain and anguish it would cause, but he felt his own motives were justified and trusted that she would not be too judgemental; there was just too much at stake.

He walked through to the room overlooking the terrace and picked up the phone. He could feel an emptiness in his stomach as he dialled Joanna's private number. Little threads of fear tightened immeasurably round his heart and he wished to God he had an alternative, but he knew he did not.

When Joanna answered the phone he wished her good-day and asked how she was feeling. She reciprocated and the subsequent conversation lasted a few moments and was full of banalities.

'Joanna, *mein liebchen*.' He faltered momentarily. 'There is something I need to tell you.' He could sense a frisson of shock coming from the earpiece and guessed Joanna was expecting the worst kind of news. 'It isn't about little Manny,' he hastened to add. 'It's about a decision I have reached.' He told her hurriedly about the news he had received from Israel. 'It means the kidnappers have started killing to learn the whereabouts of the Covenant.'

'They've already killed several people,' was Joanna's short reply.

'No, I don't mean those poor members of my staff who were murdered during the kidnap, I am talking about others.' He paused, wondering how he could mollify the shock of his decision. 'The Covenant is too important to squander now. So. . . .' He drew in a long breath through clenched teeth. 'I will be instructing my lawyers to proceed in forty-eight hours.'

The tirade came as he expected it would; surprise first, shock, then anger. He couldn't blame her. She had every right to insult and abuse him because he was playing God over her child.

'Joanna, Joanna, I would give my life to save Manny.' He had tears in his eyes. 'Believe me, please. But there are so many more lives.' He began to cry. 'Joanna, I swear to you they will be brought to justice. Believe me; I will spend my fortune tracking them down. They will pay, I promise.'

There was silence for a while. He waited apprehensively, the tears still running down his cheeks.

'If my baby dies, you will have killed him,' she cried down the phone. He squeezed his eyes closed and shook his head. 'No fortune on this earth will bring him back if you let him die.' He slumped into a chair, listening to her voice, compressed and nasal in the earpiece. 'Don't let him die, Manfred. Give in. For God's sake, let them have the Covenant.'

He shook his head. 'Your countrymen did not give in to the Nazis. It still cost many lives, but it saved many, too. I will not give in to them either. I'm sorry, Joanna. I am an old man now. I hope when I have gone you will remember me not with hate and resentment, but with affection and understanding. I love you Joanna.' He put the phone down.

Deep in the pine-covered slopes below Schiller's residence a dull grey van had been parked relatively unobtrusively in the trees. Inside the van was a host of technical equipment being watched over by two men. One of the men was wearing a headset. Beside him a small, cassette tape recorder whirled and recorded the conversation that had just taken place between Schiller and Joanna. He switched the tape off, ejected the cassette and handed it to his companion.

*

When Hoffman and Jansch arrived in Dortmund, the doctor had been in custody for little over an hour. Naturally he was in a reflective mood and not too happy about the lack of reason for his enforced incarceration in the local police station. An hour after Hoffman's arrival, the doctor was feeling even less happy and facing the prospect of an indefinite stay in one of the country's prisons, to say nothing of the loss of his practice and freedom.

Hoffman's attitude to the doctor had an affected ambivalence about it, whereas Jansch had been positively threatening. It was a fairly standard approach to this type of interrogation where they had no official reason to hold the doctor other than suspicion of complicity. But he didn't know that.

'Show me the house,' Hoffman had asked him, 'and I will show you leniency.'

The first glimmer of hope had raised the doctor's expectations. All along he had protested that the prescription had been a forgery. Or the signature even. Not much wrong with that claim, Hoffman had supposed. Proving it was the doctor's signature would not have been too much of a problem, as he pointed out to the man. Pointing the finger at him publicly in such a high profile case as this would have drawn unnecessary attention from the medical council.

'What do you mean leniency?'

Hoffman reached forward and turned the tape recorder off. He turned to Jansch and the uniformed officer who was in the room with them. 'Leave us.'

When they had gone, Hoffman spelled it out for the doctor.

'I don't want any of your crap or bullshit. You prescribed medicine for that baby. You show me where the house is and I will have no further interest in you.' He put his hand over his heart. 'You have my word on that.'

'Nothing? No further harassment?'

Hoffman agreed. 'You have simply practised medicine on a sick child. It was your duty. Now, where is the house?'

The doctor's pale face showed some shame when he answered. 'It is in Düsseldorf.'

150

Hoffman nodded. 'We know that.' The doctor's features sharpened in surprise. Hoffman grinned at him. 'You see, Doctor, we are closer than you realize. Much better you save your scrawny neck now than have us find you out later. There would be no deals then, would there?'

The doctor looked suitably chastened. 'I cannot tell you where the house is,' he told Hoffman, 'but I can show you.'

Hoffman straightened. 'Suits me.' He went to the door and called the two men back in. 'We are going to Düsseldorf,' he said. 'The doctor has agreed to co-operate.'

Frau Lindbergh opened the front door and saw a young, good-looking man on her doorstep. There was an older man with him. Both were smart and appeared quite personable. The young one smiled and greeted her.

'Frau Lindbergh? Good day. I am Detective Weller and this is Sergeant Vogel.' He flashed his warrant card at her. 'May we come in please?'

Frau Lindbergh placed a hand over her ample bosom. 'My word,' she cried. 'Whatever's wrong?'

'Oh, nothing, nothing,' he quickly reassured her. 'Just a routine investigation; there is nothing wrong at all.' He smiled again. 'May we?'

She glanced quickly up and down the street. 'Well, come on then.' She ushered them with haste, not wanting her nosy neighbours (so she thought) to put two and two together and come up with five. 'Through there.' She pointed down the hallway and closed the door swiftly behind her.

'Now,' she said when she had got them safely seated in her sitting-room. 'What can I do for you?'

The young one opened a briefcase and extracted a sheet of paper. He handed it to Frau Lindbergh.

'Tell me, does this represent the current list of your tenants?'

She scanned the page quickly, handing it back with a flourish. 'It is. Why, is anything the matter?'

He put the list back in his briefcase. 'Nothing that we know of,' he told her. 'What it is we are doing is a random check of tenants. How they arrived, where from, how they pay. Are they prompt?' He settled back in his chair, looking comfortable. 'It's part of our "Safety in the Community" project,' he went on glibly. 'And, of course, rather than speak to the tenants themselves, we feel it would be more discreet if we spoke directly to people like you. You do understand, don't you?'

Frau Lindbergh warmed to him. 'Oh, of course I do. Now, I'll get you both a cup of coffee and then we can chat.'

'That would be lovely,' he told her, 'a nice, quiet chat.'

An hour later the two men were shown out by Frau Lindbergh. Most of what she had told them had gone in one ear and out of the other, but she had at least positively identified Conor Lenihan as one of her tenants.

The house was very much the same as the others in the street. It was detached, reasonably large and with a substantial garden. A functional gravel drive swept up to the front of the house. It looked well kept, suburban.

Hoffman had ordered back up units to be strategically placed. He wanted none in sight other than plain clothes units. His car was parked twenty metres from the house and he watched in nervous anticipation as the doctor walked up to the front door.

The man's instructions had been clear. Gain entry and get the baby out of the house without endangering lives. Hoffman was banking on the girl being caught off guard by the doctor. He would claim he had been concerned for the baby and decided to make the long journey back. It was thin, but Hoffman was prepared to risk it.

He watched the doctor pause at the door and ring the bell. A minute later he rang it again. He cocked his head and listened at the door. Then he rattled on the door with his knuckles. He turned, helplessly, towards Hoffman's vehicle. Hoffman started getting nervous. Either the house was empty or the kidnappers suspected something and had flown.

After a while it was clear that there was never likely to be any response to the doctor's knocking. Hoffman got out of the car, signalling Jansch to remain where he was, and walked up the driveway. The doctor shrugged. There was no need to say anything.

Hoffman went round the back of the house and peered cautiously through the windows. Already he was dropping his guard because he knew there was nobody in the house. He went back round the front of the house and signalled Jansch to come up.

'There's nobody in there,' he told the Inspector. 'Get an armed unit up here and break the door down.' He turned to the doctor. 'You come back to the car with me.'

By now a small crowd was materializing on the pavement. It worried Hoffman for all sorts of reasons. If he had the wrong house he would look stupid. If shooting started some innocent bystander might get killed. And crowds attracted the press and he would bet his last Euro that someone was already on the phone to the local newspaper.

He gave the order to the armed response team to go in. They approached the house and took up positions around its perimeter. Two of the team stood either side of the front door while one man attacked the door with a heavy ram. Two strikes and the door flew open. He immediately stepped aside as the first pair went in, their arms outstretched and weapons at the ready.

Hoffman watched the others follow them in and could clearly see them moving about the house through the windows. After a few minutes, one of the team came out of the house, his weapon back in its holster and he walked towards Hoffman's car. By the man's body language, Hoffman could tell it wasn't good news.

'If you would like to come into the house, sir,' he suggested. 'We have a body in there.'

Hoffman and Jansch followed the officer into the house. He took them through to the kitchen. Schneider lay there. Around him was the dried pool of blood that had seeped from his wound. There were signs of water stains. His face was white but there were clear marks of something that suggested he had been scalded. On the floor lay the remains of the pasta jar, shattered into a thousand pieces.

He glanced around the kitchen. Whoever had walked out of that kitchen had not stayed long enough to clear up. A saucepan lay upended on the floor. There was a half prepared meal on the sink drainer. Perhaps more disturbing were the tins of baby food and milk powder on the side.

He went through to the front room. Like the kitchen it had been left untidy. Upstairs was the same, except for the smell of soiled baby diapers mingling with the scent of baby powder. The cot was unmade. The double bed too.

The question burning in Hoffman's mind was who had taken the baby? And if it was Breggie de Kok, where had she taken him?

He turned to Jansch. 'This case,' he said with a touch of rancour, 'like the kidnapper's plans, is coming apart at the seams. If we're not careful, we're going to lose the bloody lot.'

CHAPTER ELEVEN

Joanna opened her eyes and wondered how many times she had done that during the night. Schiller's news that he was going to instruct his lawyers to move on the Covenant had been a fierce blow to her mental state, and she had spent the night in complete despair. Moments of sleep had come briefly. Treasured as they were, they could not compensate for the anger that ravaged her brain at what she believed was a betrayal. She had lain like a slab at times, begging sleep. Her eyes would snap open suddenly and the carousel of doubt, fears and anger would come round again, and with it the skull-thumping pain of tired consciousness.

Joanna spent much of the morning trying to make sense of Schiller's decision. She had phoned him, but he was not to be moved. As apologetic as he was, there was no point in Joanna trying to convince him he was wrong. She had slammed the phone down and gone back to pacing the floor.

Eventually, after much anguish and self argument, Joanna decided to phone Dr Kistler and tell him of Schiller's decision. She doubted if there would be any kind of repercussion, and in Kistler's position he would have to respect her confidence. All she could hope to achieve was to instil a sense of added purpose in the search for her son's kidnappers. She was quite sure that this highly confidential piece of information would remain safe with the President of the North Rhine Police.

Later that morning, Joanna was feeling marginally better. Her telephone conversation with Dr Kistler had left her feeling a shade more optimistic. She had made him promise not to reveal any of this conversation to a living soul, particularly not her father-in-law. After that she was ready to eat a very late breakfast.

Joanna rang through to her kitchen staff and ordered a light breakfast with coffee. When it came, the housekeeper brought with it the daily papers and one letter that had been marked personal and had been delivered that morning by the Bundespost. Joanna recalled her conversation with Hoffman about incoming mail and how he wanted to scrutinize all correspondence. Joanna had given him short shrift, insisting that nobody, absolutely nobody was to interfere with her mail. If there was anything she considered might be of interest to the police, she promised that he would be the first to know.

Intrigued, Joanna slit the envelope open and took out the single, folded sheet of paper. The writing was in English but there was no address on the letter. She took a bite of toast and began to read.

Frau Schiller. Please do not throw this letter away nor show it to anybody. The woman who kidnapped your baby is Breggie de Kok. She has killed her lover and gone into hiding with your son. No one knows where she is. I believe you and I can find her. I have to tell you that I do not know where your son is, but I might be able to convince you I can help if I tell you I was on the team that hit your convoy and kidnapped the baby. The de Kok woman murdered four of the team shortly after the kidnap. I was lucky; I escaped the bomb which she intended should kill all of us. Please believe me when I say I can help. I can't give you my reasons here, but if I can talk to you, I know I will be able to convince you. To show my bone fide, I will put my trust, and my life, in your hands. I will be standing with the media people outside your gates at noon today. If you want to denounce me, you only have to phone the police and tell them of this letter. I promise you that if I am arrested, the police will learn nothing, and I suspect you will probably never see your son again. I have to tell you that it is imperative you get me into your house without suspicion from your security guards. It's the only way I can help. Remember, I am putting my trust in you. If you are not prepared to go along with this, I shall know when I am picked up by the police. My name is John. Don't show this letter to anyone. Destroy it.

Joanna still had a mouthful of toast when she finished reading Conor's letter. She had barely moved a muscle as she read the astonishing note. For a moment she just sat there, dumbfounded; the letter in one hand, and a slice of toast in the other.

She looked up, looked around her as if she was expecting to see people standing there waiting for her reaction. Then she looked back at the letter and read it again. Then she put it down like it was contagious. She couldn't believe she had actually touched something that had been tainted by one of the kidnappers and a murderer. For all she knew he could even be a schizophrenic; someone who believed he was actually one of the kidnappers.

No. She dismissed that because he had actually named Breggie de Kok. He had to be genuine. How else could he have known the name of the woman? She picked the note up and read it again. What should she do? She wondered. If there was a chance she could do something to get her beloved baby back, she would have to co-operate. She had no choice.

She sat there for a long period, going over various scenarios in her head. One of them was to tell the police and let them handle it. But he seemed so cocksure of himself that the police would learn nothing.

What if she got him into the house and he attacked her? But why would he? She argued with herself. What could he gain? She could get some defence, she thought. There must be a gun in the house. But would she know how to handle a gun? Of course not.

Suddenly she jumped to her feet. 'Stop bloody waffling, you stupid bitch. Get him into the house and get Manny back!'

She looked at the clock. It was thirty minutes past eleven o'clock. She went to the window and prised open the short, vertical blinds that hung at the window. From there she could see the phalanx of pressmen standing outside the gate. They looked bored. Some were chatting among themselves. Others were reading. They all looked as though they belonged there.

Joanna finished her breakfast. She didn't have much of an appetite, but the feeling of anticipation was enough to encourage her to eat. Having done that she went through to her bedroom and changed into a pair of jeans, a Jaeger sweatshirt and a pair of soft, leather sneakers. She allowed herself a smidgen of make-up before checking the time. It was noon.

With a nervousness plaguing her stomach and a slight feeling of sickness, Joanna went to the front door. She took a deep breath to steady her nerves and pulled it open. Even though the press were fifty metres away, their anticipatory senses were alerted and they all turned quickly in her direction.

As Joanna walked down the drive she could feel a hundred demons pulling her back. But her will held and she advanced on the flashing lights and tried a limp, but gracious smile for the television cameras.

Immediately the media started hurling questions at her through the gate. Joanna heard none of them, her eyes searching for a face that she would have to recognize. She could see no one who fitted the image she had of the letter writer. For a moment she felt foolish, not sure of what she should do. Then she held up her hands and asked them all to be quiet.

'Good morning, gentlemen,' she began. 'I know you are all doing your job, and I wish I could bring you some news of my son.' She scanned the faces. No one. 'Unfortunately I have to say that neither I, nor Herr Schiller has had any contact from the kidnappers.' They became impatient at their enforced silence and began another barrage of questions.

Then she saw him. He was standing a couple of metres from the journalists and TV men. He had dark hair which fell over a hard, bruised face. The nose looked as though it had been broken more than once. A scar arced across his temple, and his mouth, sensuous and hard, was just parted in a warm smile. He looked unobtrusive standing there alone, but to her he stood out like a beacon of hope.

Joanna tried to show surprise on her face mingled with delight. She hoped she could carry it off because she had to convince these people her reactions were natural.

'John,' she called to him. 'Is that really you?'

Immediately all the reporters turned their attention to where Joanna was now looking. They saw an average man looking rather sheepish, as though he didn't belong there.

'John,' she called again. 'It is you.' She went towards the gate, beckoning him to come closer. He edged his way through the small crowd and stood at the gate.

'Hallo, Joanna.' He shrugged. 'When I heard, I was devastated. I'm sorry, I truly am.'

'Oh, John, it's so nice to see a friendly face.' The questions drowned out the next sentence. She beckoned him to come to the security gate. Conor edged his way along until he was standing at the pedestrian gate.

Joanna spoke to the security guard who unlocked the gate and searched Conor for weapons. Joanna apologized to Conor for the inconvenience, thanked the security guard and slipped her arm through Conor's. They walked up the drive to the house, arm in arm like two old friends in animated conversation pursued by a barrage of wordy questions from beyond the gate.

When they were inside, Joanna stopped talking and took her arm from Conor's. He followed her across the hallway and into a room which, he supposed, would be reasonably private. They continued through that room and passed through a door at the other end. She closed the door and turned towards him. As he went to speak, Joanna slapped him across the face.

'Where's my fucking baby!'

She slapped him again, driving a fierce blow on to the side of his head.

Conor's instinctive reaction was to raise a hand and chop Joanna across the throat. It would have been a killing blow to a woman. But as quick as his reaction was, so was the speed at which he stopped himself and held his arm down by his side.

Joanna slapped him again, demanding to know where her baby was. Conor had expected something like this. It was her right. She was totally justified in punishing the man she knew had kidnapped her son. Soon the slaps became blows with her fists. She rained them down on him until he crouched into a stoop and threw his hands up to protect himself.

'Where's my baby. Tell me you fucking murderer!'

She punched, kicked and scratched until she had driven him to the floor, curled up in a ball to protect himself. She aimed her kicks at his head and his back and then threw herself on to her knees and pummelled him with all the strength she could muster.

Conor let it go on. If she wanted to vent her anger and spite on him, he would let her. As severe a beating as it was, he had suffered worse. And they had been inflicted by professionals.

Soon, Joanna's strength waned and she was reduced to loose slaps on his shoulders and cries of: 'Tell me where my baby is.' She sobbed and broke down, literally collapsing on top of him. 'Please tell me where my baby is.'

Conor rolled out from under her and knelt up. He felt compassion for her but remained detached from her feelings. He took her gently by the elbows and helped her to her feet. She allowed him to take her to a chair and lower her into it. He then knelt beside the chair and waited for her to finish sobbing.

When Joanna looked up, her face was streaked with the wetness from her tears. Her eyes were red rimmed and her hair clung to her cheeks. She looked into the eyes of a man she despised but saw no malice in them. There seemed to be friendliness and warmth. There was also a great deal of blood from the terrible scratches she had inflicted on him. Great, red weals lay in leech like patterns across his face and the backs of his hands. To her he looked an absolute mess.

'Why did you let me do that?' she asked. 'Why didn't you stop me?'

'You had to do it,' he answered gently. 'I would have done the same.'

'I can't believe I had the strength in me,' she told him shaking her head. She wiped her tears. 'Where's my baby?' There was no vehemence or anger this time, just an inherent plea in the question.

He shook his head. 'I don't know. I swear to God, I do not know where your son is.'

'But you think you can find him?'

'I'm hoping *we* can.' He emphasized the word 'we'.

'How?'

Conor looked down at his hands, examining the backs. Then he looked back up at Joanna. 'Do you mind if I get cleaned up first? And perhaps a cup of coffee? Then I will tell you what I know and how I hope we can find your son.'

Conor's photograph hit the late editions with accompanying headlines such as: *Who is the mystery caller? Is this a contact? One of the kidnappers?* There followed articles based on supposition and editorial creativity which brought the kidnap back on to the front pages. It smacked of editors sitting in their ivory towers with little else to feed the general public, so they had little recourse but to milk it for all it was worth.

It also brought the face of Conor Lenihan into the heart of the police investigation and Hoffman immediately had it sent to Meckenheim and Interpol. If this was one of the kidnappers, and he had previous form, they would know within a few hours.

As Hoffman was warming to the investigation again and no longer worrying over trails that had gone cold, Jansch came into his office with some disturbing news.

'Has Dr Kistler spoken to you today?' he asked. Hoffman shook his head.

'No. Why?'

Jansch looked over his shoulder at the open door. He closed it. 'Does Kistler know about the phone tap?' he asked. Again Hoffman shook his head.

'I haven't broken that piece of news to him. Probably won't. Why?'

Jansch was thoughtful for a while. 'Remember Schiller phoned his daughter-in-law and told her about this "covenant" he intends signing?'

'Yes. Go on.'

'Well, she phoned Kistler this morning and told him. She made him promise not to tell anyone; said it was imperative we found her son within forty-eight hours and Kistler was to find some way of speeding it all up.' Jansch then affected a look of surprise. 'And he hasn't said anything to you?'

It was Hoffman's turn to be thoughtful. Ordinarily the doctor would have come into his office, taken him into his confidence and urged him to throw everything into the investigation; so why not now?

'Perhaps Dr Kistler believes we are doing the best we can,' he suggested to Jansch, tongue in cheek, 'and is ignoring the pleas of a desperate woman. Perfectly normal thing in the circumstances, wouldn't you say?'

Jansch had to agree. Perhaps his boss was right and Kistler was simply being reasonable and discerning.

'Well, perhaps you're right,' he admitted. 'I just thought it strange, that's all.'

Hoffman thanked him anyway, but in his own mind, his boss was beginning to worry him. It was true, however, that Kistler was in the fortunate position of being able to control his own situation: he could quietly distance himself from any scandal if it looked as though he was about to be compromised. And it was unlikely, unless he was very unlucky, that Hoffman could produce factual evidence against him.

'We'll concentrate on the central points of this kidnap, Uwe. Worry about Kistler later.'

As Jansch left the office he stopped and looked as though he was about to say something. Then he thought better of it and closed the door behind him. But Hoffman was worried. Jansch was a very observant policeman, perceptive and shrewd, and he could smell a rat.

And the rat was occupying the highest office in the North Rhine Police Force.

Conor told Joanna everything, leaving out his part in the deaths of Jürgen and Oscar. The expression on her face had slowly turned to one of abhorrence as he revealed the depths of deception and violence that had permeated the lives of all those involved, voluntarily or not, in the kidnap. She could not help but remember that her dead husband, Hans, would have been a willing party to the sickening methods employed by Molke's thugs.

When Conor had finished, Joanna shuddered. It was more like a spasm and seemed to shake her from the mood that gripped her. She felt the need to reciprocate Conor's honesty. She didn't like him. Detested him even, but she found herself believing him and recognized the risk he had taken in coming to her.

'Do you know why you kidnapped my son?'

He shook his head. 'It was none of my business.'

She visibly gasped. 'I can't believe you said that.'

He was sitting in a black leather armchair, looking quite relaxed and comfortable. For all the world he could have been a friend paying a social call. He opened his hands in a gesture of resignation.

'It's what I am trained to do. I'm a mercenary, I work for money, not for a creed. I do the job, they pay me, and I go home.' He put his hands back on his lap. 'It's as simple as that. Don't try to understand it, because you won't. Now, tell me why they wanted your son kidnapped.'

Joanna noticed he referred to his former paymasters as 'they'. Perhaps he was trying to distance himself from them, she wondered. Not that it would have made any difference to her feelings about him.

If she could find a way of handing him over to the police without risking her son's life, she would.

'Well,' she began, 'my father-in-law is going to sign a Covenant handing over his entire business empire to the Israelis. Franz Molke wants control of that empire.' She looked down at the back of her hands and began massaging her fingers nervously. 'He will almost certainly become Chancellor of Germany.' She raised her head rather haltingly and tossed her hair back over her shoulder. 'So, with the Federal Government now in the new Reichstag building in Berlin, Molke will be Chancellor and will dominate a united Europe once the European Constitution is signed by the member States, which it probably will be within a few months, especially since Molke employs thugs like you to intimidate people.'

Conor ignored the barb.

Joanna stopped speaking and got up from her chair. She folded her arms and began pacing up and down.

'I simply cannot believe my baby is the key to the domination of Europe.' She paused and glanced sternly at Conor. 'There's more to it than this, you know. Do you realize that?'

Conor continued to stare at her. 'Why do you say that?'

Without answering, Joanna walked over to the wall safe. She opened it and took out the computer discs. She went across to the computer and inserted one into the disc drive. The computer hummed into life. 'This,' she said, tapping in the correct password, 'is one of my husband's files. It's a letter to Franz Molke, Minister of the Interior and head of the Volkspartei. Read it.'

Conor did as he was asked. For a man who had operated on the dark fringes of politics where governments played their dirty war games, Conor saw more than just a political dream and one man's quest for absolute power. But there was something that bothered him more than the aspirations of a political demagogue.

'You say your father-in-law, Manfred Schiller, intends handing over his entire empire to the Israelis?'

'Yes. But don't ask me why; it's too complicated.' She went back to her chair and sat down, tucking her feet up beneath her.

'How much is Schiller's empire worth?' Conor asked.

Joanna pursed her lips. 'Pick a number, add as many noughts as you like and you're not even close. No one knows. He owns several satellites and is planning to put more into orbit. They must be worth at least four hundred million each. He has a great deal of control over world communication traffic. He owns shipping companies, airlines, and a massive electronics industry. He owns armament manufacturers, pharmaceutical companies. He's involved in food production, oil, gas. . . .' She tapered off and remained silent for a moment.

'Is there anything he doesn't own?' Connor asked.

Joanna smiled ruefully. 'I suppose it would be easier to tell you what he is not in.'

Conor whistled gently through his teeth and went back to the black armchair. He lowered himself into it slowly.

'You can't give control like that to the Israelis,' he said.

Joanna cocked her head to one side. 'Why not?' she replied phlegmatically. 'What does it matter who owns it?'

'You cannot give control like that to the Israelis,' he said with more urgency in his voice. 'You just cannot do it. It isn't just a matter of who owns what, but the power it places in someone's hands. The Israeli people, as nice as they are, belong to a country born out of violence. They have fought and suffered for everything they have since the beginning of time. They will go on suffering because of the unique position they hold in the world of religion and Middle East politics. At the moment they depend a great deal on America for ideological and financial support. They have a powerful Jewish lobby in the senate and in congress in America, but the Muslims are gradually weakening that power base and will certainly weaken Israel because of it.'

Conor was quiet for a moment and thoughtful. Joanna waited but said nothing. Conor went on, 'Take away the need for America's help and indulgence; put complete independence in the hands of an extreme, right-wing Israeli Government – and that could happen with Schiller's empire in their possession – and they would turn world politics inside out. The Middle East would become a war zone and drag the entire world into another conflict.'

Joanna was unimpressed. 'It's nothing to do with me,' she rebutted haughtily. 'It's my father-in-law's business, not mine. I'm more interested in getting my son back,' she reminded him.

'If we get him back, then Schiller will be happy and sign over to the

Israelis, right?' Joanna nodded. He went on, 'So we get your baby back and we don't tell him.'

She shook her head in despair. 'I don't think my baby is a key in my father-in-law's plans anymore. And keeping my baby's safe return a secret will not do any good at all. I can't keep my child's return a secret for long, you know. Couple of weeks and the world will know.' She leaned forward. 'Like I said, it will not make any difference; Schiller has decided to sign whether my baby is back with me or not.'

It didn't surprise Conor. The life of an infant did not weigh heavily against such an enormous handover of power. And why Molke's people had believed they could sway the old man's position by kidnapping his grandson, he had no idea. He thought about the boy's father Hans, who was now dead. In him Molke had seen the future. Now that way was closed perhaps he was getting desperate? Perhaps Molke thought he could use the baby as a lever. He decided not to dwell on the reasons why. The fact was the baby had been kidnapped and he, Conor, needed to find out where Breggie was so he could resolve two issues: revenge and rescue.

'If I get your son back, will you try to persuade Schiller not to go ahead with his plan?'

'I'd be wasting my breath,' she told him. 'He didn't become the most powerful businessman in the world by listening to people like me.'

'You underestimate yourself. You are closer to him than anyone else.'

She pulled a face. 'Not where his business interests are concerned.' She was about to say something else, but suddenly checked herself. She studied him for a while, an expression of curiosity on her face. 'Why are you so concerned about what happens to my father-in-law's interests?'

He leaned forward, his hands held together as though to make a point. 'Look, the Israeli people have lived with violence for a good many years. Everyone knows that. They have shown no fear when it comes to protecting their land. They have even gone to war to annexe other people's land.' He ticked some off on his fingers. 'Egypt, the Sinai desert, Syria, the Golan Heights. They redefined the Jordanian border and established a secure zone in southern Lebanon. They call it "protecting their borders".' He said that with a lot of cynicism. 'They are lovely people, but they are as hard as nails and will put up with no

165

nonsense from anybody. The only reason they have returned some of the land they occupied is because of pressure from the West, particularly the Americans.'

'What's all this got to do with my son?' she asked testily. 'I didn't get you in here to listen to a history lesson.'

'Just let me finish and maybe you'll see why it's just as important that you try to use your influence and stop Schiller.'

'And hand it to Molke instead?' she questioned scornfully.

'No. If Schiller doesn't sign his empire over to the Israelis, it will be handed down to his grandson after Schiller's death. It will still be a corporate empire. The point is' – he shuffled in his seat – 'governments are more dangerous than business empires. I've killed people on behalf of the British Government. On behalf of the British taxpayer,' he said pointedly. 'Think about that. And not all Irishmen, I might add. A government will seek to influence others by strength, and it will do it covertly if it has to. A businessman will only seek to influence others if he is going to make a profit. If he sees a loss, he'll move out. Once the Israelis have enough financial independence to drop their reliability on the Yanks, they will assume a more proactive role in the affairs of others.' He thrust a finger towards her. 'And when the Arabs find out, the whole Middle East will blow up, believe me.'

'I think you are talking nonsense. And I don't know why you are telling me all this anyway. It has nothing to do with me.'

He got up. 'Fine, let's forget about the Israelis for now and figure out where your son is.'

Joanna looked relieved for a brief moment. 'OK, so why does this "Dutchman", whoever he is, think he'll find Breggie de Kok's whereabouts here?'

Conor shook his head. 'I don't know. I was hoping you could tell me that.'

She uncurled her legs from beneath her and rubbed some life back into them. Her hair fell forward over her shoulder and she brushed it back. 'This Dutchman obviously knows more about the de Kok woman and my husband than we do.'

'Were they having an affair?' he asked. Joanna's head shot up. Her eyes glared at him in such a profound way that he knew he had touched a nerve. 'Were they?'

'And what if they were?'

He shrugged and lifted his hands in the air. 'Well, I don't know. Perhaps there will be some letters among his personal effects. Perhaps they had a love nest somewhere.'

They both snapped to the same conclusion at the same instant. Conor stopped in a statuesque pose as Joanna sat bolt upright in her chair.

'There was, wasn't there?' he said.

Joanna got up without saying a word and went over to the computer. She closed the current file and opened the one titled 'Breggie'. Conor watched over her shoulder. Joanna sensed his presence and became very self conscious as she scrolled through the file. She could feel her cheeks warming with uncomfortable embarrassment as the depth of her husband's indiscretion with Breggie de Kok was revealed. But if this was the way to find her baby, she was prepared to suffer any humiliation.

Twenty minutes later, after switching from one file to another, Joanna sighed and let her head drop in a kind of exhausted triumph.

'Koblenz, on the river.' She glanced up at Conor. 'I know the place.'

His eyebrows furrowed deeply. 'Really? He didn't take you there, surely?'

She shook her head and laughed a little. 'No, nothing as bizarre as that. We drove past the apartments once and he told me he wanted to buy one for me. I didn't like them, so he didn't buy one. At least,' she corrected herself, 'not for me it seems.'

She got up from the desk and stretched. 'I'm hungry,' she declared. 'And I suppose you are too.'

'I could eat the proverbial horse,' he told her. 'But I didn't think you would be willing to feed me.'

Her eyes, deep pools of pure joy in which Conor would happily have immersed himself, held his gaze.

'I'm not,' she said levelly. 'But I can hardly eat on my own.' She picked up the phone and ordered sandwiches and coffee. 'Well,' she said, putting the phone down, 'while we wait for those, you might as well tell me how you intend getting my son back.'

They walked over to the chairs and sat down again. As Conor opened his mouth to speak, an alarm tone sounded from the computer.

They both turned towards the direction of the noise. Conor was mildly curious but Joanna was far from being curious. She gasped and leapt from her chair.

'Some bastard's hacking in,' she shouted, and ran across to the desk. She hurled herself into the chair and began tapping the keys furiously. From where Conor was sitting he could only see the screen changing. Joanna kept looking from the keyboard to the screen. Whatever it was she was doing, she was working with tremendous speed.

Conor watched transfixed as she ejected the disc from the drive. Then she opened a drawer in the desk and searched furiously for something. Suddenly she pulled a disc out and read the label. With a little body movement of triumph, she inserted the disc into the drive and loaded its contents into the computer's memory bank.

Then she sank back in her chair. 'Bastard!' she said again.

Conor was transfixed. Somehow Joanna had changed her character in an instant. It was almost as if he had witnessed a metamorphosis in which the desolate young mother had become a different person. A rage had filled her and her reaction had been swift and pointed.

'What was all that about?' he asked, surprise still colouring his face.

She turned sharply, and then looked back at the screen. 'Someone was hacking in. I don't know what they were after.' She typed in a few more instructions to the computer. 'Might have been some computer nerds surfing. Seeing who was on line.'

'You weren't on line though.'

She looked round again. 'I was.' She looked irritated. 'My husband always disliked having to instruct the computer to go on line, particularly if he was working on low grade stuff, so the computer is programmed to go on line automatically as soon as it's powered up.' She gave a little giggle. 'It only takes a few moments to go on line, but, that was Hansi; time was precious.'

'What was that disc you put in?'

'Oh, my retribution.' She was looking back at the screen now. 'It's another programme I wrote. It seeks out the hacker and plants a very nasty virus in his software.'

'Always?'

'Not necessarily. First you've got find him. Then you've got to hope he's not as smart as you are, otherwise he would have built some kind of firewall to protect himself against little nasties like that.'

Conor's warring instincts were heightened by this sudden insight into conflict on the internet. 'You're quite happy to do that to each other?'

'Wouldn't you?' she asked. Then she said with bland irony, 'Well, maybe you wouldn't. You would take a gun and blow their brains out.'

He ignored her jibe. 'You know how to write programmes then?'

She gave him a withering look. 'It's what I do. I have an honours degree in Computer Science. I cut my teeth on advanced computer technology.' Her expression changed. It became wistful. 'That's how I met my husband; at Cambridge. He was there on some post graduate course.' She let the moment drift away.

A knock at the door made them both turn quickly. The sound had intruded on them, cutting through the irony of Joanna's attitude towards the hacker. One of the staff came in and placed a tray filled with sandwiches and fruit on the table. Coffee came with it too. She made a little gesture and left the room.

Conor put old-fashioned courtesy aside and attacked the food with relish. He hadn't eaten since breakfast that morning. Joanna poured coffee and put some sandwiches on a plate for herself.

They ate in silence for a while until Joanna brought up the subject of the hacker.

'I hope they didn't get anything,' she said to herself more than to Conor. His jaws were still rotating with a mouthful of food so he said nothing. 'There was some pretty delicate stuff on those files.'

'Or indelicate,' he observed wryly. Then, as quickly as it had entered his head to say it, another, more worrying thought, replaced it. He stopped eating. Joanna noticed it immediately.

'What's the matter?' she asked.

He put his plate down. 'Shit!'

Joanna started getting worried. 'What's up?'

Conor put his hand to his forehead. 'The hacker.' He nodded towards the computer. 'The Dutchman knew the answer to Breggie de Kok's whereabouts was in this house somewhere. It's been puzzling me how he intended finding it. There was no way he was going to break in, not with the protection you've got here, and with the Press outside.' He shook his head. 'No way.'

Joanna locked on to his train of thought immediately. 'You think that might have been the Dutchman?'

'It has got to be,' he surmised. 'There's no other way he would find out. And he must have known your computer would go on line automatically the moment you powered up.' He made a thumping gesture with his closed fist. 'Damn.'

Joanna knew from Conor's reaction and his body language that it could be serious. Indeed, it could be dangerous. 'He might not have got the information he wanted,' she said, trying to calm her own, growing alarm. 'He wasn't in the system long enough.'

Conor held her fixed stare. He didn't want it to be true, but he had to assume the worst. 'How long would it have taken for the computer to detect someone was hacking in?'

She lowered her eyes. 'It would depend how sophisticated his programme was. I once wrote a stealth programme that could get into most systems and lay undetected.' She raised her head. 'It was only advancing technology that rendered it obsolete.'

He repeated his question. 'How long?'

'I would say he would have had enough time to suck all the information out of the file that was open before he was detected.'

He leaned back and expelled a long breath in exasperation. 'That means they know.'

'Know what?' The question was unnecessary. Joanna knew what he was going to say.

'The apartment in Koblenz. It means they know where Breggie de Kok has taken your baby.'

CHAPTER TWELVE

It was late and the open-plan office was filled with the police officers who were involved in the hunt for little Manfred Schiller's kidnappers. At one end of the room a wall had been used to display important features of the case. Photographs of suspects had been pinned up, notes, algorithms tracing possible avenues of thought. A blackboard and easel leaned incongruously amongst the high tech equipment, scrawled with the last thoughts of whoever had used it in chasing an idea. This was the incident room, the heart of the inquiry, where nerves jangled and tempers flared. It was where little bursts of excitement sounded occasionally and drew the attention of others searching for that moment where the smallest clue would bring the greatest success. This was where Hoffman co-ordinated his Fuhrungsgruppen, his leader group, and from where, if necessary, he could pull strings throughout the entire Federal Police force.

Hoffman was standing beside the blackboard. The room was quiet now as all his officers sat facing him. They were all clutching a copy of Hoffman's brief. It was a summary of what evidence they had and pooled all the information that was posted on the wall. There was no formality. They perched wherever they could find room; on stools, on the edge of desks, on the floor. At least half of them in the room had been co-opted by Hoffman from other units in the Federal Republic and it gave him a power, albeit temporary, that few could dream of.

'Right, gentlemen,' he began. 'And ladies.' He smiled across at the two female officers in the room. 'I wanted you all here so we could review our position and consolidate what we already know. Most of you have uncovered facts that might not seem to impinge directly on the kidnap, but which now, I believe, have a far greater significance than we have so far understood.' He nodded at Jansch who dimmed the lights in the room and turned on a stills projector. Immediately a face appeared on a pull down screen against the wall.

'This chap,' Hoffman said, pointing at the face, 'has been identified by the people at Meckenheim as Conor Lenihan. He served in the British Army as a corporal in the Second Parachute Regiment. He later joined the SAS and distinguished himself in Iraq, Colombia and other areas where such forces conduct their operations, including Northern Ireland.' He gave a little emphasis to that last statement. 'On discharge from the army he returned to Ireland where he remained on the payroll of his *original* paymasters, the IRA. His usefulness to them ended when a hit team from his former SAS colleagues failed to eliminate him in an assassination bid. His paymasters moved him to Germany where, we believe, he was allowed to operate as a free agent.' He paused and Jansch changed the picture. It was the one taken of Conor going through the gates at Joanna's place.

'At this precise moment he is in Frau Schiller's residence at her invitation. Naturally we do not know why he is there but strongly suspect Herr Schiller has employed him to get his grandson back. Now, so far nothing illegal has taken place, but—'

'Excuse me, sir.'

The interruption came from one of the men in the room. Hoffman looked across at him. He didn't know the young man too well, but he knew he was working with Oberkommissar Lechter.

'What is it?'

The man pointed at the shot on the screen. 'That's John Buck,' he said. 'He lives in Cologne.'

Hoffman, who had been resting his hand on the top edge of the blackboard, let it fall as the surprise registered clearly on his face.

'He's known to you?'

The young officer shook his head. 'Not in that sense, sir, no. The inquiry you instigated on the counterfeit bills?' He more than had Hoffman's attention now. 'His name has come up as a suspect.' He explained the two addresses and the one-hour chat he had with Frau Lindbergh. 'At the moment we are very interested in him, but we are under orders not to move yet.'

Hoffman looked across at Lechter. 'Otto?'

Lechter's expression, his hooded eyes giving him the look of some-one half asleep, was unchanged. He nodded. 'Preserve the status quo at the moment. He flits in and out of the picture. Just not quite enough,' he offered economically.

'Jürgen?' This was to the operations head of department KK11, the serious crimes division. 'Could this tie in with what you have?' Hoffman asked him.

Jürgen shrugged his shoulders and sat up. 'It's a little tenuous,' he replied, non-comittally. 'We had the two bodies turn up in the one flat in Cologne. One of them was a local hood, member of the Volkspartei youth group. The other was also a member, but didn't have any form. We managed to link him with Jan Kloojens, known as "The Dutchman". Kloojens has strong links with the Volkspartei. We also turned up a source who has confirmed Kloojens' connections with the Davidian group in the States.' He cast around as others reacted with growing interest to his revelations. 'Karl Trucco, one of the dead terror-ists, was a member of the Davidian cult. But,' and here he shrugged again, 'there's no crime knowing the suspects and so far, none has been proven. We are working on it though. And, naturally, we will show more interest in this Conor Lenihan.'

Hoffman thanked him. The meeting progressed in this vein, trying to link the bones of one investigation with another, looking for a thread that would tie them together. The murder of Joseph Schneider was discussed and generally accepted that Breggie de Kok was responsible and had fled with the baby. Beyond that was a blind alley and they liter-ally had no nowhere to go.

At midnight Hoffman brought the meeting to a close. 'Apart from your own investigations, gentlemen, we have little choice but to hang on to Lenihan. If Herr Schiller has hired him to find his grandson, we're not likely to know about it. But my strongest guess is that Lenihan is talking to Frau Schiller for that reason and none other.' He glanced at his watch. 'I've got a specialist team from G9 watching the house now. When Lenihan leaves, we'll be with him. Thank you gentle-men; that will be all.'

The meeting broke up. Some of the officers hung around for a while discussing elements of the case, but within fifteen minutes they had all left, except Hoffman. He waited just long enough to clear the desk in his own office before locking the door and leaving the incident room. As he passed the board displaying all the relevant information on the case, he paused and looked at the photograph of Conor Lenihan.

'Well, Herr Lenihan,' he muttered. 'From your record I suspect you have a better chance of finding that baby than we do. Good luck to you.'

He walked away and prayed that the watching members of the G9 team would not lose him.

Conor checked again. The alarms on all the doors and windows had been armed. All that the security guard had to do now was arm the front door. Joanna assured him this would not be done before midnight. Then the dogs would be brought in to patrol the grounds. If Conor was to stand a reasonable chance of getting out of the house, he had to do it before midnight.

'Why can't you go out the way you came in?' Joanna had asked him.

'My picture will be posted up in every police station in Germany by now,' he pointed out. 'Whether they want me or not, they'll pick me up for questioning.'

He explained to Joanna exactly what he wanted her to do. 'When you throw the switch, all the lights will go out. The TV screens will go blank and whoever's monitoring the screens won't have a clue for about five seconds. The back-up systems will probably cut in fairly quickly. Given that both the back-up system and the guards will need time to react, I'll be out of the front door and halfway across the lawns. The floodlights won't come on until the back-up power supply kicks in, and by the time you close the switch again, I'll be over the wall.'

She faced him with a look of bewildered surprise on her face. 'Are you sure?'

He smiled. 'Trust me. I know what I'm doing.'

She handed him the black stocking he had asked for which he slipped over his head. His nose squashed into his face and she thought he looked quite comical. As he was about to leave he reminded her of her promise. 'I give you the baby and you stop Schiller.'

Joanna had been reluctant at first. Conor's argument that the trans-fer of Schiller's empire to the Israelis would provoke a Middle East war

174

which would suck the Western democracies in did not hold water as far as she was concerned. But his persistent and cogent argument finally won her over.

'You believe you'll never persuade him?' he had asked her.

She had shook her head. 'Never. And certainly not if we have my son back.'

'But the key to his empire are those satellites, correct?' He was thinking furiously, several steps in front of himself. 'Where does he control them from?'

'There are two control centres. One at his house in the Eiffels, which you know about,' she added acidly, 'one at his business headquarters in Frankfurt. There is only one ever on line though.'

'What about satellite control officers?'

'They work at whichever centre is on line. At the moment it will be where my father-in-law is.'

'Could you hack into the computer's systems?'

She smiled. 'It isn't simply a question of hacking in. Satellites are controlled by codes. These have to be keyed in to initiate a link with the satellite. You have to know the codes to get in. There would be all kinds of firewalls and security programmes installed to prevent any illegal interception and transmission.'

'What about all the companies he owns? Don't they use them?'

She agreed. 'Well, naturally. But all their transmissions are electronically isolated from the motherboards inside the satellites mainframe computers.'

Conor swore. 'So it's got to be that one. But you could do it, couldn't you?' She didn't answer but appeared to be hesitating over something. Conor felt elated. 'You can. I know you can. And you can do it from here, right?' He pointed at the computer sitting on the desk.'

'It's not that simple, damn you.'

'But it can be done, can't it?' he pressed.

In the end Joanna agreed. 'Yes, but only if you can get in at the precise moment. You can't just walk in with a set of new codes and take over. You have to wait until the master codes have been keyed in.' Suddenly her eyes flared and she looked angry. 'It's a tricky operation, damn you again.'

'So is getting your baby back. I could wind up dead.'

She was silent for quite a long time. 'I would have to write a programme. I can't do that without hacking into my father-in-law's systems first. If I'm not caught then, well. . . .'

Joanna was recalling their conversation when he lifted the stocking from his face, cupped her face in his hands and kissed her. It was a momentary touch, a mere brushing of his lips on hers. 'I'll get your baby back,' he said, 'and you stop Schiller.'

Joanna walked down the stairs to the cellar. It was quite empty and well lit. As Conor had explained when they had come down earlier, the distribution boxes were fed from the electricity company's feeder cable which had its own main switch. All she had to do was pull the switch down, count to fifteen slowly, and push the switch up again. Then she was to walk back upstairs and return to her bedroom. He promised that in that short period of time, most of the security men would assume there had been a mains failure. Once the lights had been restored they would all settle down to another 'normal' night.

Conor eased back the handle of the front door but kept his foot against it so it didn't move. He had been in the entrance hall for five minutes without lights. His eyes were now fully accustomed to the darkness. He could see a faint glow from outside filtering beneath the door and was going to use this to let him know when Joanna had pulled the switch.

It seemed as though an age had passed when the glow beneath the door vanished. He pulled the door back, stepped out on to the front porch, closed the door and sprinted around the side of the building. He broke away from the house and crossed the open lawns in complete darkness. Reaching the far wall he jumped as high as he could with his arms outstretched and grasped the top of the wall, the leap giving his legs the momentum to carry them up on to the wall. He pulled himself over and dropped to the ground as the floodlights came back on.

Conor used that moment to cast around for signs of any movement. Seeing none, he sprinted for cover to trees on the far side of the road. He stopped there and regained control of his breathing. There was no noise to intrude on his hiding place save that of his own making. Two minutes after making the trees he stood up and walked swiftly and silently from the deep cover.

Ten seconds after Conor had cleared the wall; a member of the G9

176

surveillance team lowered the single lens night sight and nodded his head in thoughtful satisfaction.

Several hours later, Conor was sitting in his car on the north side of the Mosel River just at its confluence with the mighty Rhine. He was oblivious to the water traffic on the river, the cruise ships, the smaller craft and the barges being towed out in mid-stream. Oblivious to the men fishing along its banks, to the dog walkers and joggers and to the mothers pushing baby buggies along the embankment while chatting with one and other. He was oblivious to all of that as he studied an apartment block through a pair of binoculars from the inside of his car, parked about 200 metres from the building.

And from another car, two men from G9 surveillance team watched carefully.

Conor knew Breggie de Kok was in that apartment block with Joanna's baby son, but he didn't know where. By logical reasoning he had decided that the odds were her apartment was one of the penthouse suites. He couldn't accept that a man of Hans Schiller's wealth would settle for anything less, particularly as it was a love nest for his mistress.

There were sixteen apartments in all. Eight on either side of a central stairwell and lift shaft. Access to the apartment block was through a prestigious front entrance which allowed an observer walking by to see through the glass doors. Conor had walked by that morning. Through the doors he had seen a desk and a uniformed member of staff. No doubt the man's job was to act as a barrier and allow no unauthorized access to any of the apartments. It was a classic aspect of security in this kind of building.

From Conor's vantage point he could not see the front of the apartment block and, from what he could see there was little scope for an unobserved entry. Above the penthouse suites was the flat roof with outlets for air conditioning.

Earlier that morning, from a higher vantage point, he had seen what appeared to be the top of the lift shaft where the lift motor would be housed. There was also a roof access stairwell visible and obvious because of the closed door built into it, almost certainly used by maintenance technicians for access to the roof. But, more interestingly, from

Conor's point of view, was the fire escape. There was one at each end of the building, cleverly designed to blend in with its style and almost neatly concealed from view. There would have been a fire door at each level, and Conor had a wire coat hanger in the boot of his car that he would probably need if he had to go in through any one of those fire doors. Judging from the rooftop construction, it was obvious that the two penthouse apartments had their own access on to the fire escape.

Without the benefit of seeing it, Conor assumed there would be a fire door at the rear of each penthouse which opened out on to the roof.

He folded his arms for a while, considering how best to gain entry into the building without raising the alarm. Going through the front entrance was out of the question without proper planning. He might have been able to achieve it by using a diversion, but he was operating alone and dismissed that option. And because his knowledge of any of the residents was nil, with the exception of Breggie, he was unable to concoct some outrageous lie and feed it to the security man inside the front entrance.

He was wrestling with the problem when something caught his eye. It was a BMW car with smoked glass windows slowing to a halt in the road about fifty metres from the building. The front door of the BMW opened and a tall, well-built man got out. He was wearing sunglasses. Conor raised his binoculars. The rear door then opened and another man, similarly dressed, got out. As he turned to close the door, Conor saw the figure sitting in the rear passenger seat. The size of the man was unmistakable, such was his bulk. That brief, fleeting moment was enough to tell him that the Dutchman had turned up.

Conor lowered the glasses again. This was a development that was not altogether unexpected, but what was unexpected was that the Dutchman should turn up in person. He brought the glasses up again and followed the two men. From the car he was just able to make out their features through the binoculars. He found himself nodding gently. He had recognized one of the Dutchman's gorillas from the nightclub.

Conor knew then he had little time to scheme or plan. Those men were going into that building for one reason only. And what bothered Conor was that they looked like two men who were not expecting trouble.

He had no option but to go. He started the engine and pulled out into the traffic, intending to drive beyond the Dutchman's car and park it further along the road. To pull up too close to the Dutchman was to invite recognition from the fat man, so he continued driving until he found a convenient space.

As Conor made his move, the surveillance team from G9 saw him go. The driver of the car tried to pull out but was held up for a moment by traffic. He cursed loudly because he had to watch the oncoming cars and try to keep Conor in sight all the time. His partner made a call on the radio to say the target was on the move and in which direction he was driving. The reply was simply to maintain contact and observe. By then it was too late; they had lost sight of Conor.

Hoffman was in another car parked further along the north side of the river. He heard the voice of the surveillance operative through his headset telling him of Conor's movements and subsequent disappearance. Hoffman swore loudly.

Conor parked his car in the first convenient space. He slipped out of the car and sprinted down towards the river then ran towards the apartment block. He reached it about two minutes after the Dutchman's men had walked in through the front entrance. He slowed to a trot, then a walk and strolled past the front entrance of the building. Through the doors he could see one of the Dutchman's gorillas leaning against the desk. There was no sign of the other one. Conor threw caution to the wind and worked his way round to the rear of the block until he was standing beneath the fire escape.

The spiral ladder was designed so that it fitted in a column, rather like a chimney but with one side open. Conor was aware of the security cameras mounted on high stanchions at strategic points but kept his head down and, using a knife and the hooked end of the old, wire coat hanger he slipped the hooked end of the coat hanger between the doors and pulled back on the panic bar. The doors opened and he slid between them.

He sprinted up the stairs, ignoring all the doors that opened directly on to the fire escape until he reached the top. He opened the door there and lay flat on the roof to catch his breath. Two minutes later he sat up and began edging his way along the rear wall of the penthouse.

*

Breggie de Kok started her day in a bright mood. Little Manny was responding well to the antibiotics and she was formulating a plan to return the baby for a ransom which would leave her in clover for the rest of her life. For a while, Breggie had imagined that the baby was hers and Hansi was her husband. She acted out little scenarios with the baby, telling him that Daddy was at work now and he would be home soon. There were promises that they would all go to the Eifels for the weekend and go boating on the lakes. Later they would go to Cologne Zoo and see all the animals.

The mood fed her hopes for her future. Once out of this she would return to South Africa. Things were a little better there now, and there was no future for her in Germany. She would join the movement for an independent homeland for the whites. It was a banner that she could rally to. It had its appeal and she found herself humming a tune.

She opened the windows of the penthouse, letting the breeze flow through. She opened a rear window, too, thinking how thoughtful the architect had been to build a decorative screen wall to hide the ugliness of the flat roof. Not that they used the rooms at the back of the penthouse. They were mainly guest rooms. Hansi had never invited guests in anyway.

She walked through to Manny's room. The baby was sleeping peacefully. Breggie thought it would be nice to have a bath and, maybe, take Manny out for a walk. She went into the bathroom and opened the gold taps. She poured some very expensive foam bath into the water which Hansi had bought her and always insisted she use. Then she stripped off and stopped. The soft, downy hair on the nape of her neck lifted as she heard an unfamiliar noise immediately behind her.

Breggie was poised, one foot on the edge of the bath, half turned, when the gorilla walked in. For one, very brief moment, Breggie was too stunned to say anything. The gorilla couldn't believe his eyes or his luck.

Suddenly Breggie jerked out of her stupefied state. 'Who the fuck are you?'

The gorilla was a big man, well over six feet tall and probably 200 pounds in weight. His eyes were glued fast to Breggie's superb figure.

'Oh baby,' he drooled. 'I'm going have some of this.' Before Breggie could move he had reached out and grabbed her throat in a vice-like grip.

Breggie kicked out at him, but he was so strong she was no more than a rag doll in his bear like hand. He lifted her off her feet and carried her through to the first convenient room he could find. Breggie had tried to scream but his free hand was clamped solidly over her mouth.

He threw her on to a bed and swiped her across the face with the back of his hand. The sheer force of the blow knocked her out and she went limp. The gorilla smiled lasciviously. He took his jacket off, removed his gun and laid it on the table beside the bed. Breggie started groaning as he straddled her. He slapped her face gently.

'Wake up, baby. Look what daddy's got for you.'

Breggie started struggling again and lashing out at him, but he was strong enough to ignore her blows. He unbuckled his belt and opened his fly. Breggie screamed again and he clamped a hand over her mouth.

'Oh, baby, I'm sure going to enjoy this.'

He entered her and Breggie screamed and shouted filth and derision on him, but his huge, walrus like bulk drove the breath from her body with each thrust of his penis.

Eventually it was over. He pulled out and groaned but didn't roll off. Breggie thought she was going to die beneath his dead weight. She couldn't breathe properly and was genuinely in fear of her life.

He eventually sat up, but still kept his weight on her. He smiled and reached over for his gun. 'Don't move, honey. If you do, I'll kill you. Now that I've fucked you, you're no good to me.'

He stood up beside the bed and tidied himself up. All the while he held the gun on Breggie and she knew that to move would invite the killing shot. She had to bide her time.

'Now,' he said at last. 'Where's the baby?'

Breggie snarled at him. 'Fuck off!' she snapped.

He whipped the pistol across her face and opened the flesh to the bone. It was the last thing he ever did: Conor shot him through the head.

At that moment, Breggie had covered her face and she was unaware that her rapist had been shot. She wasn't even aware that Conor had entered the room. All that was in her mind was the blinding pain and the fear of another blow. As she screamed in agony she heard the shot. It didn't register at first, but when it did she pulled her hands slowly away from her battered and bleeding face.

Her first glimpse of the gorilla was him falling away from her. Then she saw Conor standing in the doorway, legs apart in that classic stance of someone who knew how to kill with a gun. He wore gloves on both hands.

It was all too much for Breggie to take. She recognized Conor almost immediately, but the questions in her head piled into each other so quick she couldn't speak.

Conor said nothing to Breggie. He picked up the gun dropped by the dead man. Then he put his own gun away. Breggie found her voice.

'How?' He knew she was referring to the bombed house.

'Lucky, I guess.'

'Why have you come here?'

He shook his head. 'You don't want to know that, Breggie.'

Breggie groaned and covered her face with her hands. She rolled off the bed on to the floor. Conor moved away from her, edging round to the foot of the bed. As far as he was concerned, she was still dangerous.

'We can do a deal,' she said.

'No deals.'

'We can split the ransom.'

'No deals.'

'Conor,' she pleaded through bloody lips, 'I'll do anything. We'd be great together.'

'No deals,' he repeated.

Suddenly Breggie moved. It was quick, snapping round like the wounded animal she was. She squeezed the trigger as soon as the gun was lined up on Conor's body, and at that moment, Joseph's words came back to haunt her: 'One of these days Breggie my darling, you will make a mistake.'

She had left the safety catch on.

Conor shot her. The bullet went straight into her mouth and drove up into her brain. She was dead before she hit the floor.

Conor sighed. He had hoped he could have learned more from her, but the trail had now ended. It stopped there. He went over to her body and took her gun out of her hand. He assumed she had pulled it out from under the mattress, or maybe it was lying beneath the bed. It was academic anyway; she had got the gun and was going to kill him.

He took his own gun out and pressed it into Breggie's dead hand. Then he put the gorilla's gun beside him on the bed. There was nothing left to do, so he walked out of the room and went through to check on the baby. Little Manny was sleeping, blissfully unaware of the violence that had blown like a storm through his short life.

He smiled at the infant and touched him gently on the cheek with the tip of his finger. Then he went back into the apartment and picked up the phone.

'Put me through to the police, please.'

The next thing Conor did was to leave the apartment by the front door. Outside the door he found the fire alarm as he expected. It was fixed to the wall in easy reach, should it be needed by the occupant of the penthouse. He smashed the glass and immediately the apartment block was filled with the jangling bedlam of alarm bells.

One minute later, Conor was climbing down the fire escape. He had to go down two floors before he came to a fire door that had been opened. The people who had opened the door were already halfway down the fire escape. He went inside and closed the door behind him.

The streets around the apartment building came alive with flashing blue lights and wailing sirens as police cars and fire engines converged on the area. Hoffman made it to the front of the building five minutes after Conor had made his phone call. He was greeted by a phalanx of curious onlookers, residents from the apartments, firemen and the local police. He battled his way through until he found the senior fire officer who quickly informed him that no one was allowed to enter the building until his men had located the fire and declared the building safe.

Hoffman was furious but no amount of argument would persuade the senior fire officer to let either him or any of his men through.

'We believe there's a kidnapped baby in the top floor apartment and a suspect killer in there somewhere,' Hoffman had told him angrily.

'Are you armed?' the fire officer asked.

Hoffman shook his head irritably. 'No, of course I'm not bloody armed.'

'Well, get someone who is and they can protect my men.'

It was another two minutes before Hoffman had secured two plain-clothes police officers from his own group with weapons. They went

into the building with the firemen. Ten minutes later the senior fire officer received a call on his radio. He turned to Hoffman.

'You'd better go up,' he told him. 'Your men have the baby, but there
are two dead bodies in the flat. There's no fire, so you can use the lift.'

Hoffman was gone before the man had finished speaking. When he
reached the penthouse apartment one of the firemen pointed to the
smashed fire alarm on the wall.

'It was triggered from here, sir.' He glanced back at the open door
of the penthouse. 'From what we've seen in there, it must have been a
diversion.'

Hoffman thanked him and went into the flat. One of the plain
clothes policemen was holding the baby. He looked at the sleeping
child.

'Get an ambulance,' he said to the officer, 'and have the baby taken
to the nearest hospital. Then contact Frau Joanna Schiller, she's at
Godesberg of course,' he added, 'and tell her we have a baby whom we
believe is her son. She will have to come to the hospital to identify the
child and claim him. Get on to the local boys and have them provide
an escort. And make sure the baby is guarded all the time.' He laid
emphasis on the last sentence, his eyes burning with a threat that left
nothing unsaid.

'Now,' he said to the other police officer. 'Show me what you've
found.'

CHAPTER THIRTEEN

The late editions had a field day. They carried photographs of Joanna Schiller with her baby, her face transformed into one of joy and beauty. With her in the pictures were some of the hospital staff who had received the baby and checked him over. Manfred Schiller's personal secretary was also there representing the great man, as was Erich Hoffman who had been prematurely blessed by the German press for the safe return of the infant. The television channels carried news bulletins reporting on the dramatic events leading up to the rescue, and there were several reports of burning buildings and western style shoot outs between the cops and the kidnappers.

The only man who knew exactly what had happened in that penthouse watched the events unfolding on television with amusement. Conor had returned to his apartment in Cologne, choosing not to use the Frau Lindbergh's bed-sit. He had soaked in a bath, eaten a take away Chinese meal and contemplated his next move.

He got up from his chair and switched the television off. His options were quite clear: remain in Germany and risk running into the Dutchman, or leave. He knew the latter was the only course open to him, but not until he had finished with Joanna Schiller. But before that he had to clear the apartment of his few possessions, pick up his stuff from the bed-sit and find somewhere else to stay until the job was done.

He went through every room thoroughly, trying to eradicate all forensic trace of him being there, although he knew it was virtually impossible to leave the place clean; but he did what he could before walking out the front door with his bag. He slipped the key through the letter box and made his way across to Frau Lindbergh's place.

He didn't see her when he went in through the front door. He made it to the bedroom, breathed a sigh of relief and began collecting his few bits together. Barely a few minutes had passed when a knock came at the door and Frau Lindbergh's voice came through the woodwork.

'Herr Buck? Do you have a minute please?'

Conor swore mildly under his breath and went to the door. When he opened it he saw Frau Lindbergh standing there with two men. Conor knew, instinctively, it was the police.

'Herr John Buck?' one of them asked politely. Conor nodded. 'May we come in?' Conor backed away and the two men walked into the room. They both flashed their warrant cards at him. They were big guys; not that it had ever stopped Conor before, but now was not the time to show his talents. Now was the time to bluff and keep on bluffing until they knew they had no good reason to hold him.

'Herr Buck,' one of them began, putting his warrant card carefully into his pocket. 'You are under arrest on suspicion of handling counterfeit money. Anything you say. . . .'

They produced a pair of handcuffs and took him away. In passing, Conor looked at Frau Lindbergh's shocked features and winked at her. Then he was in the back of a police car and being driven at speed to Hoffman's headquarters.

The heat from the burning sun did little to spoil Levi Eshkol's day. He was in a contented mood, walking happily among the hills of the Negev Desert, south of Hebron. There were no faxes, no phones, and no high pressure business meetings among the changing colours of the mountains. Here he could be lost in quiet solitude, absorbing nature's peaceful remedy for stress.

That morning Eshkol had received a phone call from Manfred Schiller. The transfer of power would begin in one week. Once the national press had exhausted all its interest in the kidnap and safe return of his grandson, he would have a clear field. They would have no further interest in him and there would be no more delays.

Eshkol, who had been in Hebron securing a deal with the Palestinians on behalf of the Israeli Government, had decided to motor down from Hebron to Eilat on the Gulf of Aqaba. He had planned a few days, on his own, swimming in the warm waters of the Gulf. Take in some scuba diving and a little sailing, and then he would fly back to Jerusalem.

Schiller's phone call had changed Eshkol's plans, but he deliberately took a day off to soak up the inestimable benefits of the desert peace. Tomorrow he would notify the team. One week from now, on behalf of the Israeli people, he would control the most formidable, private corporation the world had ever seen.

Conor's vista was not so grand. He had little else to stare at except the four grim walls of his prison cell. He had studied the graffiti of previous incumbents, that which had not been painted out. Deeply scratched names and dates, postulations about the police and all their bastard offspring; many of these slogans had survived the paint brush and were still readable beneath the glossy coating of an uninspiring grey paint.

The light from the high, barred window did little to brighten the gloom, but Conor had no quarrel with that. He had been in far worse prison cells than this. The Middle East variety did nothing for the health and welfare of the inmates, and Conor had been in the best (or should that be the worst?).

His predicament was nowhere near as serious as some of his earlier incarcerations. From what he knew of interrogation techniques, he could last the distance until there was no longer any reason to hold him. He had nothing to fear from a physical beating because it was extremely unlikely the German police would stoop to such tactics. He had also prepared himself well, mentally, and couldn't think of anything they could, legally, lay at his doorstep. If he'd forgotten anything, he didn't know what it was. And it was too late anyway.

They had taken most of his things including his belt and shoe laces. They had left him with his shoes, trousers and T-shirt; nothing else. He wasn't unhappy with that either. He had lain naked once, in stinking filth, at very low temperatures for several days at the hands of jailers who had been determined to break him. But Conor was a tough bastard which was why men like him were employed by governments to do their dirty work.

The door to his cell opened and a policeman hooked a finger at him. Conor got to his feet and walked in front of the policeman. He went up a flight of stairs and into an interview room. There was a table and a couple of chairs in the room. Against one wall was a mirror which Conor assumed was one way. It allowed others to witness the interrogation. There was also a tape recording device on a bench. A uniformed policeman stood at ease against a wall. Conor sat down, his back to a reinforced frosted glass window and waited for his interrogator to come in.

A few minutes later the door opened and Hoffman walked in. He paused for a moment studying Conor. He seemed to make up his mind about something and switched on the tape. He gave the date, time and names of all those present in the room including Conor's pseudonym, John Buck. Then he sat down opposite Conor.

'Do you smoke?' Conor nodded. Hoffman produced a packet of cigarettes and a lighter. Conor lit a cigarette and blew the smoke out of his mouth, directing it away from Hoffman. 'Do you want a drink? Tea? Coffee?'

'Tea please, milk and sugar.'

'It's out of a machine,' Hoffman warned him.

Conor shrugged. 'So be it.'

Hoffman leaned back in his chair and asked one of the officers present to fetch a cup of tea for the prisoner.

'How long have you been in Germany?' Hoffman asked.

'Six months.'

'Have you worked at any time during those six months?'

Conor shook his head. 'No.'

'Do you have any friends here, people who could vouch for you?'

'No.'

'So you're a loner?'

'Yes.'

'Why are you here?'

Conor shrugged. 'I like the country.'

'You don't work, have no friends, but like the country which is why you stay. What do you do for money?'

'I have funds.'

'Counterfeit funds?' Hoffman suggested.

'Not as far as I know.'

They had searched Conor's bed-sit and his apartment, but had found no counterfeit money, nor evidence of any.

'What is your relationship with Frau Schiller?'

'She's an old friend.'

'A special friend?'

'No.'

'Why did you visit her at Godesberg the day before yesterday?'

'Just wanted to say hallo.'

'You were seen leaving her house just before midnight, in darkness and in what can only be described as "unusual circumstances". Why did you do that?'

'I wanted to avoid the press.'

'You then made your way to Koblenz. Why?'

'I heard it was a nice place to visit.'

Hoffman didn't say anything for while. He just studied Conor, without expression, wondering how tough this man would prove to be.

'You were seen at the Hoeffler Apartments. Why were you there?'

'No particular reason. They were on my way, I guess.'

'And did you go in to the apartments?'

Conor shook his head, took another lungful of smoke in and blew it away.

Hoffman took two photographs from his pocket. One was of Jürgen Krabbe, the other of Oscar Schwarz. He pushed them across the table to Conor.

'Do you know, or recognize either of these men?'

Conor studied the two photographs at length. His expression didn't change until he screwed up his face. 'No,' he said, pushing them back across the table at Hoffman.

'Let me try some names on you.' Hoffman kept his eyes on Conor's, hoping to see some small blink of a memory. 'Breggie de Kok?' Conor shook his head. 'Joseph Schneider?' The shake of the head again. 'Karl Trucco?' Same result. Hoffman knew he was wasting his time. The door opened and the police officer came in with Conor's tea. Hoffman waited until Conor had the tea and continued with the questions.

The interview went on for another two hours. Hoffman tried every subterfuge he knew to unbalance and trick Conor into some kind of admission that he could work on. But Conor's answers were resolutely economic, almost monosyllabic, and bloody hard to break down. Hoffman terminated the interview and switched the tape off.

'Can I have something to eat now?' Conor asked before he left. 'And am I entitled to a phone call?'

Hoffman laughed quietly. 'We'll get you something to eat, naturally. But a phone call?' He left it hanging in the air for a moment. 'You want to contact your solicitor, right?'

Conor shook his head. 'I don't have a solicitor.'

'We could get you one,' Hoffman informed him.

Conor laughed. 'I bet you could, but no thanks. I may want the phone call later though, but not yet.'

Hoffman tipped his head in a mock bow. 'Very well, Herr Lenihan, as you want. You will be taken back to your cell now and some food will be brought to you.'

'My name is Buck,' Conor reminded him. 'John Buck.'

Hoffman nodded. 'My apologies, it was a slip of the tongue.' He had hoped Conor might have reacted normally to his real name, by not reacting in the way that he did. Because Hoffman's department had identified Conor, there was no reason, no legal reason why Conor couldn't have changed his name to John Buck. He decided that it was not important. For the moment.

'Oh, there's one other thing,' Conor said.

Hoffman smiled. 'One other thing?' he repeated mockingly. 'Why not?'

'When can I go?' Conor asked him.

It was Hoffman's turn to laugh. 'Go? Never, I hope. Why?'

'I want to know when to make that phone call.'

Hoffman was intrigued. 'I don't understand.'

Conor sat upright in his chair. He held one hand open and tapped its palm with the finger of his other hand. 'You can only hold me for so long, right? Then you either let me walk, or release me on bail. How long?'

'We can hold you for quite some time yet, Mr Buck. We can get a magistrate's order to extend the period if we believe we have sufficient grounds. But as far as releasing you on bail, who would post it and where would you go?'

Hoffman couldn't help chuckling at what he believed was a dilemma for Conor. But somehow he had an uneasy feeling that Conor was already one step ahead of him. He shook his head despairingly and walked out of the interview-room.

Uwe Jansch and Otto Lechter had sat behind the one-way mirror for the entire length of the interview. The room was thick with the smoke from Lechter's cigarettes. The debris from potato crisp packets and chocolate bars littered the table, mingling with the stained plastic coffee cups that had fortified them throughout Conor's skilful handling of their chief.

Jansch pushed himself up from his chair when he saw Hoffman leave the interview-room and arched his eyebrows at Lechter. The message was left unsaid but it carried a great deal of meaning. Lechter nodded his unspoken reply and they left the room together.

Hoffman was on his way back to his office. He glanced back over his shoulder and waited for the two men to catch him up. They said nothing, not even as they went up in the lift to Hoffman's operations room, keeping quiet until they were all seated round the desk, the door closed behind them.

'Well?' Hoffman asked. 'What's the verdict?'

Jansch waited for Lechter to speak, giving way to his seniority.

'You're not going to break him, Erich. He's too clever.'

Hoffman conceded that. 'So he should be; he's been trained by the best in the world.'

Lechter signalled his disbelief with a quick shake of the head. 'He has no alibis, not one person to vouch for him, yet he oozes confidence. He has nothing to fear.'

'I don't think *fear* is the right word for his kind,' Hoffman observed. 'It's milked out of them before they are released on to an unsuspecting world.'

'He doesn't appear to have done anything wrong,' Jansch put in. 'But we know he has.'

'Do we?' asked Hoffman. He looked at Lechter. 'Your men couldn't find any counterfeit money at either of his places, could they?'

'We know he had some, but, it's like he said, he could have got that from anywhere.' Lechter looked bitter. 'It's all circumstantial. We could never take him to court on what little evidence we have.'

Hoffman flipped open a file that lay on the desk in front of him. It was a report from the forensic laboratory on Conor's clothing. 'No powder burns. So we cannot link the deaths of Krabbe or Schwarz to him. We are confident he entered the apartments, but not that he was involved in the rape and murder of Breggie de Kok, nor that of Kleiber.' Kleiber was the gorilla who had killed Breggie. 'It looks like a straight-forward case of rape, self defence and both dying as a result.' He closed the file. 'Which we know is bullshit!'

'You think Lenihan killed them, sir?'

Hoffman tapped the desk hard with his fingers. 'I don't know. How could he?' The question was largely rhetorical. 'But I just have a feeling he was involved.'

'It's the same with the kidnapping, isn't it?' Jansch said. 'We are pretty confident he was involved, but cannot prove it. All the terrorists are dead.'

'Except Lenihan,' Hoffman reminded him.

'But we don't know, do we?' Jansch countered. 'We've got no proof. The only witnesses we have to the kidnap are the Schillers, and they can't tell us anything except Breggie de Kok was the leader. She's dead. They're all dead. End of story.'

Hoffman sighed heavily. 'I know what you're saying, Uwe. We'll just have to hope something turns up.'

'Mister Micawber,' Lechter observed.

Hoffman looked puzzled. 'What?'

'Charles Dickens? Micawber?'

'Oh yes, the eternal optimist; would have made a good policeman, but a poor detective.'

They all laughed. If nothing else, it had done something to lighten the mood. And at that point, the meeting broke up for a late lunch.

Joanna was standing by the large window overlooking Schiller's magnificent view of the southern Eifels Mountains. Their verdant slopes dipping down to the Mosel, gently meandering through vine-yards, their vines casting lengthening shadows in the evening sun. It was always a beautiful and peaceful place to be.

Joanna was happy and content now. Her darling Manny was back with them, safe in the nursery. He had been declared fit and unharmed by the kidnap. She had a crooked doctor to thank for that. And although she didn't know how, she was sure Conor had found some way to let the police know where her baby was being held. She hadn't seen him since he left her place under the cover of darkness, and wondered if she was likely to. At other times, and in different circumstances, she knew she would have liked to have known him better. She felt ashamed of that because he was a killer, but he had a certain atavism that attracted her feminine instincts.

She felt a movement at her side. It was Manfred Schiller. He had a glass of Krug in his hand. 'Penny for your thoughts, *mein liebchen.*'

'Oh,' she started wistfully. 'I was thinking of the reason for Manny's kidnap.'

'The Covenant?'

'Yes, the Covenant,' she replied. 'I was thinking of how many people have died because of it.'

'Not because of the Covenant, dear Joanna' – he raised his glass as he made his point – 'but the people who chose to commit those barbaric acts.'

'But the Covenant is the catalyst. And it will go on being the catalyst.'

He smiled: it was patronizing. 'Don't worry your pretty head about the Covenant. It will give control to those who want peace. To those who deserve peace.'

She regarded him with a sense of pity. 'And feed the hatred of those who will destroy that peace and the peace of others.'

He wrinkled his brow. 'Who, the Arabs?' He laughed, teasingly. 'Dear Joanna, what nonsense. The Israelis are almost Arabs themselves. The Covenant will serve them all.'

Joanna thought of Manny and others like him; newly born into a world torn apart by hatred, religious dogma, ethnic cleansing and xenophobia. Into that the Covenant would put the tools of Satan and the insidious weapons of modern man.

'You still intend to transfer your power, despite my arguments,' she asked him, 'and despite all my pleas?'

He placed his hand on her shoulder. 'Joanna, I love you and our little Manny more than I love life itself. I would do nothing I thought would harm either of you.' He let his hand fall to his side. 'But I must tell you that your arguments and your pleas have fallen on deaf ears. I will sign the Covenant and transfer control of my satellites three days from now. And there is nothing anyone can do to stop me.'

193

*

Jansch was reading through the statement provided by the security guard who had been at the front desk when Breggie de Kok met her untimely death. He claimed that two men, one of whom had been found dead in Breggie's apartment, had walked into the building and shown him a Polaroid photograph of his wife. She was sitting on a sofa. Beside her was a masked man holding a gun to her head. She was holding a copy of the daily paper. There was no mistaking the implied threat, so when they demanded to know which apartment Breggie de Kok was in and that he hand over a master key, he didn't argue. One man, the one who died, went up to the apartment, the other remained at the desk to ensure the security guard did nothing foolish.

When the guard had been shown a photograph of Conor Lenihan, he told the police he had never seen the man. Asked what had happened to the second man, the guard told them he had vanished during the commotion caused by the fire alarms. A check with the man's wife confirmed his story which the police had expected it to, but the couple remained on the suspect list.

When Jansch had finished reading the statement, he took a video from the same file box and inserted it into the machine. It was a fire department video recording of the incident at the apartment building. There was something puzzling Jansch, something niggling away at him that he had seen somewhere. He watched the recording which lasted about thirty minutes.

He had watched the video the first time earlier that day because he had hoped to see something which might help to incriminate the Irishman, Lenihan. But he had been disappointed. The second run was no better than the first. He gave up and moved on to the surveillance photographs which clearly identified Conor at the scene. Because he had never denied being by the apartments, there was little point in trying to prove Conor was lying about his movements.

The photographs also contained stills from the Fire Department video. He shuffled them about on his desk, scanning each one, looking for something, when Hoffman walked in. Jansch looked up and glanced at the clock on the wall. It was almost midnight.

'Hallo, sir. Can't you sleep either?'

Hoffman helped himself to a cup of coffee from the vending machine. 'What are you doing, Uwe? Looking for inspiration?'

Jansch leaned back in his chair. 'Something like that.'

Hoffman walked over to the desk. He looked at the photographs, sipping his coffee.

'Nice motor.' He pointed in the general direction of the desktop.

Jansch leaned forward and picked up one of the stills. Caught neatly in the middle of a shot was a BMW. It was a Seven series. It had darkened windows. Jansch picked up a magnifying glass and scanned the shot. What caught his eye was the figure of a man on the far side of the road whose body position suggested he was about to cross over towards the car.

He glanced quickly at Hoffman, an unspoken question forming on his lips. Then he reached across to the video player and rewound the tape. Hoffman watched with growing curiosity as Jansch punched the play button.

The film fluttered into life and, once again, Jansch sat back to watch for something significant. The video began indistinctly because the camera was being held by one of the fire crew inside the cab of the fire truck. The figure of the man standing on the far side of the road came into view almost within seconds of the fire tender passing the parked BMW. He was obviously waiting for the fire truck to pass him before crossing the road. As the crew member holding the camera stepped out of the fire truck, the camera swung back towards the rear of the tender and caught the figure climbing into the open door of a BMW motor car.

'Look!' Uwe exclaimed suddenly, and touched the screen, pointing at the image. The car rolled smoothly away from the kerb as soon as he was in and disappeared off the screen. The reason Jansch had not seen it earlier was because he had been concentrating on the building.

He rewound the tape and froze it at the point where the man was about to cross the road. He then pulled the photograph of the BMW in front of him. He pointed at both the screen and the photograph.

'We need to identify that guy and that car.'

Hoffman picked up the photograph. The number plate was clear enough to be read through a magnifying glass. He tapped Jansch on the shoulder.

'Better put a trace on it.' He dropped the photograph back on the desk. 'Perhaps we are in for a little luck.'

Jansch turned to the computer and keyed in his personal password authorizing access to police files and traffic records. He tapped in the number plate of the BMW when asked what his query was and requested details of its registered owner. The answer was flashed on to the screen inside a minute and made both of them whoop for joy.

The car was registered in the name of Jan Kloojens, otherwise known as the Dutchman.

Levi Eshkol arrived in Germany the following morning and was met by one of Schiller's limousines. The Covenant had been brought over in the diplomatic pouch and Eshkol had been given diplomatic privileges accordingly. In the limousine with Eshkol when it left the airport were two armed bodyguards. Following the car was a nondescript Opel estate, occupied by armed Mossad agents.

Eshkol felt relaxed and at ease, no longer fearful of any attempt by Molke's thugs to secure the Covenant from him. The journey to Schiller's residence was uneventful and he was greeted most cordially by the great man himself.

Eshkol steepled his fingers and tipped his head forward slightly. '*Shalom*,' he said warmly.

'*Shalom*,' Schiller replied. Then they shook hands and hugged each other.

'It has been a long and torturous road, my dear friend,' Schiller said to him as he showed him into the house. 'Please understand how deeply I was affected by Alf Weitzman's death; such barbarism.'

'Another Nazi atrocity,' Eshkol answered with venom. 'One more reason why we should strive to curb their growing power. The Covenant will do all of that.'

Schiller took him through to the room overlooking the terrace. 'Goldman and Binbaum will arrive tomorrow,' he said. 'But Hess has decided to distance himself from the transfer. He feels that in his position it would not be politic to be involved in such a coveted circle of influence.' Schiller smiled. 'Something like that anyway.'

Eshkol laughed. 'Coming from the next President of the Bundesbank, I would think he is an expert on such matters.' The laughter subsided. 'I think he's right,' Eshkol conceded. 'But he will always be a useful ally. If not, we can always use some friendly pressure.' They both laughed again.

And what neither of them realized was the subtle shift in Eshkol's position with that last, remarkable statement.

Jansch came into the operations room in something of a hurry. In his hand he was carrying the statement made by the desk clerk at the apartment building. There were not so many officers in the room now that Hoffman had wound the case down to a lower priority, and none of them bothered to give him more than a glance as he went directly to Hoffman's office.

The chief looked up at Jansch's knock on the door frame. Hoffman's door was rarely closed.

'Yes, Uwe, what is it?'

Jansch laid the statement on the desk. 'The desk clerk has identified the second man as the one in the photograph. It links Kloojens with the kidnap by direct association. We can lay this at the Dutchman's feet, no trouble.'

Hoffman had been reading. He removed his glasses and laid them on the table. 'It's all coming together too neatly, isn't it?'

'Sir?'

Hoffman tapped the report in front of him. 'This is the report from ballistics.' He stopped and pointed to the vacant chair opposite. 'Sit down Uwe, sit down.' Jansch did as he was asked and waited for his boss to continue. 'The bullet that killed the de Kok woman was fired by Kleiber after he raped her. Somehow she managed to kill him. Interestingly, the gun that she used was also the same gun that killed Jürgen Krabbe and Oscar Schwarz. We are fairly confident that she killed Joseph Schneider before she fled the house in Düsseldorf.' He leaned back and stretched his arms upwards. 'So,' he said, expelling his breath explosively, 'add that to the evidence, circumstantial or otherwise, and we can lay the blame for the deaths of all the terrorists at the hands of Breggie de Kok, which means you don't need the brains of a rocket scientist to work out that Fraulein de Kok intended to do a runner with the Schiller infant and claim the ransom for herself, much to the chagrin of the Dutchman.'

Jansch let the discourse run over him for a while.

'You haven't mentioned Conor Lenihan,' he pointed out.

Hoffman threw up his hands. 'How can I? Much as I hate to say it, we have to accept that our evidence is quite flimsy. We cannot prove he had anything to do with the kidnapping, nor with any of the people I have mentioned.' He leaned back in his chair, one elbow pressed into the armrest, his other hand extended. 'He was watched going towards the Hoeffler apartment block, but he was not actually seen going in there because G9 lost sight of him. The security camera tapes were bloody useless so we can't prove he went in. And if he did, nobody saw him come out. He led us to the baby. People got killed, but we are not convinced of the "whom" as much as we are of the "manner". We believe Lenihan was involved but,' he shrugged, 'we can't prove it.'

'But we know he is up to his neck in all this,' Jansch said pointlessly.

Hoffman agreed. 'Yes. I know it. You know it. We all know it. But can we convince a court?' He shook his head. 'Unlikely.'

Jansch opened his mouth. Then he shut it again. It was fairly obvious that, apart from trying to pin some minor felony on the Irishman, it would be a complete waste of police time and money in trying to prove a case against him: all the witnesses were dead.

'You mean he's free to go?'

Hoffman nodded. 'I'll interview him again. You know, go through the motions. Otherwise, yes: Conor Lenihan is free to go.'

Jansch knew Hoffman would never let a criminal go if he had just a micron of proof of the criminal's guilt. And here, he had nothing. Jansch, like Hoffman, knew it was over. He nodded his understanding to the chief and walked out of the office.

Hoffman watched him go and waited until he had closed the door before reaching for the phone. He held his hand over the instrument and thought about what he was going to do. It was unethical, criminal even. Then he thought back to that day he had looked upon the carnage wrought by Breggie de Kok and her fanatical killers, and the promise he had made to himself. He thought about the bodies of those who had been gunned down with no mercy. The young woman whose only crime had been to be a member of Schiller's staff, employed as a nanny to the baby, to have her life cut off because of some evil fanaticism. He had promised himself that day that he would bring the killers to justice and, were it possible, see them dealt with by their own kind of justice in a place where the arm of the law courts could not reach. His hand touched the phone. He felt he had no alternative: Conor Lenihan was as guilty as sin, and by freeing him he had released on to the world another terrorist who was ready to kill again.

'Get me Meckenheim, British desk. Yes, thank you, I'll wait.'

CHAPTER FOURTEEN

Conor stood on the steps of Police Headquarters, a free man. A limousine with blacked-out windows waited at the kerb exactly as she had described. There were no media men, no press photographers nor TV cameramen. No one gave him a second glance as he hurried down the steps and crossed the pavement to the limo. He pulled open the door and climbed into the rear seat. The car was empty except for the driver, who glanced in the rear-view mirror. With barely a sound the car pulled out and settled into the steady flow of traffic.

The ringing phone startled Joanna. She had just walked in from the nursery where she had spent some time with Manny. He was sleeping now and Joanna's mind was on her son and how close she had come to losing him and, perversely who she had to thank for his safe return.

She picked up the phone. 'Frau Schiller.'

It was Hoffman. '*Guten tag*, Frau Schiller. This is Herr Hoffman.'

'Good day, Herr Hoffman,' she continued in German. 'What can I do for you?'

'Frau Schiller, now that you have your son back, I imagine you might feel that the case is now closed. All settled, so to speak.'

Joanna frowned. 'Well, apart from tying up loose ends as you people often say, yes, I would think that the case is closed.'

'For you, yes, but for my department there is still much work to be done. The investigation will continue until we have caught all those involved in your son's kidnap.'

Joanna sat down, curious now. 'So what can I do for you, Herr Hoffman?' she asked.

'Frau Schiller, we know that there is still one suspect unaccounted for; one member of the terrorist gang who attacked you. It is my duty, and my desire, to catch this man. I intend stopping at nothing to see that justice prevails.'

'Very commendable, Herr Oberkommissar,' Joanna replied, 'but why are you telling me this?'

'Frau Schiller, let me be frank. You are an intelligent woman and I am sure that, without being a policewoman, you probably understand what is meant by the due process of law.' He didn't wait for a reply. 'Whether I continue on this case or not is immaterial, but the case will never be closed until all those who were involved, before or after the kidnap are brought to justice.

'We know there is still one killer out there, and we know that he has received shelter from a member of the public.'

Joanna began to sense warning bells ringing in her head.

Hoffman continued, 'We believe that member of the public is a foreign national, which would mean prison and deportation for that person should he or she be caught, tried and found guilty.'

'Herr Hoffman,' Joanna interrupted. 'Why are you telling me this?' She could feel her hands beginning to tremble.

'Frau Schiller, is your phone secure?'

Joanna nodded. 'Herr Schiller is very sensitive about that. It's secure. Unless your department has put a tap on the line,' she said testily.

'No taps, Frau Schiller, I can assure you. So,' he paused, 'I will speak frankly. We know that Conor Lenihan was a member of the team that attacked you and kidnapped your baby. We know that he is guilty of the murder of those members of your staff who died, including Helga.'

Joanna gasped, not from surprise but at the heart-rending reminder of Helga's bloody death. Hoffman droned on.

'We know that Lenihan has been in your house, under your care and protection, and we believe it was because you had reached an agreement with him to return your baby.'

'That's nonsense!' Joanna stammered.

'Harbouring a known killer is a federal offence prosecuted by a term in prison of at least ten years,' Hoffman continued. 'On release you would be deported, by which time your son Manny will, no doubt, have been placed in the care of somebody appointed by Herr Schiller. Your son would not know you, Frau Schiller, and I have no doubt that you would not be allowed access to him because of your known association with the killers and your subsequent term in prison.'

Joanna was sweating now. The phone began to slip through her fingers. She hastily wiped her fingers on her jogging bottoms. She could feel her hands trembling. She cleared her throat and tried to remain calm.

'You're clutching at straws, Herr Hoffman, there is no way in the world my father-in-law would allow you to prosecute such a case on the flimsiest of evidence. His lawyers would laugh you out of court. It wouldn't even reach court,' she added in a flourish.

'Frau Schiller, I have spoken to Irmgard Ballack.'

Joanna felt herself weaken at the knees. Irmgard Ballack was Helga's mother. She had been with the Schiller family for years. 'Yes?' she barely whispered.

'Frau Ballack lost her daughter. Killed by Conor Lenihan. Imagine how she would feel if she learned of your connivance in the kidnap.'

Joanna stood up. 'That isn't true Hoffman,' she shouted. 'You are making this up. Why?'

'Frau Schiller, I want Lenihan to pay for his crime. He is a killer and must be stopped. At the moment he is free and appears to have powerful friends. I know he is on his way back to your house right now. How else will this look when we compile a dossier of evidence against you?'

Joanna couldn't answer for a while. She could understand everything Hoffman was saying. She knew that even being linked to Lenihan was dangerous. Guilt by association, some would call it. No smoke without fire, they would say. Probably even claim that she had conspired with the killers to have her baby kidnapped in order to bring pressure on her father-in-law into paying a huge ransom. None of it would be true, of course, but she knew exactly how the media and consequently the German public would look at it.

'What can I do?' she asked eventually. 'All I am guilty of is knowing this man. I only met him a couple of days ago. If you press those kind of charges, Herr Hoffman, you know they will not be proved, but you will damage me and my reputation for ever. Why? What will you gain from it?'

'Think of Helga. Think of another eighteen-year-old girl, or boy, caught up in the crossfire of some murderous association. There will be others, Frau Schiller, I can assure you. Maybe not in Germany, but certainly elsewhere. These men hold no allegiance to anybody but the highest bidder, believe me. They have neither morals nor scruples. You ask what will I gain from pressing charges against you? The answer is I will gain nothing. But you will lose everything.'

Joanna took a deep breath to steady her beating heart. 'Herr Hoffman, why did you ring me? Was it to frighten me? Was it to make me feel ashamed of something I haven't done? Was it to bargain with me?'

'Yes!' he said quickly. 'To bargain with you. And in return I will guarantee that this conversation and everything I have mentioned will be history: it will never see the light of day again.'

'So what is it you want?' Joanna asked hesitantly.

Hoffman told her, and his voice became persuasive, using subtle argument and reasoning. There was no way in which her name could be revealed or ever discovered, for obvious reasons. He fell short of saying it was her duty, but reminded her of the torn and mutilated bodies, of the young girl, Helga who was to have been Manny's nurse. He used very powerful words. All Joanna had to do was 'deliver the parcel', nothing else.

Joanna was still trembling as she replaced the receiver. She couldn't believe what she had just agreed to do as she drew her hand away from the phone, but added to what she already knew, and the conversation she had just had, there was no doubt in her mind what had to be done. It was justice. It's what governments do, Conor had said.

She heard the sound of the car through an open window and hurried out to meet him. She felt nervous and now just a little afraid. She hoped he wouldn't notice. Conor didn't; he was just pleased to be there and mentally fired up for what they had planned to do. He smiled at Joanna, thanked her and followed her into the spacious lounge.

'You would like tea, I take it?'

He liked the way she flicked her hair back over her shoulders as she turned to speak. 'As ever,' he answered.

Joanna rang for tea and sat herself down on the leather Chesterfield facing Conor. He sat down opposite her.

'Now,' she began, 'I spoke to my father-in-law this morning and asked him to delay his plans, even if he wouldn't cancel them, but I'm afraid he will not budge.' She pushed her hair back. Conor thought she looked a little nervous, which was understandable considering the import of what she was about to do.

'You couldn't appeal to his sense of duty?'

'He's a Jew,' she told him testily. 'He sees it as his duty.' Then she apologized. 'I'm sorry; I shouldn't have spoken to you like that. It irritates me though.'

'Only "irritates"?' He sounded suitably amazed. 'It bloody well infuriates me. The man's playing with millions of lives.'

'He doesn't see it that way,' she told him.

'More like a mission?'

She nodded. 'Definitely.'

'But you *will* be able to stop him?' he asked tentatively.

Her black hair glistened and shimmered as she nodded. 'I think so.'

'What will you do when you have the codes? How will you handle that?'

Joanna was quiet for a moment and didn't answer directly. 'I've spoken to my lawyers.' She put her hand up to ward off Conor's protest. 'I asked about the possibility of getting an injunction against him. If it's heard in the judge's chambers, it will not get into the press. I also spoke to Dr Kistler. I know now he's not the best man to talk to because he's in thick with the Volkspartei, but I need an influential ally. I didn't tell him too much; just my suspicions.'

Conor approved. 'Well, I think you can summon up enough muscle to protect yourself. And I'm not talking about my kind of muscle,' he added, laughing. 'I presume you've said nothing about breaking into the satellites to anyone?'

She shook her head. 'No, absolutely not.'

The tea arrived. Conor waited until the maid had left. 'When does the transfer take place?'

She shook her head sadly. Her hair shimmered and Conor found himself again wishing he was there with her for another reason. 'I'm not sure. It will be some time tomorrow, but I don't know exactly when.'

'And that presents you with a problem?'

'It means I've got to get into Schiller's system and sit there, undetected, until they begin their transmission.'

'And there's a risk in that, right?'

'Yes. If his systems men are any good, they'll spot me and blow my software to kingdom come.'

Conor winked at her and lifted his cup. 'I've got every faith in you Joanna. The worst that can happen is you lose face.'

'No. What I am about to do is a crime,' she answered angrily. 'I could go to prison.'

Conor yawned. It was past midnight and Joanna had been working on a programme for much of that time. Conor's input had been more of moral support than anything else. In the coming battle, Joanna would be in a league of her own, a commander directing the war game, whereas Conor might be used as an orderly, to fetch and carry.

Joanna had rigged up a second computer which she was using to hack into Hansi's computer in a simulated attempt to insert her alien software. Conor had watched in total fascination, understanding little but learning a great deal about this beautiful woman. She had suffered a wounding trauma on discovering the extent of her dead husband's infidelity and involvement in Molke's Volkspartei. The fear generated by the kidnap of her infant son had, to a certain extent, mollified the effect, but now that her son was returned to her safe and well, the mental paralysis had ebbed away to be replaced by a desire and need for retribution.

Joanna had told Conor she felt she had been used by both her father-in-law and her husband. Manfred Schiller's decision to hand over control of his empire to the Israelis despite his grandson's kidnap had been a deep blow to her. Coupled with her complete innocence of Hans Schiller's dreams and aspirations, and the natural anger any cuckolded woman would feel, it had fuelled her desire for vengeance.

He finished yawning and stretched himself back into some semblance of life.

'If your computer has legitimate access to Schiller's, why do you have to go in like a thief in the night?'

She glanced up and leaned back in her chair, probably thankful for a little respite. 'If I went in through a modem, like going in on the Internet, I could not establish the correct protocols for access to confidential files. The target system will have security procedures in place.

Firewalls will have been set up to deny unauthorized access. By using the legitimate access I have with Hansi's computer, I can achieve a deeper, legitimate penetration into the target computer.' Conor nodded, hoping he looked as if he understood. Joanna went on. 'But the target system would still not allow me to retrieve, or interfere with any secure file or software that I have no right of access to.'

She pointed to the second computer she had rigged up alongside Hansi's main computer which sat on the desk in front of her. 'So, what I'm doing here is using this computer to hack into this one.' She pointed back to the main console. 'This is known as the host. What I do is put a programme into it, one I call piggy back, so when the host is talking to the target computer, which is Schiller's, my piggy back thief is sitting there reading, but not retrieving information.'

'So how do you get access without retrieving?'

She sighed deeply. 'With a lot of luck.'

'You don't mean that, do you?' he asked encouragingly.

She smiled. It had a cheeky countenance to it, like that of a child in a sweetshop, full of expectation.

'Not really. I would back myself against the most sophisticated systems anywhere in the world because, basically, they are all programmed by people like me.'

'You're enjoying this, aren't you?' That much was evident. 'So how do you get access to those satellite control codes?'

'Well, up to a point, it's quite straightforward. I have all the passwords Hansi used for access, including those for the most sensitive files, but I have to use them in the correct sequence. For the less sensitive files I can afford a couple of incorrect passwords before the alarm bells start ringing. So, by logic, I can eliminate those passwords that are unnecessary. Are you with me so far?' He nodded lamely. 'Good. Once I have the correct sequence of passwords, I copy them on to my piggy back programme as deleted files. It means I have to set aside some of the host system's non volatile storage area so I can hide them there. Then I transfer the sequence on to my second computer, remove the piggy back temporarily, and leave the host computer on line. If anybody thinks they've detected unauthorized access, they will find only Hansi's system reading low grade data.'

She smiled at him again. She knew he wasn't taking it all in, but he was so attentive. Conor wanted, more than ever, to take her in his arms and hold her.

'Coffee break?' he suggested. Joanna looked at her watch.

'Is it really as late as that?' she asked. She got up from the chair and massaged her legs and thighs. 'I'd better freshen up while you get us some coffee. It's going to be a long night.'

'I thought you'd finished.'

'No,' she replied, shaking her head. 'Believe it or not, everything I've told you is true, except that my piggy back programme will be detected unless I make it polymorphic.' This time Conor's mouth just fell open. 'So you get the coffee, and I'll freshen up and think about the best way to pull a rabbit out of a hat.'

'Undetected,' he said.

'Exactly.' And she left him thinking thoughts that had nothing to do with software.

Conor woke. He wasn't sure where he was for a brief moment, but when he saw Joanna, her head cradled in her arms at her desk, he remembered. It had been a bizarre night. He had watched in helpless admiration as Joanna had struggled to fend off the onslaught of almost overwhelming tiredness, and complete the task of writing a programme that would ensure, as far as possible, that her piggy back remained undetected. She had forced Conor to sit at the second computer and feed in commands, according to her directions, that would hack into the system in her own computer while she tried to detect it. The polymorphic files she had created as the framework of her piggy back would, she had explained to him, continually mutate themselves into an amorphous mess that would remain undetected but not lose their functionality. As each file or part of a file slipped though her defences and avoided each security sweep, she would clap her hands and clench her fist. But whenever they were detected, she would curse, grab her pen and rewrite part of the analogous arithmetic that went into the heart and interlocking soul of her stealth software.

The night had dragged on until it embraced them both in the welcome sanctuary of sleep. Neither of them moved from their respective places and so they woke in the same manner they had slept.

Conor stood up and stretched the stiffness from his body. He walked over to Joanna and laid his hand gently on her shoulder. He gazed down at her as she stirred.

'Morning, Joanna.'

She lifted her head, her eyes still heavy with sleep and turned towards him.

'What time is it?'

He checked his watch. 'Seven o'clock.'

She sat up and stretched. 'God,' she said, yawning. 'What a night.' Then she leaned forward and punched a few keys on the keyboard in front of her and extracted the floppy disc from the computer's disc drive. She then went over to the second computer and did the same.

'I guess we'll have a couple of hours before they start,' she told him, 'so we'd better freshen up and have something to eat. I'll order breakfast for seven thirty. We'll eat in the breakfast-room.'

Conor watched her leave and found himself wondering if she thrived on the adrenalin from her computer wizardry in the same way he thrived on adrenalin. But the big battle was to come and he wondered if she had a breaking point.

He doubted it.

Manfred Schiller was feeling decidedly better than his daughter-in-law, although he was not aware of the difference. He had eaten a hearty breakfast in the terrace room overlooking the valley. With him was Levi Eshkol. And beside them both was the pile of folders that made up the Covenant.

Schiller's lawyers had been through the Covenant with a fine tooth comb. Nothing, it appeared, had been left out. All laws of the individual countries had been checked previously by Schiller's own lawyers in those respective countries working as part of Eshkol's team. All risks of breaking any aspect of any peculiar legislation, particularly in the United States where they were so hot on anti-American activities, had been dealt with. All monies had been paid to each member's nominated bank account, many electing to use Swiss banks, and everyone had been sworn to secrecy. The threat of Schiller's power had been left unsaid but was implicit. The fact that Schiller was dissolving his own power did not alter other people's opinions of him. His personal wealth would still be intact and was omnipotent. The unspoken threats remained.

When they had breakfasted, Schiller and Eshkol went through to the central control room. It was from here that the satellites were controlled. Eshkol, naturally, had never seen it before. He had expected something quite large, technical and straight out of the science-fiction books. But modern technology, miniaturization, sophisticated design had rendered all that unnecessary.

Schiller introduced Eshkol to the senior control officer. He was a middle-aged man, slim and balding. He shook Eshkol's hand and went back to his monitors. From his position at the desk, the officer could see the tracking dish located in a small, aerial plot in the grounds. Alongside the dish he could also see the communication dish and various radio antennae. In front of him were two keyboards, four computer screens and other pieces of ancillary equipment. It looked about as high tech as the average supermarket security post, although he couldn't see the equipment and the servers which were housed in a separate room. A second man was introduced to Eshkol as the senior computer technician.

'It doesn't look very busy,' remarked Eshkol.

'It doesn't have to be. But those machines are processing an incredible amount of traffic.' He smiled and put his hand on Eshkol's shoulder. 'And it's all done with numbers. Amazing, isn't it?'

Eshkol continued to look round the room. Apart from the screens and an oddment of small, indicator lamps on the consoles, the only lighting in the room came from four florescent tubes mounted on the ceiling. He could hear the hum of cooling fans somewhere. Probably the air conditioning, he decided. And there was no carpeting on the floor. Instead the floor covering was some kind of high grade linoleum, polished to a perfect finish.

'Well,' he said after a while. 'Something of an anti climax really.'

Schiller laughed. 'In that case we'll go back to the office and ask the others to make ready. We'll begin with the paperwork and complete the satellite transfer about noon.'

Conor was sitting in front of the second computer. Taped to the edge of the screen was a sheet of paper. On it were several makeshift codes that Joanna had written in large print. These were code words she would call out to Conor to which he would respond by hitting the correct key or combination of keys as fast as he could. They were simple words: *hit, run, hide,* etc.

Joanna was sitting at the other computer. Both machines were on line and Joanna was looking at Schiller's system in legitimate access mode. Conor was simply staring at the sheet of paper trying hard to memorize the correct keys.

There was a knock at the door and one of Joanna's staff came in. She handed Joanna an envelope. 'Special messenger delivered this,' she told her and left the room. Joanna felt her heart beating heavily as she took the envelope. She glanced across at Conor who was studying his screen intently. She ran her fingers over the envelope and felt the unmistakable shape of a barrel-type door key. She almost froze at the memory of the telephone conversation. The voice had been persuasive, promising no comebacks; her name would never be involved. Absolute secrecy, he promised. Joanna knew that by hacking into Schiller's satellites, whether she was successful or not, was a crime. The voice on the phone didn't know anything about Joanna's plans, but Conor was privy to them and he could always use that knowledge as a lever. He could be dangerous. She breathed in deep to steady her nerves and got up out of her chair.

Conor looked across at her as she walked across the room to where she kept her purse. She tore the envelope open, removed the key and dropped it in the purse. Conor went back to studying his screen. Joanna went back to her desk. Her legs felt so weak she was grateful for the safety of the soft chair. She closed her eyes and prayed to God that she would have the strength to carry it through.

Schiller sat facing the consoles, his mind at ease with what he was about to do. His recompense for atrocities committed by the Nazis against his own people was about to begin. It was payback time. No more would Israel suffer the indignity of American purse strings. No more would Nazi Germany rise up against the Jewish nation. No Arab nation would set its heart at war against the peaceful ambitions of his true country. The power he was handing to the people of Israel would ensure their elevation to one of the truly great nations on this planet. He looked at the men assembled around him. It was God's will, he thought. For God's people, God's will.

Joanna watched her screen closely. Communication protocols had been established between her and Schiller's system. The piggy back was scooping up a stream of data which was being downloaded on to Conor's computer. It was being encrypted on to his file access table and rendered irretrievable by any other source. Joanna would number crunch the information she required at Conor's keyboard and transmit it back to Schiller's system. The two-way flow of data would go on for approximately thirty minutes. Thirty minutes in which they were at their most vulnerable.

The lawyers had asked permission to remain until the transfer was complete. Schiller was in a good mood. He had agreed. They were in place now as the satellite control officer, the SCO, opened up communications with two satellites which were in geostationary orbit, 28,000 miles above the earth, encircling the globe at the same speed that the earth was rotating.

'They're in.' Joanna felt her pulse quicken. 'Read the digits back to me. I want to compare them with what I have; make sure there's no mistake.'

Conor could feel the tension rising. His flesh prickled with nervous apprehension. A number one appeared on the screen, followed by a nought. More digits appeared as if at random until there were thirty-two sprawled across the screen. Another row blossomed in front of him and he read those across as he had done with the first block. Some rows appeared that included letters as well as a string of numbers. He read them all back.

The SCO waited for a protocol command from the first satellite. When it came he keyed in a password. Joanna followed him in. The second satellite asked for a separate protocol command. In it went. Joanna swore gently.

'What is it?' Conor asked, barely raising his voice above a whisper.

'They're about to do a satellite cross check. We'll be blind while they do it.'

'But you knew this.'

'Yes, but don't worry. It's just me being nervous,' she reassured him.

The SCO nodded his satisfaction and checked with the second control officer who was sitting at the console and controlling a separate computer.

211

'We're getting some noise here,' he said quietly. The SCO watched as he tapped in an enquiry code. Then he turned to Schiller. 'Sir, didn't you authorize a transmission ban?'

Schiller looked at his watch. 'Yes. The ban is on for another thirteen minutes. Probably some idiot hasn't read his mail shot. Check it out anyway.'

The second control officer turned back to his console. 'Ah, it's gone now.'

Joanna whistled through her teeth. 'Damn.'

Conor's head jerked round. 'What is it?'

Joanna's fingers flowed over the keyboard. 'It looks like we're the only system on line. Schiller must have banned all communications traffic until the transfer is complete.' She clucked her tongue angrily. 'Makes it a touch more difficult.'

The SCO turned to one of the Israeli contingent. Eshkol, ever attentive stepped forward. 'You want these, I presume?' He handed the SCO the new codes. In his briefcase was another set of codes which he intended putting in once the SCO had completed the transfer. It was part of the agreed procedure. The SCO typed them in to a file box.

'The new codes,' Joanna said. 'When they're complete I'll write the complement codes.' This was Joanna's Trojan horse: the numbered codes would be interpreted by her computer. Joanna's piggy back had an amorphous copying programme which substituted the opposite numbers. When the satellites' command system asked for verification it would automatically return Joanna's numbers, but these would be changed back to the original numbers for transmission to the screen.

'They're back on line again.' The second control officer almost jumped out of his seat. He looked across at the SCO. He could feel his cheeks getting hot. 'I think someone is trying to break in.'

The SCO shrugged. 'Probably a kid. See if you can track him down. Feed him some shit.'

'They're doing a search!' Joanna almost screamed. 'Go for a run.'

Conor hit the combination of keys written alongside the paper taped to the side of his screen. This was a diversion which, Joanna had hoped when she wrote it, would distract the searcher and send him on a wild goose chase.

'Bastards!' The second control officer punched a medley of keys.

'They want us to chase them.'

Schiller stiffened in his chair while the others in the room were now aware that something was unsettling the controllers.

'Is something wrong?' Schiller asked.

The SCO called back over his shoulder. 'Somebody is still on the line sir. We are trying to identify them.'

'Well, let me know who it is the moment you find them.'

The second controller muttered under his breath and fed in a virus. If he located the intruder, the virus would sit in that intruder's software and destroy it. He had already given up the wild goose chase and was searching for the source of the illegal traffic.

The SCO went to the next step of the communication protocol and fed in the codes for both satellites. The response on the screen was to ask for the codes to be fed in again. As this was done the screen changed and the codes were put there for verification. The SCO acknowledged and then instructed the satellites that the control codes were about to be changed.

'Here we go!' Joanna called nervously. 'Keep your fingers ready Conor.'

The codes came up on the screen exactly as they had on the main control computer in front of the SCO. The next instruction was that the new codes should be typed in.

'Now Conor! Open!'

Conor hit the combination and looked across at Joanna.

'Shut!'

Conor closed transmission.

Eshkol watched the SCO feed in his codes. It entailed a thirty two bit encryption which Joanna's Trojan horse was busy transmuting into a junked version of the Israeli codes. The computer reproduced the new code numbers for verification and transmitted them to the satellite. At least, it looked that way, but in reality, Joanna's converted figures were busy winging their way across thousands of miles of space and being returned to the SCO's console. And there they were transposed back to the original numbers.

The SCO confirmed the new codes had been entered and grinned up at Eshkol. 'Codes confirmed, sir,' he said triumphantly.

A cheer went round the room followed by general back slapping and hand clapping. Champagne appeared as if by magic and euphoria began to envelope them all.

Except the second control officer. He had been within seconds of identifying the hacker only for the itinerant to close down communication.

'Got them!' Joanna leapt up from her chair and danced around the room.

Conor felt elated too. But tinged with that elation was an element of sorrow. It was over. Soon there would no longer be any reason for him to continue his association with Joanna. As much as he wanted to, he knew he had more chance of flying to the moon.

He got up from his chair. 'Is that it?' he asked.

'Yes,' she sang. She continued to dance and suddenly waltzed her way over to Conor. She threw her arms around him. Conor almost stumbled backwards. Then he felt Joanna's lips on his and he returned the kiss hungrily.

Suddenly she pushed him away. She looked away from him brushed herself down. It was a defensive kind of gesture.

'I'm sorry,' she said hurriedly. 'I shouldn't have done that.' She looked up quickly and then looked away again. 'I'm not usually given to spontaneous gestures like that.'

Conor nodded. 'I understand,' he told her unhappily. 'So,' he said, changing the subject. 'what happens now?'

She turned to the computers. 'Well, first we have to unplug because in a little while the balloon will go up.'

'What do you mean?'

She gave him a lopsided smile and picked up a disc from the desk. 'This is a time bomb.' She removed the disc from the computer's disc drive and inserted the one she had shown Conor. 'Right, transmit to me then pull your data lead out.' She nodded. 'Do it now, Conor.'

He did as he was asked and transmitted. Then he closed down and pulled the communication lead from his computer. Joanna loaded the disc in and transmitted.

'Got them!' The second control officer was jubilant. 'Yes!' He clenched his fist.

The SCO looked round. 'Are they still transmitting?' he asked. His colleague checked the screen.

'No, they've stopped. But I have them. Next time they come on line. . . .' He snapped his fingers.

Schiller had his back to the consoles. He was talking to Eshkol. Suddenly the man's expression changed. Schiller frowned, turned towards the direction of Eshkol's source of confusion and saw, from the body language of the two computer men that something had gone wrong.

'What is it?' He barked the question out. He was no longer thinking of irritating hackers playing games. Something told him this was serious. The two control officers were transfixed by a message on the screen. It dominated the two computers, emblazoned like a banner.

WARNING!! You have a virus time bomb in your software. The active boot partition of your system has been encrypted. You must respond to this message within fifteen minutes to prevent detonation. Failure to do so will result in a total reformat of all your hard discs. You are at liberty to challenge me and attempt to find and destroy the virus. To acknowledge me and halt the clock, please type the word Freiheit.

There was silence in the room as each man clustered round the consoles. The SCO typed the word in. Another message flashed up on the screen.

Thank you. You now have sixty seconds to attempt communication with your satellites. You will find this impossible. The clock will start after that unless you type in the word Lebensraum.

The SCO looked frantically at Eshkol who was now, or should have been, effectively in control. He was still trying to come to terms with this frightening development. He nodded.

The SCO typed in the passwords for access to the satellites' control computers. Once in he was then asked for the codes. Gingerly, all eyes on the screen, he typed in Eshkol's new codes. The reply on the screen was like a knife turning in their stomachs.

INCORRECT CODES. ACCESS DENIED.

Schiller slumped to the floor, his frail heart unable to take the shock. Although he was still alive, his breathing was quite shallow. Suddenly pandemonium broke out. The Israeli contingent immediately suspected some kind of collusion by the Germans with another group, which was ludicrous in the extreme. There was no reason why Schiller need play the Israelis for fools.

Schiller's personal secretary pushed aside any concerns for his master's satellite system and ran from the room to call for medical assistance. All Schiller's house staff were trained in first aid and there was always at least one paramedic on duty.

Above the noise and confusion, the SCO called for quiet. He had their attention immediately. He went back to the screen and typed the word Lebensraum. Another message appeared on the screen.

The clock has stopped. When you next press a key, the clock will start. You will have precisely thirteen minutes to find and destroy the virus. Try if you dare. To stop the clock again type Himmel. *I will communicate again soon.*

The message disappeared. Immediately the SCO attacked the keyboard and began typing in commands which would set in motion torpedo programmes to search out and destroy enemy viruses. As he did, a digital clock appeared on the screen and began counting down from thirteen minutes.

Schiller was struggling to his feet after someone had produced a glass of water. His secretary returned and helped the old man up. Schiller's complexion was wan and pale, and there was genuine concern for his wellbeing as he was lowered into a chair.

'What is going on?' he seemed to ask nobody in particular. 'Why are they doing this to me?'

There was no one to answer for him; no one to offer any comfort other than to stare and wonder as obliquely as the poor, frail old billionaire was staring and wondering.

He drew in a deep breath and struggled to his feet. His secretary helped him walk over to the consoles where he could see the one-sided battle being waged. It was obvious though which side was losing.

The clock eventually ticked down to fifteen seconds when the SCO typed in the codeword to stop the clock. The inevitable message appeared.

I knew you wouldn't do it, but tomorrow is another day. You will now retain control of your satellites for one week. I'll be in touch.

The screen went blank.

There was a collective murmur of incredulity. All of them in that room were intelligent enough to realize they would have to rely on the expertise or guile of others to resolve the situation. There was little or nothing any of them could do.

The SCO sat there feeling helpless. 'Whoever he is, he's a clever bastard,' he admitted. 'Really clever.' He turned to his colleague. 'Did you track him down while I was on line?'

His colleague grinned and wiped his hand across his forehead. 'You won't believe it,' he warned him. 'Because I don't.'

Schiller pushed forward. 'You mean you know who did this?'

The second officer regarded Schiller carefully. 'I know where it came from, sir. But not necessarily who did it.'

'Where, man? Where?' he demanded to know.

'Whoever hacked into our system did so from somewhere inside the Volkspartei headquarters.'

CHAPTER FIFTEEN

Conor was sitting beside Joanna in the noiseless interior of her Mercedes. Behind them, secure in his baby car cot, was little Manny. The three of them were like a small family and Conor found himself surprisingly content with that.

They had left behind the frenetic highways of the industrialized heartland and were motoring gently on well-made roads that turned and twisted through the beauty of the Black Forest. The lush green of the pine and cypress trees dipped their foliage against the sunlight and lined their route in graceful symmetry.

Conor had no idea where they were going. Joanna had been surprisingly reticent about revealing the details. He had been even more surprised when she had suggested, in emotional, faltering tones, that they go away together. She hadn't wanted it this way, she'd told him. It appalled her to think she felt even a trace of emotion for him, but she felt the need for his company. Somewhere quiet. Somewhere peaceful.

Naturally, Conor showed no reluctance at all. In his wildest dreams he would never have imagined that Joanna felt something for him. The realization elated him, and he was quite happy to ride the wave to its blissful conclusion.

After their battle on the field of computer technology, he had embraced Joanna. The adrenalin rushes had driven them both to a high degree of warmth and good feeling. It had been this, Conor decided, that had moved Joanna to ask him to come away with her.

They wasted little time. That morning, the day after Joanna had planted the software time bomb in Schiller's system, she had gathered up her son and told her staff she would be away for a few days. None of them were told where she would be.

Conor wondered how she intended to continue her battle with Schiller and how she intended to resolve the outcome. It was then she told him how she had planted the identity code of the Volkspartei computer in the machine Conor had been using.

'I hacked into the Volkspartei HQ,' she had explained. 'I was able to go in legitimately using Hansi's communication protocol. I used the piggy back to extract the data I needed. So, when they were trying to trace the source of the software time bomb, I let them find you. They thought they had found the culprit.'

Conor whistled through his teeth. 'Clever girl. So Schiller will go after the Volkspartei with all guns blazing. And that means Franz Molke.'

'Should sort them out,' she had remarked laconically.

Conor watched the trees flashing by in silence. His thought wrapped around the beauty beside him. The intelligence of the woman staggered him, and she had shown tremendous mental agility that would have matched any physical prowess shown by many of his previous comrades. He was looking forward to their association and hoped it would be more than just a fleeting affair.

Joanna had not spoken for some time. She seemed nervous. Conor thought he could understand why. She had asked him to be patient; to show some understanding. It wasn't going to be easy for her under the circumstances. But he had made up his mind to follow her lead; not to push. He knew his patience would be more than justly rewarded.

'Is it far?'

Joanna almost jumped out of her skin. In truth she wasn't too sure just how far they had to go yet. 'I don't think so,' she answered hopefully. 'Last time I came this way, Hansi was driving.'

He let it go. What did it matter how far they had to go? So long as he was with her, he would travel as far as she wanted.

It occurred to Conor that Joanna had relinquished control of the satellites quite readily to Schiller after inflicting such a crushing defeat on the man. It wasn't the kind of thing that a man of Conor's persuasion was used to. He needed to know why, just to satisfy his own curiosity.

'You're taking a bit of a gamble though, aren't you, Joanna?'

The question startled her. She could feel moisture gathering on her fingertips. 'Why? What do you mean?'

'You handed control of the satellites back to Schiller. What's to stop him going ahead with his plan and handing that control over to the Israelis as he'd already planned? Or do you still have control of his codes?'

He watched her driving as he spoke. Her eyes did not leave the road. She flicked a quick, nervous glance at him. Then she smiled a little lopsidedly; almost triumphantly.

'Look, there is no way I could keep control by denying my father-in-law access to his codes. Any programme I left in their system would eventually be found and purged.'

She was quiet for a while. Then she looked at him again before concentrating on the road ahead.

'Conor, computer hackers can get into a system and destroy it or try to control it, but they can only retain control for so long. I had control of Schiller's satellites for a comparatively short time. I was playing a very dangerous game with them, Conor; I was on the edge. I wanted them to believe the impossible. Or perhaps I should say the improbable. The truth is, I lied,' she told him. 'I didn't deny them their codes. I couldn't deny them their codes without destroying their whole system. But they will spend the next week tearing their hair out wondering how on earth I could do what I threatened when the truth is, I can't. What I have done though is to sow a seed of doubt. It's like putting a virus into their collective minds. They will spend a lot of time and energy trying to solve a problem that doesn't exist. All I did was to put a message on their screen before we left; let them think they only have control for a while.'

She raised her chin in a kind of superior gesture. 'I decided to let them stew a little. I worded it with enough Volkspartei arrogance to convince them who was running the show now.'

He smiled and looked back through the windscreen. The road curled languidly, following the line of trees, past flowing streams rushing over rocks that churned the water into minor rapids. The car ate the miles up effortlessly and smoothly. Above the forest canopy the sun was losing height and casting streamers of gold through the foliage.

'Will you make contact with Schiller?'

Joanna shook her head. 'Someone else will do that.'

'Who?'

'It's best you don't know.'

He let it drop. Joanna knew what she was doing. Whoever she asked to make contact with Schiller would need a lot of clout. Schiller was like a man without his crutches; capable of standing, but not capable of walking. But the endgame was disposal of Schiller's empire in a more parochial fashion. Conor knew that Schiller would have to agree terms. One word to the national press and all hell would break loose. Once the Arabs got a whiff of Schiller's plans there would be bedlam. He would have lost the advantage and be accused of being a threat to world peace. Any label attached to him would stick. Yes, he decided, Joanna knew exactly what she was doing.

The road ahead forked. Sitting at the beginning of the fork was an old man. He was wearing a Loden cape which Conor thought was unnecessary in the pleasant, autumnal weather. Joanna's heart skipped a beat when she saw him. She could feel her mouth drying and she prayed Conor would not ask her a question because she didn't think she would be able to speak.

She took the right fork, looking nervously now for a track on the right-hand side of the road. It appeared after about a hundred metres. It was exactly as she had been told. She could almost hear the voice over the phone.

Joanna signalled and slowed. She made a brave attempt at small talk but the words piled up against her arid vocal chords. The noise she made was more of a croak.

'What's up?' Conor asked.

'Nearly there,' she stammered.

'You're nervous, aren't you?'

'Mmm!' It was all she could manage.

Joanna drove the car along the track which climbed lazily through the trees. Eventually they came to a hunting lodge. It looked a trifle incongruous in such a setting; a throwback to days of German aristocracy. But it still looked magnificent.

Conor had seen places like this in many parts of Germany and Austria. Stout, log-built lodges, pine smoke drifting from the chimney, mingling with the scent of the forest. It seemed perfect for a secret tryst with Joanna.

She swung the car round in front of the lodge and stopped so that the car was facing back the way they had come. She took a deep breath and turned the ignition off. The gentle throb of the engine, barely discernible in the plush interior of the Mercedes, died. Joanna sat back in her seat, her hands stretched out on the wheel.

'Here we are,' she said at last.

Conor unbuckled his seat belt. 'It looks magnificent.'

Joanna retrieved her purse from the door recess beside her and opened it. As her hand touched the barrel key, its coldness seemed to rifle through her. She trembled and fumbled with her seat belt.

Conor touched her gently. 'Don't be nervous,' he said softly. 'I won't rush you. Take all the time you need.'

Joanna threw him a half-hearted glance and a wan smile. She then opened the door and got out of the car. Conor followed her. They walked up a narrow path leading to a few steps. Joanna felt her legs shake as she climbed each step. She wondered if she would make it to the top without collapsing.

They stepped on to the veranda, their footfalls noisy on the wooden floor. Joanna approached the front door and inserted the key. She hoped Conor couldn't see how violently her hand was shaking.

The door swung open, creaking on its hinges, to reveal a magnificent lounge made entirely of pinewood. Around the walls were various hunting trophies, the pride of which was a huge boar's head over the magnificent fireplace. Joanna walked to a beautifully carved coffee table and dropped the key on to its top. She straightened.

'Kiss me, Conor.'

He needed no second bidding. He stepped forward and took her in his arms. She melted in to him, her stiffness softening as their lips met. He crushed her mouth beneath his and drew her against his body so that he could feel every soft curve of her flesh.

She pulled away. 'I'll go and get Manny. He'll need feeding.'

He let her go and watched as she closed the door behind her, the vision of her loveliness held like a photographic still, black and white, fixed in his brain.

'Hallo, Conor!'

The deep voice shattered the moment and Conor spun round. Facing him was a man he recognized. He was standing with his legs apart and his arms thrust outwards. Between his hands, Conor recognized the silenced barrel of a Browning 9mm automatic. He felt the thud of two bullets in his chest before the sound came to his ears. The force of the shots threw him backwards and he crashed into the coffee table. He slid off the table and sprawled on the polished wooden floor.

Conor turned his face to look upwards and opened his eyes. His vision blurred, but he was vaguely aware of a second SAS man standing over him. Conor knew what was coming. But before he felt the impact of the bullets, he thought once more of Joanna and then he died.

Joanna hurried down the steps, tears streaming down her face. She didn't hear the thud of the silenced gun. Hoffman was standing beside the car. He was alone, the Loden cape discarded. Joanna couldn't bear to look at him. She reached the passenger door which he was holding open and climbed in. Hoffman got into the driver's seat. He looked at Joanna. Her chin was pressed deep into her chest and she was sobbing uncontrollably. He waited patiently until she had calmed down. He said nothing, but put a comforting hand on her shoulder.

When she felt able, she reached into her purse and took out an envelope. Inside was the computer disc with the satellite codes on. It also contained all the information he needed to wreck the Volkspartei's chance of forming the next government and ensure that Franz Molke would be discredited and forced to abandon his political career.

Joanna gave him the disc. From that moment, Hoffman held the key to Schiller's empire. He slipped the disc into his pocket, moved the gearshift forward and the Mercedes rolled quietly away from the hunting lodge.